They were two blocks u[...] happened. Clooney had [...] walking in the street, be[...] times blocked by Killou[...] a shadow move at the m[...] shal passed by. What occ[...] only seconds, and yet from Clooney's perspective, everyone was moving in slow motion, and he saw it all quite clearly.

The shadow turned out to be a man, clad in black, wearing a sombrero. Even in the darkness, the shape of the sombrero was quite distinctive. He had his back to Killough and Clooney, looking after the unsuspecting Ethan, and Clooney realized that this had to be Willie Creed, and that he was about to spring an ambush.

But before Clooney could react, Killough leaped forward, and in the same instant, the man Clooney assumed was Creed whirled, sensing that someone was behind him even before he heard a sound. Clooney shouted a warning intended for Ethan a heartbeat before muzzle flash lit up the night. Clooney heard two gunshots and saw Killough going down, giving him a clearer view of Creed, who was spinning around to face Ethan, bringing his matched set of pistols to bear on the marshal.

But Killough had distracted him just long enough—Ethan had his gun drawn, and when Creed turned on him, the marshal fired without hesitation. Falling backwards, Creed triggered one of his pistols, and Ethan fired again—for a few seconds, the crashing of gun thunder filled the street. Clooney had the derringer in his hand, but there was no need for that, not anymore.

ST. MARTIN'S PAPERBACKS TITLES
BY JASON MANNING

GUN JUSTICE
OUTLAW TRAIL
GUNMASTER
FRONTIER ROAD

TRAIL TOWN

JASON MANNING

St. Martin's Paperbacks

TRAIL TOWN

Copyright © 2002 by Jason Manning.

All rights reserved. No part of this book may be used or reproduced in any manner whatsoever without written permission except in the case of brief quotations embodied in critical articles or reviews. For information address St. Martin's Press, 175 Fifth Avenue, New York, NY 10010.

ISBN: 0-312-98203-8

Printed in the United States of America

St. Martin's Paperbacks edition / December 2002

St. Martin's Paperbacks are published by St. Martin's Press, 175 Fifth Avenue, New York, NY 10010.

10 9 8 7 6 5 4 3 2 1

CHAPTER ONE

When Ethan Payne rode into Abilene, Kansas, on a lanky coyote dun, the dry summer wind was casting a pall of red dust over the town. The sun-bleached sky played host to an anemic wisp of clouds. Ethan wondered if he would ever feel rain on his face again. Not that he much cared one way or the other, but old-timers were talking drought, and the lack of rainfall had turned his long trek from the mountains of Colorado into an unpleasant ordeal. He'd found many a water hole and even a few rivers drained bone dry.

Having circled wide around a couple of herds held out west of town, he expected to see Abilene brimming with Texas drovers, especially since the long hot day was, mercifully, drawing finally to a close. But the streets were oddly empty. There were just a few cow ponies hitched to the tie rails; they weren't stacked stirrup to stirrup as he had thought they might be, based on all the stories he had heard about this place. Abilene was a town that, by all accounts, was as wild and woolly a place as any one would likely find in the west. Ethan's first impression of it, though, was a real disappointment for a man who longed for excitement. He'd crossed hundreds of monotonous miles of empty plains from the Colorado goldfields, haunted every step of the way by bad memories, and had hoped to find a

few distractions in this place—and instead Abilene looked
as tame as a Sunday prayer meeting.

Riding into town, Ethan wondered if there was a funeral
going on somewhere. Or maybe some deadly epidemic had
struck the inhabitants. All the people he'd heard talk about
Abilene couldn't have been wrong. A lot of the folks who
came to the Colorado goldfields passed through Kansas,
and since the new Texas cattle trade was a development of
indubitable importance to the frontier, it was quite often the
preferred topic of conversation around a crackling cook fire
or felt-covered saloon table. Ethan reviewed what he'd
heard about Abilene, thinking maybe he had somehow gotten his facts wrong.

With the Civil War over, Texans had found themselves
with a lot of land, a lot of cattle, and no money. Things
looked bleak, until they heard that back east there was a
growing demand for beef. So it made sense to the Texans
to round up their half-wild longhorns and drive them north
to the railroad that ran through Kansas and connected east
coast to west. The Indian Territory was in the way, but the
Texans had never let Indians stop them from doing what
they wanted to do, and they weren't about to start now.
Most of the tribes settled for the payment of *wohaw*, a duty
usually paid in cattle and given in exchange for a herd's
safe passage across their lands—irrefutable evidence that,
if nothing else, the Indians had learned to be pragmatic in
their dealings with white men. Those groups that tried to
keep the Texans off their lands altogether, or opted for trying to purloin the longhorns by hook and crook and night
raid, were summarily dealt with.

Still, the Texans had plenty of other problems. Chief
among them was that their cattle were prone to carry the
lethal splenic fever, more commonly known as Spanish Fever. The drovers found themselves blocked from entering
Kansas or Missouri by quarantine lines established by the
state governments at the behest of citizens who did not care
to see their own livestock infected by the Texas cattle. A
compromise struck in 1867 opened the western third of

Kansas—the part of the state that was largely unsettled—to the Texas herds. Beyond the quarantine zone's "deadline" the longhorns could only be moved along a trail that connected the zone to the Union Pacific rail line. To keep the Texas cow trade, the Kansas politicians who pushed the necessary legislation for this arrangement through the state assembly also formed the Topeka Livestock Company and tried to entice the Texans to sell their herds to stockyards they owned. What no one had counted on was the Indian trouble that flared up and disrupted everything. These weren't the Civilized Tribes of the Indian Territory, either. They were Plains Indians, who had made the waging of war a lifestyle. And that made them a real handful for the Texas drovers, and very nearly killed the entire Texas cattle industry stillborn.

Then Joe McCoy showed up in Kansas. A tenacious entrepreneur, McCoy cut a deal with the Union Pacific. The railroad would pay him five dollars for every railcar he could fill with cattle. The UP was in dire need of eastbound traffic. Its westbound trains were filled with emigrants and gold seekers and goods destined for a frontier starved for merchandise of every description. But its eastbound trains rolled mostly empty cars. Texas cattle could correct that costly imbalance. All the UP had to do, said McCoy, was prevail upon the United States Army to come in and make the Indians of western Kansas behave themselves. The railroad had a lot of influence in Washington, and before long the Texans discovered that their Indian trouble had been handled for them.

McCoy decided that the town of Abilene would be a prime location for his stockyards. The fact that Abilene actually stood on the wrong side of the deadline did not long deter him. He convinced the Kansas governor to endorse his plan. The governor wasn't sure but that the quarantine law was unconstitutional anyway, in that it infringed on interstate commerce, so he was willing to go along with McCoy, who, it was said, could sell fire to the Devil. In September of 1867 the first carloads of Texas cattle clattered eastward on

Union Pacific rails, bound for Chicago slaughterhouses. Texas—and Kansas—would never be the same again. Though some Kansas farmers and stockmen objected strongly to the influx of disease-laden longhorns—not to mention the presence of the "unreconstructed Rebels" who pushed them north—about thirty-five thousand head reached Abilene during the abbreviated season of '67. This was a mere dribble compared to the flood that was coming.

The following year, the Texans pushed their cows up a trail through the Indian Territory that had been blazed by a half-breed Cherokee trader named Jesse Chisholm. By early summer the Union Pacific had to admit that it was having difficulty supplying enough rolling stock to transport all the longhorns that McCoy was holding in his stockyards and roaming the uplands near Abilene, waiting their turn. Meanwhile, the Abilene farmer who had precious few cattle to begin with and no money with which to replace livestock lost to Spanish Fever became increasingly hostile to the Texas trade. But for the action of the Texas drovers, who taxed themselves five cents per head of cattle owned in order to contribute to a fund that was used to reimburse the locals for their livestock losses, an open gun war would have resulted. By the end of the 1868 season, nearly sixty thousand head of Texas cattle had passed through Abilene on the way to eastern markets. Abilene's success as a trail town was secured.

As a consequence, the town grew at an incredible rate. Texas names were prominent on saloons and other establishments in an effort to make the drovers feel more at home. There was the Long Horn Mercantile, the Alamo Saloon, and a dozen Lone Stars of every description. Groceries and clothing were commercial products of supreme importance; a cowboy's first major expenditure when he hit town with three months' worth of wages burning holes in his pockets was for new duds, decking himself out from hat brim to boot heel so as to impress the dance hall girls. Clothiers reaped enormous profits. The Great Western Store on the corner of Texas and Cedar Streets was the grandest of many such businesses. Boot makers were in high demand, as a Texas drover would pay up to twenty dollars—nearly a month's pay—for high-heeled, red-tipped boots spangled with a lone star and, maybe, a crescent moon. The Texas Store sold these footwear items, too—along with guns, ammunition, watches, brand-new Brazos lariats, cowhide bests and sheepskin chaps, Union Leader tobacco and Cuban cigars.

Hotels were in great demand. In addition to Joe Mc-Coy's own Drover's Cottage, Abilene could boast of three more hostelries and a half dozen boardinghouses by the end of 1868. Stock dealers used these establishments as business headquarters, and the hotels maintained stock registries in which drovers could advertise their livestock. Buyers consulted these registries to find the herds they wanted to purchase. Banking was another essential trail town enterprise. Texas cattle barons needed loans with which to pay off hired hands, replenish supplies, and foot living expenses while waiting for a buyer. And buyers often needed loans to make quick purchases and pay rail charges. Bankers realized immense profits on interest alone from large short-term loans and by discounting the great volume of paper that passed through their hands. The Abilene office of the First National Bank of Kansas City handled nearly a million dollars in its first two months of operation. Another bank declared a whopping ten percent dividend on its capital stock after only six short months in operation.

A trail town could not have too many saloons. In addition to the bars in the Drover's Cottage and the Planters Hotel, Abilene boasted a dozen watering holes. They ranged from the elegant Alamo, with its set of triple glass doors and walls adorned with gilded mirrors and Renaissance nudes, to the more typical hole-in-the-wall like the Bull's Head owned by Ben Thompson and Phil Coe, a pair of frontier ne'er-do-wells, with the English-born Thompson reputed to be the quickest and most accurate shootist on the frontier. All saloons offered the Texas cowboy an opportunity to try his luck at a variety of games. Poker, monte, and faro were the most popular, followed by dice games like hazard and chuck-a-luck. Professional gamblers flocked to Abilene in March and April, the beginning of the cattle season, to earn their share of the spoils. Very few remained at season's end, come November.

Like the gamblers, prostitutes flocked to Abilene during the cattle season. In 1867, a few girls showed up from points east; the next year they descended on the town like a swarm of locusts. Three permanent brothels with two dozen girls between them sprang up. And then there were the denizens of the tent town on the outskirts. They stalked their cowboy prey at the busy, rollicking dance halls. Proprietors of these establishments derived their income from dancing fees, bar sales, and the renting of back rooms to soiled doves and their clientele.

In addition, Abilene provided fertile ground for doctors, lawyers, barbers, druggists, blacksmiths, contractors, and realtors. In many cases, these men tolerated the wild Texas cowpunchers only because there was immense profit in it for them. It was, said one, like making a living in a snake pit. The Texas rowdies worked hard, and they believed themselves entitled to play hard, too. The citizens of Abilene required strong law to "keep the lid on." Too much violence tended to be bad for business. A city ordinance was drafted that established the first cattle town police force. The town marshal would operate the city jail, maintain a record of all arrests and confinements, and run the police force, which was charged with keeping the peace and was authorized to "enter any saloon, billiard hall, or other place of public resort or amusement, and to arrest and confine in the jail of the town any person guilty of disorderly conduct who may refuse to be restored to order and quiet." The town marshal was also responsible for removing any street obstructions or nuisances, including the apprehension of any swine found at large. Police officers acted as sanitary and fire inspectors, as well. For his services, the marshal would be paid one hundred and fifty dollars a month. Since whoring, gambling, and drinking were the root causes of most of the disruptions of trail town serenity, those enterprises engaged in such practices subsidized local law and order with exorbitant license fees. Gamblers, prostitutes, and saloonkeepers were regularly "assessed" on a personal basis, too.

These denizens of the Abilene underworld generally tolerated the assessments as long as business boomed. But with the 1869 cattle season came a severe drought; this, coupled with a decline in cattle prices on the eastern market, caused the Texas trade to taper off. The bar owners, cardsharps, and calico queens held on, hoping that the situation would improve, and growing ever more resentful at the high taxes they paid to provide the town marshal, "Happy Jack" Crawford, and his three deputies with their salaries. Those drovers who had made the long push up the Chisholm Trail now lingered, waiting for a buyer. Their wages long since spent, they became increasingly bored and troublesome.

Into this potentially explosive situation rode Ethan Payne, in the hot dry summer of 1869—a drifter with a few prospects, and no idea of the trouble that awaited him in this wild and woolly Kansas trail town.

He dismounted in front of the first saloon he saw, a watering hole called the Lone Star. A dog lay in the shade of the boardwalk, too lethargic to raise its head and snap at the flies that pestered it. It curled its speckled lip back and growled half-heartedly at Ethan as he mounted the boardwalk. A man sat with his back to the saloon's front wall, chin resting on chest, and Ethan wondered if he was sleeping or passed out drunk. Leaning closer, Ethan caught a whiff of rotgut whiskey. Flies lifted out of the tangled matting of hair on the man's head and then settled back down again as Ethan straightened, stepped over the man's sprawled legs, and entered the alluringly dim saloon.

He paused to study each person in the establishment before proceeding further. He'd made some enemies in his years as a troubleshooter for the Overland, and some of those people were still above snakes. A couple of customers were bellied up to the bar, behind which stood a single bartender, reading a newspaper. There were two men and

a painted percentage girl at a table near the back wall. And
then there was a gambler at another table in the corner, his
back to the wall, looking almost fatally bored as he shuffled
a pack of pasteboards. His face was familiar, and as Ethan
bent his steps in the gambler's direction the man looked up
and recognized him.

"It's a small world, after all," said Clooney, delighted.

Too small, thought Ethan sourly. Clooney reminded him
of the Overland, and the Overland reminded him of Julie,
and Julie reminded him of Lilah Webster. His past was one
big vicious circle of bad memories, memories that took him
down a back trail littered with broken dreams and unkept
promises. He had wandered up into the Colorado goldfields,
and now had wandered into this dusty Kansas trail town in
hopes of finding some way to forget, at least momentarily.
Lonesome camps on the high plains were not conducive to
forgetting. Apparently Abilene wasn't, either. He was beginning to think that there was just no escape.

He wearily draped his lean frame on a chair across the
table from the gambler. "Hello, Clooney."

"Payne." The gambler gave Ethan the once-over. He saw
a long, lean man with black hair and dark eyes and a three-
day stubble of beard on gaunt cheeks, wearing down-at-
heel boots, stroud pants, a muslin shirt under a dusty black
frock coat. "You look like you've been to hell and back.
What brings you to Abilene?"

Ethan shrugged. "Nothing in particular." There had been
no rhyme nor reason to his yonderings since leaving Ben
Holladay's employ more than three years ago. First he had
gone to Carson City and lived high off the hog, spending
every last cent of the wages he'd managed to save, indulging
in his every whim. But, in the end, he'd had to admit to himself that self-indulgence had failed to make him feel any better about himself or his prospects. Then he had wandered up
into the Colorado high country, landing a job as a hired gun
for a mining combine, but guarding gold shipments had
quickly gone stale. So then he'd flipped a coin to decide
which way he'd yonder and the coin had come up tails and

he'd turned his horse to the east—and now here he was in Abilene. He didn't feel it necessary to explain all this to Clooney. It was none of the gambler's business, anyway.

"Heard you got fired from the Overland a few years back," said Clooney. "It was a raw deal, if you ask me."

"No, it wasn't."

Clooney raised an eyebrow. He hadn't changed much since Ethan had met him on an Overland stage that had been held up by a gang of road agents. Clooney was a tall, narrow man with dark eyes and bloodless lips in a gaunt, sallow face. "They say you killed an Overland employee in self-defense, but the company didn't care that you were just protecting yourself."

"I had to kill him because he found out I'd been sleeping with his wife," said Ethan bleakly. "What else could he do but try to take me?"

It hadn't been the killing of Joe Cathcott so much as it had been the situation; Cathcott had run the Overland's Wolftrap Station until one day he'd just up and disappeared, leaving his wife Julie to run the place as best she could in his absence. One thing led to another and Ethan had found himself in Julie's bed. And she'd found her way into his heart. But he'd had bad luck with relationships in the past, and he'd hesitated to make the commitment Julie had so desperately wanted. So that when Cathcott unexpectedly returned, she'd given up on Ethan and took her wayward husband back in. Inevitably Cathcott learned of Ethan's trespass, so a confrontation had been unavoidable. Ethan could still remember the terse telegram sent by Ben Holladay—the one that had abruptly terminated his years as an Overland troubleshooter. *Killing Cathcott not in my best interests stop sure you agree stop your services no longer required stop good luck stop.*

"Well," said Clooney, "you may be wondering what I'm doing in this neck of the woods."

"Greener pastures, I'd guess."

"I'm persona non grata in California." The gambler flashed a rueful grin. "Beat a straight with a full house and won a gold mine from a young fool who decided I must have cheated him. Self-defense, I assure you, but unfortunately that tyro's father was an important man. They stuck a murder charge on me. So here I am, the proud owner of what I hear is a very productive gold mine, only I'm in no position to defend my claim. Life isn't fair, is it?"

"Do tell."

Clooney shuffled the cards. "Up for a friendly game?"

"I don't gamble."

"Oh yeah, you told me that before. And I said it was too bad—you'd be good at cards. You had the nerve and the stamina."

"Besides," said Ethan, "I'm stone broke. I don't own a gold mine. In fact, I'd have to turn my pockets out to buy one drink and a bed in a cheap hotel."

"Run into some hard times?"

"I'm as broke as the Ten Commandments."

"I could make you a small loan. Not much—I'd have more to offer except that, as you can see, business isn't booming. I give twenty-five percent to the owner of this splendid establishment, and damn near that again to the city. The 'sin tax,' as we call it."

The bartender came over. "Name your poison, mister."

"Whiskey. But I don't want the stuff you gave that fella who's decorating the front door."

The bartender gave him a funny look, and shrugged. "Happy Jack will come along and take care of him," he said, and walked away.

"He means the local law," said Clooney. "Jack Crawford or one of his badge-toting boys will haul him off to the hoosegow, take everything he has in payment for the misdemeanor fine—drunk and disorderly—and then roll him out of town."

"Sounds like you don't cotton much to Happy Jack."

Clooney leaned forward and pitched his voice in a low whisper. "A thin line separates a lawman from an outlaw. Crawford and his bunch have one foot on either side of the line, if you ask me. They're pushing too hard. Not just the

Texas boys, though that's bad enough. Bad for business, that is. More and more herds are heading over to Ellsworth on account of Crawford's tactics. Fact is, they push *us* too hard, too." Clooney made a gesture that Ethan assumed incorporated every gambler, percentage girl, and saloon keeper in Abilene. "Stick around for a while, Payne, if you're looking for some excitement. This town is a powder keg, and the fuse is awfully short."

"I don't know. I've been thinking about going back to Illinois."

The bartender arrived with Ethan's whiskey. Clooney nodded at the apron, who shrugged and returned to his newspaper without asking Ethan for payment. Ethan took a cautious sip of the amber liquid and determined that it was the genuine article and not a concoction of rubbing alcohol, tea, bitters, and tobacco—just one of several common recipes for the making of rotgut. He took a longer sip, washing away the dust of a long day on the trail.

"Illinois," said Clooney. "Is that where you're from?"

Ethan nodded.

"You've got kin there?"

"My father. But I'm not sure if he's still alive. I haven't heard about him for several years."

"That why you want to go back? To find out about him?"

Ethan shrugged.

"Might find work that suits you in Chicago," said Clooney. "It's a rough town, they say."

Ethan didn't know exactly how to explain to Clooney that it wasn't actually concern about his father that had him contemplating a trip to Illinois, but rather curiosity about a girl named Lilah. A girl he had been in love with, whom he had thought would one day become his wife—and whom he had left behind on an ill-begotten excursion to seek his fortune in California along with his friend Gil Stark. He could still vividly recall every aspect of that sunny summer day so very long ago when he had last seen Lilah, at the old oak tree on the banks of the Rock River.

There was only one problem with going home. He was

afraid of what he would find. The last word he'd had from Lilah was that she was getting married to a man named Stephen, who loved her madly and who treated her like a princess.

"I should never have left," he muttered.

"What did you say?" asked the gambler.

Ethan shook his head. "It's not important." He scraped the chair back and stood up. "See you around, Clooney. Thanks for the drink."

"Don't mention it. Try the Drover's Cottage. Tell the desk clerk to give you a room and put it on my bill." Clooney raised a hand as he saw Ethan prepare to protest. "Like I said, a loan. With interest."

Without saying yea or nay to the gambler's suggestion, Ethan left the Lone Star Saloon. Pausing on the boardwalk, he scanned the quiet, dusty street, an ironic smile curling his lips. He was beginning to think that coming to Abilene had been a mistake. But then, his life had been one mistake after another, ever since he'd made that first big mistake of leaving Illinois and Lilah. The road to hell was paved with good intentions. He'd gone to California to find gold so that he could offer her more than the dreary life of a farmer's wife. But he'd found no gold—just trouble, and heartache. Then he'd moved on to the Overland, working as one of Ben Holladay's troubleshooters, but that had turned out to be another mistake, ending with the killing of Joe Cathcott. And now here he was, stuck in a dusty and dead dull town without a dollar to his name, forced to rely on the charity of a cardsharp. Ethan Payne shook his head ruefully. There wasn't anything for it but to see how his latest mistake would play out. So he bent his steps for the Drover's Cottage. He'd swallow his pride and take the room Clooney had offered. It beat sleeping in the hay at the livery stable, or in some back alley.

CHAPTER TWO

The Drover's Cottage was the most impressive structure in Abilene, standing in splendid isolation surrounded by vacant lots overgrown with weeds. Located at the edge of town near the stockyards and the railroad, the hotel was a boxy clapboard structure, three stories in height, with fifty spacious rooms that were better furnished than your average frontier hostelry. Downstairs there was a bar, a restaurant, and a billiards room. Painted beige, the hotel sported green louvered shutters on its windows and a long veranda lined with chairs, providing its patrons with a shady place to watch the Union Pacific trains come and go. And when the wind was wrong, those patrons were treated to a strong whiff of the stockyards. Most didn't care. Cattle were the lifeblood of Abilene, and many of the guests at the Drover's Cottage depended on them, in one way or the other, for their livelihood.

Joe McCoy, the hotel's founder, had recently sold the establishment to a Texas cattle king by the name of Moses George, and George had started an ambitious undertaking: the addition of an extra forty-odd rooms to the hotel. But as Ethan rode up, he noticed that there were no workers on or near the scaffolds; Mr. George had postponed the work until Abilene's fate was resolved. There were only two men idling away the afternoon in the shade of the veranda, and they didn't look too happy. Ethan could tell they were cattlemen. They watched Ethan intently as he approached, wondering if he might be in the cattle business—or, more to the point, in the cattle business with money to spend—but as he drew closer and they got a better look at him they could tell he was just a drifter, and immediately lost interest.

Clooney was right. Rooms were cheap, and he had good credit with the management. Ethan got a room on the second floor, with a window from which he could see much of Abilene. Dusk was beginning to settle over the treeless plains, and the lights of town were warm golden invitations in the purpling gloom. Ethan figured he might as well have a bath and a shave and a good dinner, but in order to have any of those things he was going to have to sell a belonging. The only things of any real value he had were his horse, his pistol, and a rifle, and he wasn't particularly inclined to part with any of those. He wondered what kind of steady work he could find in town. The saloons and dance halls might have use for a man who knew how to use a gun. Or he could go ahead and risk his horse or guns in a game of chance, and hope he won. Faro? No. In his opinion only a fool "bucked the tiger." Three-card monte? The odds were slightly better. Poker? He'd have to be lucky to win at poker, especially with professionals like Clooney running the games, and he'd never considered himself to be a particularly lucky sort. There was that old saying about how if a man was unlucky in love he'd be lucky at cards. Ethan figured he was about as hapless as a fellow could get where affairs of the heart were concerned, but that dismal state of affairs hadn't seemed to improve his fortune at the gaming tables. And if he lost? It wouldn't be the first time he was stone broke and on foot. No, he'd be better off sticking to his guns and staying away from games of chance.

A knock on the door turned him away from the window, and his dark reflection. Instinctively he kept his hand on the butt of the Remington Army as he opened the door a few scant inches, bracing his foot against the bottom of it. These were apparently desperate times in Abilene, and he knew well that desperate times bred desperados.

The man standing in the hallway was a big, beefy fellow with rust-colored hair and small, ice-blue eyes. There was a tin star on his shirt, a Colt revolver in a cross-draw holster on his hip, and a scattergun in his hand. He looked at Ethan's Remington and then, suspiciously, at Ethan.

"You looking for trouble?" he asked.

"I've never had to look for it."

"Follows you around, does it?" The lawman looked him over from head to toe and nodded, as though he wasn't surprised to find that the man before him attracted trouble. He stepped forward, pushing against the door, and when he felt resistance his eyes narrowed and fastened truculently on Ethan. Ethan decided that even while he had taken an immediate dislike to this man there was nothing much to gain from contesting the threshold. So he moved his foot and stepped back and the lawman brushed by him into the room without so much as asking for an invite, but then that was the kind of man he was—this Ethan could tell in a glance.

"Name's Crawford," said the badge toter. "I'm the town marshal."

"Happy Jack Crawford," said Ethan. "Abilene's one-man welcoming committee?"

Crawford eyed him askance, then raked his gaze over Ethan's scant belongings—saddle, blanket roll, saddlebags, Henry rifle in its saddle boot. "Heard tell a stranger rode into town today. A stranger who had the look of a gunslinger. I came to find out if you were."

They push too hard, Clooney had said.

"I'm no gunslinger."

"Cardsharp, maybe?"

"No."

"Then what are you?"

Ethan thought it over. "I'm just passing through."

Crawford nodded. "Yeah. A no-account drifter. Your kind usually ends up behind bars, or six feet under, because you're too no-account to hold on to an honest job. But in case you're thinking of trying your hand at gambling, you can't work in Abilene without paying a license fee."

So that's what he's here for, thought Ethan. *Come to collect his money.*

"Like I said, Marshal, I'm just passing through."

Crawford grunted, threw one last quick look around the room, then showed himself out. On the threshold he paused. "You strike me as a problem just waiting to happen," he drawled. "You cross over the line in my bailiwick and you'll live just long enough to regret it. You savvy that?"

"I hear you," said Ethan, fiercely struggling to hold his temper in check.

Crawford nodded and sauntered down the hall.

Ethan gently shut the door and muttered an unflattering assessment of Happy Jack Crawford's probable ancestry.

Trying to put the town marshal's unpleasant visit out of his mind, Ethan went ahead with his plans. He hocked his saddle and rifle at the nearest pawn shop, which garnered him enough cash to buy a bath and a shave, a good dinner at the Drover's Cottage restaurant, and enough left over to get him through another day or two if he didn't squander it on cheap whiskey or cheap women.

He wandered back to the Lone Star Saloon, wondering if Clooney would still be there. He was, and his table was busy. With their herds bedded down for the night, some Texas cowpunchers had wandered into Abilene, and there were about a dozen of these dusty, rowdy souls in the Lone Star when Ethan arrived. Three sat at Clooney's table, and in a glance Ethan could tell that they were not faring well. Clooney glanced up and gave him a brief nod, which Ethan answered with one of his own before moving on to the long mahogany. He ordered a shot of good whiskey, intending to make it his one and only of the night, and, as was his habit, scanned each and every denizen of the room. Most of the cowpokes seemed harmless enough, bent only on some good clean fun. But a trio that was standing belly up to the bar bore watching. These three were drinking heavily, and by the belligerent expressions on their faces, the truculent tones of voice, and the way they put their heads together in an earnest and sometimes heated but certainly conspiratorial discussion, Ethan figured it didn't take a genius to see that these boys were probably up to no good.

Ethan nursed his whiskey and divided his attention between the three cowboys at the bar and Clooney's game of poker. Lady Luck was smiling on the gambler tonight. Clooney was winning steadily, so that in a half-hour's time he was up several hundred dollars, taking most of these winnings from a couple of cowboys and a whiskey drummer. The way the Texans at the bar were paying attention to the game had Ethan surmising that perhaps it was Clooney they were planning to roust—there was seldom any love lost between gamblers and Texas drovers. But then one of Happy Jack Crawford's deputies strolled into the Lone Star. The trio at the bar, primed to the brim with liquid brave maker, reacted to the lawman's arrival in a way that made Ethan change his mind where their intentions were concerned. Clearly they'd been waiting for the deputy, who was making his rounds, to arrive at the Lone Star.

As the deputy wandered the length of the bar, checking all the patrons, seeing how they were armed and gauging their moods, one of the cowboys abruptly pushed away from the mahogany to block his path.

"I want to talk to you, mister," sneered the Texan.

"I don't want to talk to you. So step aside."

"You're a Yankee, ain't ya?"

The deputy was a square-built, blond-headed man, with a short-cropped beard and cold blue eyes, and looked to Ethan to come from German or Scandinavian stock. There was no backing down in him; his tone was every bit as belligerent as the cowboy's had been.

"I am. And you're rebel Texas trash. So get out of my way or I'll throw your worthless hide in jail."

"I'm Tell Jenkins. I ride for the K-Bar brand. You've got my brother Clute in jail already. He's been in that iron cage of yours for a week, just 'cause he drank too much snakehead one night. Me and my pards have decided that that's long enough."

"Well, you don't have a say in the matter. The judge will decide that—when he gets around to hearing your brother's case."

"You'll set Clute free if you know what's good for you."

The deputy glowered at Tell Jenkins, then at Jenkins' two saddle pards. "Why don't you boys come and try to take him," he said, and with that, turned on his heel and walked out of the saloon. Watching him, Ethan knew what he was up to. The deputy had measured the odds against him and, finding them not to his liking, had issued a challenge that, if accepted by Tell Jenkins, would place the fight that was surely coming on ground more favorable to the star packer. Ethan shook his head. He'd spent some years as a troubleshooter for the Overland, and in his opinion didn't back down from a confrontation, regardless of how unfavorable the circumstances might be. Not if you were a figure of authority, to whom reputation meant more than anything. You couldn't step around men like Jenkins. That only made matters more dangerous. No, you had to walk right over them.

When they got over their surprise, Jenkins and his two cronies had a good laugh and ordered the barkeep to pour them another drink. Five minutes passed. Ten minutes. Ethan was about to finish off his whiskey and walk outside when Tell Jenkins reared back from the mahogany and drew his thumb buster. The barkeep disappeared behind the mahogany as the Texas drover put two bullets into the pier glass over the back bar. Curses and shouts of alarm mingled with the sound of a deluge of glass shards. From one end of the Lone Star to the other, men sought cover, except for Tell Jenkins—and Clooney, who was in the process of raking in a sizeable pot he'd just won with a trio of queens. And Ethan, who remained unmoved at the end of the bar.

Jenkins reeled into the middle of the room, the focus of attention, as he had intended with the gunplay.

"This town," he declared, "has itself a pack of yeller-bellied lawdogs. I'm Tell Jenkins, and I'm here to tell you . . ."

He put a slug into the saloon's green tin ceiling, and his two friends laughed uproariously. Standing forgotten at the end of the bar, Ethan calmly finished off his whiskey as Jenkins stumbled out of the Lone Star. His two cronies followed. The barkeep peeked warily over the edge of the mahogany.

"They gone?" he asked Ethan.

"You got a scattergun back there?"

"Well, yeah. But . . ."

"Give it to me."

The apron stood up, reached under the bar, produced the shotgun, and slid the sawed-off greener down the bar.

"Take it from me, mister. You stick your nose into other people's business and you're liable to get it shot off," warned the bartender.

"Thanks." Ethan picked up the scattergun, broke it open to confirm that it was loaded, both barrels, and went outside.

Tell Jenkins was in the middle of the street, about fifty yards away.

"Come on, you Yankee coward!" he yelled. "Come take ol' Tell Jenkins to jail—if you can! Where are you, you lily-livered snake? You ain't skeered of Texas trash, now are you?"

Ethan looked for the other two cowpunchers. They were moving down the boardwalk, in deeper shadow, keeping more or less abreast of Jenkins as he walked slowly, uncertainly, down the street. They had their backs turned to the Lone Star, so they didn't see Ethan.

Suddenly another man appeared in the street, farther down, emerging from an alley on the side opposite the boardwalk where Jenkins' saddle pards were stationed. Ethan recognized this new player. It was none other than

Happy Jack Crawford. Though he didn't look at all happy.

"Drop the artillery, cowboy," drawled Crawford. He held a shotgun at hip level.

Jenkins chuckled. "You got the drop on me, now don't you?"

"It appears so. Now do as I say, boy, so I don't have to blow a hole right through you."

"Sure thing, Marshal."

Jenkins threw himself sideways. Crawford's shotgun roared, spewing flame and buckshot from both barrels. But the Texan was quick as lightning, and he hit the ground and rolled and came up unscathed, his pistol barking once, twice—and Crawford shuddered, stepped back, made a half turn, and then toppled to his knees, gutshot. Astonished, Ethan realized that Jenkins had been play-acting; he hadn't been staggering drunk at all—no man could have been drunk and done what he had just done. Jenkins stepped closer to Crawford and raised the pistol. Ethan realized what the Texan was about to do. Realized, too, that if he rushed forward and triggered the scattergun in his hands he might be able to prevent Happy Jack's execution. But he didn't. Because Crawford was as good as dead, anyway, and if Ethan rushed forward he was as good as dead, too, because Tell Jenkins' buddies were still lurking in the shadows. Jenkins coldly put one more bullet into the back of the marshal's head, and Crawford's body slammed face-down into the dust of the Abilene street.

"Jesus, Tell," muttered one of the cowboys on the boardwalk.

Ethan stepped, cat-footed, to the end of the boardwalk at the corner of the Lone Star Saloon. Something moved in the black shadows of the alley that separated the watering hole from the adjacent building, and Ethan whirled, a hair's breadth away from triggering the scattergun. An errant glimmer of light from somewhere flashed across the tin star on the chest of the man who crouched in the alley, and as he backed away, out of the deep shadow, Ethan recognized him as the bearded deputy who had walked away from Jenkins in the saloon only moments ago.

"I don't want no part of this," whispered the deputy, his eyes wide with fear, and Ethan could tell he had witnessed it all.

A hot surge of contempt left a sour taste in Ethan's mouth. Jenkins had been right about this one. He lacked the backbone necessary to keep the lid on a trail town.

"Then shed that badge and you'll be free of it," hissed Ethan.

The deputy plucked the tin star off his shirt and let it drop from his fingers as he turned and pelted down the alley.

Ethan scanned the street. The two cowboys lingered on the boardwalk about thirty paces up the street. Jenkins stood over Crawford's corpse, staring down at his handiwork with a sour expression on his face, as though he was disappointed that it had taken so little time to kill the man. None of the Texans were, as yet, aware of his presence. *You can just turn and walk away from this and no one will be the wiser*, Ethan told himself. *You've got no stake in it.* But he knew that wasn't precisely so. It had been his choice to take the scattergun and walk out of the saloon and buy into the trouble he'd sensed was brewing. He'd done it for purely selfish gain—to advertise the presence of a gun for hire newly arrived in Abilene. But now the situation had taken on an entirely different context. The cold-blooded way in which Jenkins had finished off Crawford made Ethan's skin crawl. And now he couldn't walk away without wondering if he was spooked by just how lethal that Texas cowpuncher had turned out to be.

Spooked or not, he made up his mind to act. With strides that were long and quick and full of purpose, he stepped out into the street, closing in on Jenkins. The two cowboys on the boardwalk spotted him before Jenkins did, and they didn't miss the scattergun in Ethan's grasp, or the fact that it was aimed right at them. He was about twenty paces away, which was just about the maximum range for a greener if you wanted it to do serious damage, but the two cowpunchers had to take a few precious seconds to measure distance and odds before they risked calling out a warning to Jenkins—and that was all the time Ethan needed to come up behind the gun-happy drover. Ethan was just a few strides away when Jenkins heard him and whirled and stared, hesitating for a fateful instant. Then, a split second before Ethan reached him, panic touched his swarthy features and he brought the pistol up and pulled the trigger at point blank range.

The hammer fell on an empty chamber.

"You already spent six," said Ethan softly—and with a cold smile drove the butt of the scattergun into the cowboy's face.

That had been his ace in the hole. Tell Jenkins had fired three bullets inside the Lone Star—two into the pier glass and one into the tin ceiling. He'd fired two more into Happy Jack Crawford's belly, and yet another into the marshal's skull. The only gamble on Ethan's part was in banking on the assumption that Jenkins hadn't bothered reloading his smoke maker upon exiting the saloon.

Jenkins collapsed in a heap, his unconscious form draped over the body of Happy Jack Crawford. Ethan spun as the Texan's two friends, recovering from their uncertainty, left the boardwalk and came toward him. They had not yet drawn their pistols, but they were clearly thinking about doing just that.

"Just who the hell are you?" rasped one of the cowpunchers. He had looked for a badge and, seeing none, couldn't fathom why Ethan was buying into this dangerous brand of fun.

"Nobody," said Ethan.

"How come you done that?" asked the second man, nodding at the fallen Jenkins.

"You ain't no lawman," added the first. "And we ain't never seen you before, so it can't be on account of no grudge. Besides, Tell don't ever leave nobody alive who has a grudge against him. So this is none of your business."

"You're right," said Ethan. "I have no vested interests here. That should worry you." He pointed the scattergun at the unconscious Tell Jenkins' head. "Because I don't much care if he lives or dies. I'm betting you do, though. So back off, or I'll blow his brains out."

That stopped the cowboys cold. They weren't sure if Ethan was serious, but they weren't going to take the chance.

"Let him go," said the second man. "Just walk away."

"Your friend is going to jail. He just killed the town marshal."

"You ain't taking him to jail," snarled one of the Texans.

"It's either the jail or the funeral parlor. You decide."

"Let's go, Dusty," said the second cowboy.

"Good idea," said Ethan. "You boys are making me nervous, and this greener's got a light trigger."

"This ain't over," said the one named Dusty. "You ain't seen the last of us."

The second cowboy grabbed Dusty by the arm and pulled him away. They went to their horses, tied in front of the Lone Star, and rode hell for leather out of town, taking a cayuse that Ethan presumed belonged to Tell Jenkins along with them. Ethan didn't relax—and didn't take the barrels of the scattergun away from the unconscious Texan's skull—until Dusty and his saddle pard were out of sight. Only then did he lower the scattergun's hammers, taking a deep breath and trying to smooth out his nerves. All along the street, people were cautiously emerging from doorways. Several men converged on the middle of the street, where Ethan stood over the bodies of Jenkins and Crawford. He didn't know any of them, and they scarcely glanced at him. Their focus was on Happy Jack.

"My God, he killed the marshal," muttered one. "Who is he? Anyone recognize him?"

"I don't know his name," said another of the men, "but I've seen him around. I think he rides for the K-Bar brand. That would be McKittrick's bunch."

"Lord help us," murmured a third. "Where are the deputies?" He cast an anxious glance up and down the street.

Ethan considered mentioning that at least one of the deputies was probably on his way out of town by now. But nobody had asked him, and his mother had taught him that it was usually wiser never to volunteer information.

Finally, belatedly, one of the men rested his gaze upon Ethan and scowled. "Who are you, anyway?"

"Name is Ethan Payne."

"I think I know that name," said one of the others. "Can't quite place it, though. Were you a lawman somewhere?"

Ethan shook his head. "I've never worn a badge."

"My name is Ransom," said the first one. "I'm a member of the town council. So are these fellows. Hope you don't mind my asking, but what brings you to Abilene?"

"Just passing through."

"Why would a drifter get involved in something like this?" asked the man who thought he'd heard Ethan's name before.

Ethan tossed him the scattergun, without warning. Startled, the man nearly dropped the greener.

"You're right," said Ethan. "I guess this Texan is your problem, not mine. Good luck."

And with that he turned and went back to the Lone Star.

CHAPTER THREE

Abilene's town fathers came for him the next morning. George Washington Ransom, hero of the Civil War, a politician of which great things were expected, was currently serving as the mayor of Abilene. As mayor he had very little autonomy, but he sat at the head of the table when the town council met, and had some say in the matters that the council took under consideration. Then there was John Tyler White, representing the merchants, a man who had made his fortune launching several highly successful establishments in Independence and St. Joseph, Missouri. But it wasn't the money that mattered to White. It was the thrill of opening a business and fighting for its survival, and that was why he was here in Abilene. Finally there was William T. Langford, a man whose family had made its fortune in steam engines and who had invested heavily in Abilene. It was said of Langford that he owned a piece of more than half the businesses in town, and a good deal of the residential real estate belonged to him at one time or another, too. He, perhaps, had more to lose than anyone if Abilene faltered.

Ethan had risen with the sun, shaved, put on clean clothes, and was downstairs in the restaurant eating breakfast when the trio arrived. He saw them coming, crossing the wide, dusty street, clad more or less alike in their black broadcloth suits and white linen shirts and hand-tooled half boots. Their faces were set in grim lines. Their stride was purposeful. They were men on a mission. Ethan had been halfway expecting them.

He sat with his back to the far wall so that he could see the doorway that connected the restaurant to the lobby of the Drover's Cottage, so he saw the three enter and confer briefly with the clerk at the desk, who pointed in Ethan's direction. Ransom took the lead as the three filed into the restaurant, making for Ethan's table, sparing the other diners, of which there were a half dozen, the briefest of looks. Ethan had a hunch that Ransom usually took the lead where this bunch was concerned.

"Good morning, Mr. Payne," said Ransom, taking off his hat and fastening eyes as gray as cold steel on Ethan. "I hope you slept well."

"Pull up a chair, gentlemen."

They sat down around the table, and the waiter rushed forward, quite aware of the personages who had just arrived in his bailiwick. Ransom and White ordered coffee, while Langford declined to order anything but requested a spittoon, as he had a wad of chewing tobacco bulging in his cheek. The waiter departed, and for a moment no one spoke as the three men looked Ethan over, taking his measure in better circumstances than the night before—a dark and bloody street with the scent of powder smoke lingering in the air.

"Well, Mr. Payne," said Ransom. "That was a brave thing you did last night." He nodded gravely, like a man who was an expert when it came to bravery, and who put great store by it. "Tell Jenkins is a nasty piece of work. A cold-blooded killer. You took a big chance."

"The question is," said Langford, "why did you do it?"

"That's obvious," said White, and Ethan thought his smile was about as close to a sneer as you could get. "It was very neatly played, Mr. Payne. A couple of eyewitnesses have suggested that you might have stopped Jenkins *before* he put a bullet in Jack Crawford's brainpan. But you chose not to. Which leads one to think that perhaps you deemed it in your best interests to wait until the town marshal had been killed before intervening."

"Christ, John," rasped Ransom. "Stop beating around the damned bush and just come out and say what you have on your mind."

"I made a few inquiries last night, and received a telegram this morning in reply." White fished the telegram out of a vest pocket, unfolded it, and proceeded to read its contents aloud. " 'Ethan Payne was troubleshooter for Overland for six years stop He did commendable work until the end stop Killed one too many men and left under a cloud.' From a district manager by the name of Tattersall."

Ethan grunted. It was a far better recommendation that he would have expected from John Tattersall who, during his period of employment with the Overland, had always been a thorn in his side, accusing him of riding roughshod over the law.

"Your point being, John?" asked Ransom.

"That Mr. Payne might have come to Abilene looking for work. And when Tell Jenkins put a gun to Happy Jack's head, he saw an opportunity coming his way."

Ransom looked warily at Ethan, trying to discern from his expression what his reaction to White's accusation would be. But Ethan was inscrutable.

The waiter arrived with the two cups of coffee. He went away and came back with a spittoon for Langford, who immediately put it to good use. This gave Ethan time to consider White's words. He'd had plenty of time since the showdown on the street last night to figure out what his motives had been. He'd concluded that his decision to interfere stemmed from a hope that something would happen that would save him from having to make a decision about whether to go to Illinois. Something *had* happened, and now that Ransom and White and Langford were here he was pretty certain that Abilene, Kansas, was as close to Illinois as he was going to get this year. He wasn't yet real sure how he felt about that.

"Crawford was as good as dead already," Ethan told White, his voice flat, devoid of emotion. "Jenkins had two friends up in the shadows I needed to worry about. So I wasn't going to go charging out into the middle of the street."

"Besides," said Langford, "who could have foreseen that Jenkins would commit such a heinous act. Good Lord, he had already put two slugs in poor Crawford. Only a savage would have done what he did after that."

"That's true," said Ransom. "And, if there's any justice in the world, he'll hang for it."

"Assuming we can keep him in jail long enough to try him," said White dryly.

Langford scowled. "We must, John. By God, we must! Abilene cannot afford to get a reputation as a lawless town."

Because that would be bad for business, mused Ethan, reading Langford as the type who would worry less about justice than about profit.

"Which brings us to the reason for our visit this morning, Mr. Payne," said Ransom, relieved to be getting, at last, to the point. "You've apparently worked for Ben Holladay for a number of years, in a job that I think everyone would agree has to be one of the most dangerous in the West. Holladay put up the money for a stage route that connected California with the rest of the country long before the transcontinental railroad, but it was men like you who kept it up and running in a lawless land. You've obviously got plenty of backbone. And you've got the kind of experience that would serve a town marshal well."

"Hold on just a minute," said White curtly. "Before you go offering this man the keys to the city, G.W., I at least want to know what this Tattersall fellow meant when he wrote that Payne here had killed one man too many."

"Fair enough," said Ethan, flatly. "I killed a man. It was self-defense. But he was an Overland employee."

"Why was this man trying to kill you?" asked White, eyes narrowed.

Ethan didn't hesitate. He knew he had to be careful. These men were interviewing him for the vacancy created by Happy Jack Crawford's demise, and they had a certain kind of man in mind, and that man would be one who wouldn't lie—at least to them.

"He thought I was messing with his wife."

"And were you?" asked White bluntly.

"Yes."

Scowling, White settled back in his chair and looked at Ransom, eyebrow cocked, an "I-told-you-he-was-no-good" expression on his face. It was one thing to be a killer; on the frontier there were plenty of reasons why you might be, and most men were willing to give you a lot of slack in that regard. But being an adulterer was something else again. It was akin to being a horse thief. Horses and women were highly prized and a man who would steal one or the other was suspect.

"Why were you having an affair with another man's wife, Mr. Payne?" asked Ransom. He'd realized that Ethan would not offer information without being asked to do so.

"Her husband was a station master. He ran off and left her. She was lonely, and I liked her, and one thing led to another. After many months he suddenly returned. He learned the truth, and in my job as troubleshooter I couldn't avoid the station forever. He came at me and I shot him dead. That's the long and short of it."

"So Holladay let you go," said Ransom.

Ethan nodded. "The killing was bad for morale. A lot of rumors were circulating. I didn't blame him for cutting me loose."

It was Ransom's turn to look at White with eyebrow raised, a silent question on his face. Was White satisfied with Ethan's explanation of the events that culminated in his being fired by the Stagecoach King, Ben Holladay? White simply shrugged. Ethan sensed that the man wasn't completely sold on the idea of hiring him to be Abilene's new town marshal, but he wasn't going to throw up any further objections. White turned to Langford.

"You have any questions, Colonel?"

"Hmm." Langford extracted a long nine from his coat

pocket. "Well, I . . . I don't know. . . . Mind if I smoke, Mr. Payne?"

Ethan gestured for him to go ahead.

"Then we'd like to make you a proposition," said Ransom. "Jack Crawford was our city marshal. We'd like to know if you'd be interested in the job now that it has, um, come available."

Ethan had already made up his mind not to jump at the offer too readily. It wouldn't do to appear too eager.

"What about your deputy marshals?"

Ransom shook his head. "One of them rode out of town last night. I suspect he lost his nerve."

The bearded man who had walked away from Tell Jenkins in the Lone Star Saloon. Ethan didn't bother telling Ransom that the man hadn't had any nerve to begin with. He'd just been a bully with a badge. Such men would not last long against Texas rowdies.

"We've decided the other two deputies just aren't qualified," added White. "They were Crawford's men, you see. We didn't pick them in the first place."

"And that's why you're not sure if you can keep Tell Jenkins locked up."

"We're fairly certain the K-Bar outfit will try to break him out," said Langford over the smoldering cigar clenched between his teeth.

"I'd expect nothing less," said Ethan. "They're pretty much obliged to make an effort."

"And do you think you can stop them?" asked White.

"I'd have to. Because if Jenkins doesn't swing for what he did, wearing a badge in Abilene will just make you a target for every Texas cowpuncher with a six-shooter and a grudge."

"So it wouldn't have anything to do with justice, where you're concerned," said White dryly.

"I'm all for justice," replied Ethan. "But self-preservation is a strong motivator."

"Well, at least you're honest," said White.

"So you accept our offer?" asked Langford.

"Well, that depends," said Ethan.

"You have conditions?"

"A few."

"What are they?"

"First, you lower the assessments on the gamblers and percentage girls and saloon owners."

"Now just hold on there," rasped White. "One thing we don't need is a lawman who sides with the bad element."

"I'm not siding with them," said Ethan. "But if you don't want Abilene to dry up and blow away you're going to have to stop worrying about lining your pockets quite so fast."

"And how do we pay your salary if we do as you suggest?" asked Ransom.

"Fines alone will pay for your police force, and then some."

"You'd have to make more arrests than Crawford did."

"I would expect to. For one thing because I want an ordinance passed that prohibits the carrying of firearms within the town limits."

Ransom nodded. "In fact, we've considered just such a statute. But Crawford didn't think he could enforce it. I take it you think you can."

"Worth a try. Crawford probably concentrated on taking money from the gamblers and saloon keepers because it was generally easier."

"Jack Crawford was no coward, if that's what you're implying, sir," said Langford. "He didn't shy away from tangling with the Texans when he had to."

"I'm not saying he was yellow. I'm saying he was inclined to take the easy way. But he failed to look at the big picture. You *need* the people Mr. White here calls the bad element. If it becomes too expensive for them to set up shop in Abilene they'll just go somewhere else."

"I sometimes think that wouldn't be so bad," said White. "They give respectable merchants a bad name."

"I hate to tell you this, Mr. White, but the cowboys don't come here just to buy a new hat at trail's end. They want their fun. It's all they've been thinking about for a hundred days and nights on the trail. And if they can't have it in Abilene they'll go somewhere else, too."

"Any other conditions?" asked Langford. He sounded like he'd suddenly remembered an urgent appointment elsewhere, and was in a hurry to conclude the negotiations.

"Just one more. Don't try to tell me how to do my job. This is your town, I realize that. So if you don't like the way I do things you can fire me, and that's fine. But unless you're prepared to do that, leave me alone."

Ethan looked them in the eye, each one in turn. White didn't like it one bit. Langford looked a bit disgruntled. Ransom was inscrutable.

"We'll talk it over amongst ourselves, Mr. Payne," said Ransom, sensing, as Ethan did, that both of his comrades had reservations. "We will inform you of our decision before the day is out."

"Fine," said Ethan. "I'll be around."

The three men left. Ethan finished his meal and then went out onto the veranda to watch the wind off the high plains blowing dust and trash across the empty lots that surrounded the Drover's Cottage. He looked at Abilene with new eyes—the eyes of a man who isn't just passing through, the eyes of one who couldn't help but wonder what misery lay in store for him here. For that always seemed to be the way of it. Every time he thought he had a promising new beginning he discovered that it was really just a detour on the path to disappointment. With his good friend Gil Stark he had gone to California with dreams of striking it rich. Instead, he'd lost the woman he loved, another who loved him, and watched his friend become an outlaw. After that he'd thought working for Ben Holladay as troubleshooter for the Overland would be a step in the right direction. Only that had gone sour, too, in the manner he had just described to the three town fathers of Abilene.

Ethan didn't believe in much, but he did believe in Fate, and he didn't think it was a coincidence that curiosity had brought him to Kansas just in time to be there, in the Lone Star Saloon, having a drink, when a chain of events that culminated in the killing of Happy Jack Crawford began. No, a whimsical Fate had engineered it all. For what purpose he would discover soon enough. But Ethan doubted it would turn out well. Not very much had ever since he'd left Illinois.

He was still on the veranda, sitting alone in a rocking chair, gazing out at the half-empty stockyard when Ransom returned. The latter handed Ethan the town marshal's badge without saying anything. G.W. Ransom was not the kind of man who would waste his time stating the obvious.

"You should know," said Ethan, "that I intend to get rid of the rest of Crawford's men."

"What will you do for deputies?"

"We need to put out the word. Advertise for professional lawmen. Bring them in, let me talk to them, and if it looks like we can work together, you can hire them."

"I know a couple of good men—"

"No," said Ethan firmly. "I want outsiders. Men nobody around here knows. Men who have no interests in this town to protect."

"Then what will motivate them? A desire for justice?" Ransom sounded skeptical.

Ethan smiled. "Not really. Such men are hunters. And the badge gives them a license to hunt. It's what they live for. And it's why they generally stay on the right side of the law."

Ransom was watching him speculatively. "I think you've just described yourself, Mr. Payne. Personally, I think Abilene has found the lawman she needs. But John White does not share in that sentiment. I think, however, that he'll come around in time. You're right about the people he calls the 'bad element.' We do need them." Ransom gestured at the stockyard. "Abilene is dying before its time. We need to make some sacrifices, turn things around, or before long this will just be a ghost town. John doesn't seem to understand that. But I do. And I think your approach is the right one for the times."

"I'll try to live up to your expectations," said Ethan.

Ransom smiled and extended a hand. "If McKittrick and the K-Bar crew have anything to say about it, Mr. Payne, you won't even live out the week."

Ethan shook the proffered hand, and returned the smile.

Once Ransom had taken his leave, Ethan went up to his room to retrieve his Henry repeating rifle before heading out and down the street to the Abilene jail. Both of Crawford's deputies were on duty, and they had the jail locked down tight. They took some convincing to open the door for Ethan, and they were quick to shut and bolt it once he was inside. Both men, Ethan noticed, were armed to the teeth. And they had worried eyes. This was because of the only two prisoners in the cell block. Ethan checked on Tell Jenkins. The Texas cowboy was brooding in silence behind strap iron, sitting slump-shouldered on a narrow bunk staring at the scuffed toes of his cowboy boots. In the cell next to him was another cowboy, and he bore a striking resemblance to the first, leading Ethan to assume that the second drover was Tell's brother Clute. When he saw Ethan, Tell Jenkins jumped to his feet like his pants were on fire.

"You!" rasped Jenkins. "You're the one who did this."

He gestured at his face, and for the first time Ethan got a good look at his handiwork from the night before. The cowpuncher's left eye was blackened and swollen shut. His nose was swollen. His upper lip had been cut, and was also swollen. In fact, the entire left side of his face was misshapen.

"You're one lucky son of a bitch," muttered Jenkins.

"Lucky, I guess, to know how to count to six," said Ethan, with a smirk.

"Your luck will run out soon enough." Jenkins' eyes narrowed. "Just who the hell are you, anyway? You a lawman?"

"I am now."

"So you're the new town marshal, is that it?" Jenkins grinned. It wasn't a pretty sight. "When I get out of here I'll do the same to you that I done to that bastard Crawford."

"The day you get out of here will be the day you take that long walk to the gallows."

"My brother won't dance on the end of no Kansas rope," drawled Clute Jenkins. "I can tell you that much."

Ethan shrugged. "Reckon we'll find out, soon enough."

He turned his back on the Texans' cell and stepped out of the cell block, closing the door behind him, and focused his attention on the deputies. One was tall and lanky. The other was of medium height and stocky. "You two expecting company?" he asked.

"Yeah," said the tall one. "Company on horses wearin' the K-Bar brand."

Ethan shook his head. "Not your concern any longer." He took the tin star from his pocket and pinned it on the breast of his dusty black frock coat.

The two deputies stared at the badge in disbelief.

"How'd you come by that?" asked the stocky one.

"Mr. Ransom loaned it to me. And since he did, you boys are out of a job."

"What?"

"You heard me. Go see Ransom and collect what's coming to you. But I'll take those stars before you go."

"Who's taking our place?" asked the tall one.

"Haven't got anybody at the moment."

The tall deputy leered. "You figure you can keep that Texan in jail all by your lonesome."

Ethan sighed. "You're not reading me. It's not your concern anymore."

"Fine," said the stocky one, disgusted. He threw his badge on the kneehole desk that stood in one corner of the office. "But if it's all the same to you I think I'll stick around town for a spell. I wouldn't mind seeing your bloody carcass lying out there in the street. And that's where you'll wind up when the K-Bar outfit rides into town."

"Thanks for the vote of confidence. Now get the hell out of my jail."

CHAPTER FOUR

Ethan stayed at the jail until noon, getting acquainted with his new surroundings. The building was constructed of stone, with a door front and back, two windows in the office and only a transom above the back door to provide any natural light for the cell block. The windows and the transom were covered with strap iron, and in addition the former had thick wooden shutters with cross-shaped gun ports. Both doors were made of heavy timbers secured together with strap iron and bolts, and the bars that secured them from the inside were two-inch-thick timbers. The office was fairly small—sixteen by twenty feet—and furnished with the kneehole desk, a gun cabinet, a potbelly stove, a crate nailed to a wall and holding a few cans of beans and a bag of coffee, and a bunk nestled in a back corner. The cell block consisted of four strap-iron cells, each approximately six feet by eight feet, all in a row on one side of the room, with a passageway leading to the back door. The back door opened onto a narrow, trash-strewn alley. Located on the west side of Abilene's main street, the jail was flanked on one side by a mercantile and on the other by a photographer's gallery that also doubled as the coroner's office. Behind the jail, across the alley, was an adobe wall about five feet high—the back of a livery that fronted the next street over.

Finding a ring of keys in a desk drawer, Ethan made sure the Jenkins boys were locked up tight before leaving the jail; not only were the cells secured but also both doors to the cell block itself. Then he walked to the Lone Star Saloon. As he had hoped, the gambler, Clooney, was there. Having played cards most of the night, Clooney had slept through most of the morning, rising at ten-thirty and having a shave and breakfast before arriving at the saloon at noon. He was back at his customary table now, looking well groomed and fully rested, waiting for a likely prospect to wander in.

"Well I'll be damned," said Clooney when he saw the badge pinned to Ethan's frock coat. "It's true! They offered you the job and by God you took it. I guess Illinois is going to have to wait a while."

"I guess so."

Clooney shook his head. "You can't be any worse than Happy Jack."

"That's quite an endorsement. Thanks."

"You in the mood for some free advice? Just watch your back."

"Sure, Clooney, I need a favor."

"Really." Clooney was suddenly wary.

"I need you and a couple of other men to keep an eye on my prisoners while I'm gone. I should be back by sundown."

"You've got to be kidding."

"I just fired all of Crawford's deputies."

"They won't be missed. But you must know you're asking a hell of a lot."

"I know. But I figure you owe me. You and all the rest of your kind."

Clooney tilted his head to one side. "Is that right? How so?"

"Ransom and the others agreed to lower the assessments."

"Now how did you get them to go for that?"

"It was a condition of my taking the job."

Clooney shuffled his pasteboards a moment, thinking it over. "I guess there's no denying that I do owe you, then," he conceded. "But I don't cotton to standing in the path of those K-Bar rowdies when they ride in here to set Tell Jenkins and his brother free."

"I'm not sure it will come to that."

"For one thing," drawled the gambler, "if I kill a Texas cowboy I'm finished in this town and any other in Kansas. The word will get around and just about every drover coming up the trail will be gunning for me."

"Okay. Forget it." Ethan began to turn away.

"Hold on," said Clooney, and sighed. "I'll take care of your damned prisoners for you, Ethan. Just don't make this a habit, okay?"

"Thanks. I knew I could count on you."

"If that's true then you're the first person who ever has. But where are you going, anyway?"

"I'm going to ride out and pay a visit to a couple of those Texas outfits."

Clooney just stared at him. "That's the craziest thing I've ever heard. You go around looking for trouble, don't you?"

"That's not what I'm looking for."

"When they bring you in stone cold dead what am I supposed to do with the Jenkins boys?"

Ethan shrugged. "Cut 'em loose, if you want. I'll be dead, so what will I care?"

He reached the camp of the Rocking J outfit by mid-afternoon, the burning heart of another dry and dusty day on the plains of Kansas. Checking his horse at the summit of a low rise, he scanned the pale blue sky. Not a cloud in sight. The rains would have to come soon, he mused, or the whole state and everything in it would simply dry up and blow away.

Down below, the bawling of hundreds of cattle filled the

air. The Rocking J herd of Texas longhorns was spread out before him, partially obscured by a haze of dust. The outfit's camp was situated in the lee of a crescent-shaped hill about a quarter mile to the west; Ethan could clearly see the chuck wagon and the picket line of saddled horses. A few of the cowboys were riding the circuit around the herd, and another was keeping tabs on the remuda of horses—each drover had a string of five to seven cow ponies that he'd brought along on the push. But most of the outfit had nothing better to do than while away the hours in camp. It was that or go into town, and there wasn't much point in doing the latter until they got paid, and they weren't getting paid—at least not the full sum owed them for three months on the trail—until the herd was sold. Ethan was well aware of the fact that this situation was tailor-made to produce a gang of highly perturbed cowboys.

Prompting his horse into motion, Ethan rode on toward the camp. There was no time to waste. He'd told Clooney he would be back in Abilene by sundown and he had at least one other outfit besides this one to call on before he was done.

As he drew near he could hear that someone was blowing on a harmonica, rendering a mournful version of *Red River Valley*. Four Texans sat around a cook fire where a pot of coffee was brewing. Three more were over by the chuck wagon. They had already pegged Ethan for a stranger, and he noticed that most of them had their hands resting near their pistols. They could see the star on his coat, but Kansas law was no friend to a Texas cowpuncher.

About twenty paces from the camp Ethan checked his horse and stepped down out of the saddle. To address these men from astride his horse would be a grievous breach of range etiquette.

"Howdy, boys," he said. "Who's the big smoke here?"

The cowboys exchanged glances. Ethan could see the wariness at the corners of their eyes and mouths. A man stepped forward.

"I'm the boss of this outfit. Who are you and what do you want?"

Ethan looked him over and shook his head, smiling. "Straw boss, maybe. I want to talk to the big augur. The man who owns that herd yonder, and who pays you your wages."

Another man stepped up—he'd been one of those at the chuck wagon. He had a cup of steaming java in hand. Somewhat older than the other cowboys, the burden of command was etched deep in his craggy face. Though Ethan knew nothing about this man, he couldn't help but respect him simply for what he was. A Texas cattleman had to be one tough and determined hombre, because it took buckets of blood, sweat, and tears to carve a ranch out of the wild country. This was a man whose willpower had to be monumental, and whose ability to withstand pain and punishment was surpassed only by his willingness to inflict the same on anyone or anything that stood in the way of his achieving the goals he'd set for himself.

"I'm Jake Weller," he said, his voice raspy like a file on a horseshoe. "I own the Rocking J and everything on it." It wasn't braggadocio so much as it was a warning to Ethan that Weller was ready, willing, and able to keep possession of all that belonged to him.

"Ethan Payne, town marshal of Abilene. I'd like a minute of your time, Mr. Weller."

"Well, if you're going to ask that nice, you can have two minutes."

"Got any of that crank to spare?"

"Cookie, get the man a cup to drink out of."

The outfit's cook, a balding, white-bearded Mexican wearing a grimy canvas apron, tossed Ethan a tin cup. Ethan sat on his heels and poured some java from the coffee pot that was balanced on the stones rimming the fire. The coffee was strong enough to float a horseshoe. Weller hunkered down across the campfire from him.

"What brings you out this way, Marshal?" asked Weller. "Can't be any of my men in trouble, seeing as how I've got them all here, and they're not allowed into Abilene."

"I've come to ask a favor of you, Mr. Weller, and the owners of the other herds staked out around here."

"Even the K-Bar?"

Ethan smiled. "Figured you knew all about that by now. That's part of why I'm here. I've got two Texans in my jail. One of them is going to be tried for killing my predecessor, Happy Jack Crawford."

"Happy Jack was as low down as a snake's belly. He liked to ride roughshod over Texas boys. That's why my outfit was steering clear of Abilene."

"I understand. And what you say about Crawford may be so. But it's not the point. Tell Jenkins killed a lawman and he's going to go on trial and I suspect he will be found guilty and sentenced to hang by the neck until he's dead."

Weller's eyes narrowed. "You really think this Jenkins feller will step foot on a gallows?"

"He has to. Or we might as well shut Abilene down. They'll say the town is too lawless to let live."

"Some of these boys wouldn't mind if Abilene was shut down."

"I know. But I've come to ask you not to side with the K-Bar on this. If McKittrick wants you to buy into it, I'd be obliged if you would decline his offer."

"And why should I do that, Marshal?"

"Because Abilene needs the Texas trade, and you need Abilene. Now that Happy Jack is gone, I'm going to do all I can to make Abilene a town friendly to outfits like yours."

Weller sipped his coffee. "McKittrick sent his segundo over this morning to tell me he wants to meet with me and the owners of the other herds tonight at his camp. Seems he has in mind burning Abilene right down to the ground."

"I'm not going to let that happen."

"You're an intrepid soul, Marshal." Weller smiled. "That's what a reporter down Texas way called me once. I like the sound of it, and you riding in here bold as brass like this, seems to me you fit the bill."

"This is a bad season for all concerned," said Ethan,

"and tempers are short. I'm just trying to do my job—
keeping the lid on."

"No reflection on you, Marshal, but I think you might
be a day late and a dollar short. I don't know this Tell
Jenkins feller. But I know McKittrick. Well enough to
know he will not allow you to stretch the neck of one of
his boys, no matter how wild that boy is or what he's done.
Now it ain't that McKittrick is a lawbreaker himself, or
much tolerates his employees breaking the law. It's just that
he expects to be the one to dispense justice. And it's particularly galling to him to think of a Texan being judged—
much less executed—by a bunch of Kansans."

"I'm not asking you to help me hang Jenkins," said
Ethan. "I'm just asking you to mind your own business.
Then we'll all get along. Crawford's dead and I hog-legged
all his deputies today. Abilene will be a different place from
now on. More friendly to cowboys. I'll see to that, as long
as I'm wearing this piece of tin."

Weller took the makings from his shirt pocket and offered them to Ethan, who declined, and sat on his heels,
watching the Texas cattle king roll a smoke. He could tell
that Weller was doing a lot of thinking in the meantime.
He'd made his pitch and there was nothing to be gained by
overselling it.

Once he had the quirly rolled and lighted and clenched
between his teeth, Weller glanced around at the faces of
his drovers, who had been hanging on every word that had
passed between their boss and Abilene's lawman.

"I like a man who knows how to talk straight. What do
you boys say?"

The drovers exchanged glances.

"It's the K-Bar's fight, I reckon," said the first to speak
up. "Not ours."

"I don't cotton to the idea of a Texan hanging from a
Kansan rope," said another. "But I rode with the K-Bar—
and Tell Jenkins—before I signed on with the Rocking J.
And even back then we all kind of figured Jenkins would

come to a bad end. I won't fight against him, but I won't fight for him, either."

"We're with you, boss," said a third. "Whatever you say goes."

Weller nodded. He could look at the others and see that no one was going to voice an opinion contrary to those just enunciated. "Okay, then. We won't buy into this, Marshal. You have my word on it."

"That's plenty good enough for me," said Ethan, relieved. He finished the coffee, put the cup down, and stood up. "Thanks for the java."

Weller flicked the spent cigarette away and also rose. Standing hipshot across the fire from Ethan, he smiled lopsidedly. "Since it's you all by your lonesome against McKittrick and the K-Bar, Marshal, I reckon I better take this opportunity to say it's been good to know you."

A couple of the cowboys chuckled at that. Ethan just smiled. He didn't expect these men to like him. But he could tell that at least they respected him, because he'd had the grit to ride right into their camp and tell them straight out what he was after. No, they would never like him—not even if he managed by some miracle to prevail over the K-Bar crowd, or turned Abilene into a trail town that was every drover's dream. A man who wore a badge was a fool if he thought he'd ever win a popularity contest. Especially among Texas cowboys, who were half-wild buckers of authority and bull-stubborn in their independence.

Mounting up, Ethan rode out of the Rocking J camp and headed south, for he'd been told that there was another herd being held in that direction. He could only hope that he would have as much luck with the next cow crowd. He trusted Weller to keep his word, and that meant he'd whittled down the odds of his survival in the coming fight from impossible to only highly unlikely. If he could talk the other outfits into steering clear of the trouble that was brewing, the odds would get even better. Not that they'd ever be very good.

*   *   *

He got back to Abilene late into the night. Hitching his weary mount to a tie rail in front of the jailhouse, he went to the door and called out to Clooney, who lifted the bar and let him in. A quick glance 'round the office showed Ethan that all seemed to be in order. Pasteboards were strewn across the desk—apparently the gambler had been whiling away the time with a game of solitaire.

"I was beginning to wonder if you were coming back," said Clooney.

"Sorry. Took longer than I expected."

"So you actually rode right into the camps of those Texas outfits," said the gambler, shaking his head in wonderment. "You must be tired of life, Payne."

"I can take it or leave it," said Ethan wearily, trudging across the office to the potbelly stove and pouring himself a cup of coffee from the pot. It was almost as thick and black as sludge, but he drank it anyway.

"Oh, so that's how it is," said Clooney, returning to the desk and, sitting on the corner, retrieving his cards. "A man who has nothing to lose is a dangerous man indeed."

"I don't know about dangerous, but I *am* bone tired."

Clooney ignored the hint and made no effort to quicken his card collecting so that he could make the exit Ethan obviously hoped he would make. "They say most of the men who come out here are running from a mistake or two in their pasts. I know I am. What about you? Why are you here, Marshal?"

"My mistake was coming west in the first place," said Ethan. "I never should have left Illinois."

"And if you hadn't left, what would you be doing right now?"

Ethan smiled pensively. "Pushing a plow."

Clooney shook his head. "No. I can't see you doing that."

"What's wrong with being a farmer?"

Clooney shrugged. "I don't know. You tell me."

Ethan shook his head, thinking of his father. Abner Payne had *tried* to be a farmer. He'd tried to make a go of the old homestead. But bad luck plagued him. And the worst luck of all was the loss of his wife. After the death of Ethan's mother, Abner Payne had sought solace in the jugs of corn liquor he procured from an old ex-slave who ran a still back up in the hills. He'd become a drunk, the butt of jokes or an object of contempt in the community of Roan's Prairie, Illinois. Ethan hadn't wanted to end up like that, and so he'd headed west, seeking quick riches in the California goldfields. And the irony of it was that he'd become very much like his father, all the same—a man with few prospects, who found it unpleasant to both dwell in the past and contemplate the future.

"Thanks again for watching over things for me," he said. "I reckon you'll be wanting to get back to the Lone Star now."

Clooney slid the deck of pasteboards into a vest pocket and shrugged on his frock coat. "They're already making wagers on how long the new town marshal will live, by the way."

"How am I doing?"

"Not good. Odds are eight to one against you living out the week. This is getting bigger than any boxing match or horse race I've ever had the privilege of being involved in. There is a *lot* of money riding on the outcome of your imminent clash with the wild and woolly Texas hellcats of the K-Bar. Almost everyone has made a wager. I've been told that even the Honorable William T. Langford has bet five hundred dollars."

"On the K-Bar, no doubt."

"No doubt."

Ethan laughed. "And what about you? You placing any bets?"

Clooney had reached the door. He paused there, looked back at Ethan, and grinned. "I stand to make a lot of money if you're still above snakes on Sunday. So try to stay out of Boot Hill for my sake, if not for your own, okay, Marshal?"

"Well, I'll be," said Ethan. "And I thought I was the biggest fool in Abilene."

CHAPTER FIVE

There was no doubt in the mind of anyone in Abilene that the K-Bar outfit would come and try to free Tell Jenkins and his brother. It was merely a question of when. Neither was there much doubt that they would accomplish their goal. What chance did their new town marshal have, standing alone against a Texas wild bunch? Especially a marshal who had fired all his deputies and then seemed in no big hurry to hire new ones. Several men had applied—some with local reputations as being better-than-fair hands with shooting irons—but the marshal had turned them away, every one. Some folks were even of the opinion that Ethan Payne would hightail it out of town before the K-Bar riders showed up. Of course, these people were careful never to say any such thing within earshot of the marshal.

John White was among those most anxious about Marshal Payne's apparent lack of concern for what was about to happen, both to him and to Abilene. He pointed out to his friend G.W. Ransom that all Payne seemed inclined to do was to sit in a chair on the boardwalk in front of the jail, the chair tilted back against the stone wall, the brim of his hat pulled down over eyes that ceaselessly scanned the street. He would just sit there all morning long, and round about noon would rise and cross the street to the Alamo

Saloon where he would have a drink. Then he would return to the jail in time to meet the boy who brought the meals for the marshal and the prisoners from the Silver Spur Restaurant down the street. Just before sundown he would make his second foray into the Alamo and indulge in another shot of Old Nash.

"Who does he think he is," asked White, "that he's set on facing the K-Bar crowd all by himself? But he won't take on any deputies. And when I suggested that he deputize every able-bodied man in Abilene he just shook his head no and said that wouldn't help matters any. Wouldn't help matters!"

Ransom shrugged, trying to mask his own anxiety. He liked to maintain the fiction that he was a man consistently in control of his emotions, unlike White, who tended to go off half-cocked. "Leave the man be, John," he advised. "He's a professional, after all. Let's give him the benefit of the doubt, and assume he knows what he's doing."

"Sure," replied White, dryly. "Let's do that. And before we know it, Payne will be eating dirt in Boot Hill and Tell Jenkins will be scot-free and on his way back to Texas and that will pretty much be the end of Abilene."

"We'll see."

White squinted suspiciously at Ransom. "You've got something up your sleeve. You can't fool me. I've known you for twenty-five years, G.W."

"Let's just say I've taken the precaution of contacting my friends with the UP, and they're sending a few good men to help out. Pinkerton men, in fact. They should be here on tomorrow's westbound."

"Payne won't like it."

"Probably not. But Mr. Payne will simply have to remember who he's working for, won't he?"

On the third day of his vigil at the jailhouse, Ethan was visited by a bespectacled young man wearing a tweed suit and bowler hat. He approached the marshal—who was en-

sconced, as usual, in the tilted chair in front of the jail—
with considerable trepidation.

"Pardon me, Marshal," he said, nervously doffing his
hat. "My name is Lewis. Eben Lewis. I'm a correspondent
for the St. Louis *Democrat*. May I have a few moments of
your time?"

"I guess," said Ethan, without enthusiasm.

The newspaperman could tell that he wasn't really welcome, but ambition got the better of timidity and he pressed
on.

"Is it true, Marshal Payne, that you intend to face down
fifty Texas cowboys?"

"Fifty?" Ethan had to smile. "There are only fourteen
drovers in the K-Bar outfit, and that's counting the owner,
McKittrick, and the two men I have locked up."

"Still, sir, if you don't mind my asking—how do you
expect to survive against such steep odds?"

"I don't expect anything. You say you're from St.
Louis? What brings you to Abilene?"

"I was in Ellsworth when I heard about what was going
on here, so I dropped everything and bought a ticket on the
next train. This is a great frontier story, Marshal. Just the
kind of thing our readers enjoy. Blazing guns, one man's
indomitable courage and commitment to law and order, the
eternal battle between good and evil. If I could have the
story of your life, sir, why, I'd be immensely grateful."

Ethan looked away, gazing off into the hazy distance,
his brow furrowed. "The story of my life? I'm a man with
an ugly past and a dim future."

Eben Lewis waited, expecting more, but Ethan seemed
lost in thought, and no longer even aware of his presence.
After a moment the newspaperman discreetly cleared his
throat.

"To be honest, Mr. Payne," he said, tentatively, "I really
need this story. It would do me a world of good, you see.
I'm . . . rather new at this. That's why they sent me out here
to write a series of articles about life in the Kansas cow

towns. Nobody else on the staff wanted the job, frankly . . ."

"Kid," said Ethan, "I'll make you a deal. If I'm still alive Monday morning you'll get your story. The whole story of my life, if that's really what you want. How does that sound?"

Lewis wilted, unable to conceal his keenly felt disappointment—and Ethan had to laugh.

"I see you don't expect me to be in any condition to tell a story on Monday," he said.

"Nothing personal, Marshal, but . . . well, I mean . . . twelve to one?" Lewis shook his head morosely.

Ethan nodded. "But look at it this way. If I lose, nobody's going to care two bits' worth about me."

Lewis sighed and planted the bowler hat back atop his head. "I very much hope to see you on Monday, sir."

Ethan consulted his stem-winder and discovered that it was close on noon. He crossed the wide, rutted street to the Alamo Saloon and lingered over his drink in the dim, cool interior of the watering hole. He dwelled on the prospects of fame, and found it ironic that after all these years Lilah Webster might finally hear of him in the pages of a penny dreadful. He had somehow wandered into a situation that, if he managed to survive it, would likely acquire for him a reputation that would make his a household name, like Kit Carson or Jesse James. And would fortune come with fame? Would he finally, after all these years, find the fortune he had come west to make? A reputation could become a real asset where making money was concerned. But it could also be a liability. Especially the kind of reputation he would get if he faced down the K-Bar. He could expect the gunslingers to come looking for him then—men seeking to make their own reputation by sending him to his grave. One thing was certain. He had no choice but to see this matter through. If he turned tail and ran he was finished. There was one thing the frontier could not abide, and that was a yellow coward. There would be no place he could hide to escape the consequences of running from a fight.

His drink finished, he left the saloon. No one had spoken to him, or even approached him. It was as though an aura of death surrounded him, and others feared it might be contagious, so they kept their distance. He didn't blame them for doing so.

He was in the middle of the street, bending his steps for the jailhouse, when he first felt the vibration coming up from the ground, through his boots, into his legs, and he looked north, up the street, and saw them. Eight—no, make that nine men, riding in two ragged lines abreast. Even before he could see the brands on their ponies he figured this had to be the K-Bar outfit. Part of it, anyway. A few drovers would have had to stay behind to watch over the herd. They would be the ones who had drawn the short sticks, because every last K-Bar cowboy would want to be in on the fight.

As soon as they spotted him the cowboys checked their horses, holding them to a walk. There was something very grim and purposeful about the way they came down the street, a street that cleared as if by magic. Wagons and riders hastily turned down intersecting streets. People on the boardwalks disappeared through the most convenient doorways. In less than a minute Ethan Payne was alone in the street with the men who had come to challenge him.

With long strides, Ethan entered the jailhouse office. He moved quickly to the gun rack and took down the scatter-gun, checked to make sure both barrels were loaded, and filled the pocket of his frock coat with buckshot shells.

"Lawman!"

It was a gruff, stentorian voice, the voice of a man accustomed to giving orders, coming from the street. The Texas riders were out in front of the jailhouse, their hard-run horses fiddle-footing nervously, kicking up a cloud of dust that partially obscured them. This Ethan could see through the front door, which stood ajar. But first he went through the door into the cell block. Tell Jenkins was standing at the door of his cage, grasping the strap iron with a white-knuckled grasp, his eyes bright with excitement.

"That's Mr. McKittrick," he rasped. "They've come for me, haven't they? What did I tell you, Clute? I knew they'd be coming to break us out of this hole."

Ethan glanced at Clute, in the next cell. Tell's brother was stretched out on his bunk, hands behind his head, hat pulled down over his eyes. "We're not breathing free air yet, Tell," he said from underneath that hat.

"We will be, soon enough." Tell let loose with a piercing Rebel yell. "Come and get us, boys!" he yelled, clearly addressing his K-Bar compañeros in the street. "Take me across that old Red River to home!"

"If you cross a river anytime soon," said Ethan, "it'll be the Jordan, not the Red."

Jenkins leered. "Say your prayers, lawman. If you know any."

Ethan left the cell block, locking the door behind him and then tossing the keys onto the kneehole desk as he crossed the office and stepped out onto the boardwalk. The scattergun was cradled in his arm. He scanned the riders arrayed in the street before him. They formed a shallow semi-circle from one end of the boardwalk to the other, and they sat their horses in belligerent silence, some of them staring at Ethan, others warily scanning the street, looking for signs of an ambush. Ethan recognized two of them as the cowboys who had been with Tell Jenkins the night Jenkins had killed Happy Jack Crawford. A horse whickered and sneezed, an unexpected explosion of sound in the tense silence, and a couple of the cowboys jumped. Ethan repressed a smile. He wasn't the only one with a bad case of frayed nerves. He just hoped he was looking calm and confident, and not scared. His mouth was as dry as Kansas dust, and his stomach was a little unsettled. He just couldn't let his true feelings show. There was a slim chance that if he stood firm the Texans might back down. But a glimmer of fear, the slightest hint of a lack of resolve on his part, and they would fall on him like a pack of wolves.

A voice inside his head—the voice of self-preservation—
screamed at him to run. *Run, you fool, and live*, it said.
*You've got no stake in Abilene, or in seeing Tell Jenkins
hang.* But he did have a stake. A huge stake. If he lived
he'd have made a place for himself, and for a yonder man
that was more important than even fame or fortune. If he
walked away he'd not only be a worthless drifter for the
rest of his days, but he'd have lost the one thing he could
call his own—his own self-respect. Without self-respect, a
man might as well curl up and die.

"You boys must not be aware of the new law," he said
quietly. "Nobody goes heeled inside the town limits. We
haven't put up any notices as yet, so I won't fine you for
riding through town with your guns. But I'm telling you
now, so you might as well check your irons with me, and
pick them up when you're finished in Abilene and you're
on your way out."

"By God," breathed an older man, sitting squarely in the
middle of the semi-circle of Texas toughs. "You've got
plenty of hard bark on you, don't you." His tone was one
of grudging admiration. "My name is McKittrick. I'm boss
of the K-Bar. But I reckon you know that. Now listen close,
mister, 'cause I ain't one of those who likes to repeat himself. You let Tell and Clute Jenkins go, and in return I'll
let you and this town live."

"We might be able to work something out where Clute
is concerned. But Tell Jenkins stays right where he is. He's
charged with murder. And I expect he'll hang for his
crime."

McKittrick straightened in the saddle, wincing as old
bones and stiff joints complained about the punishment in-
flicted during the long ride from the K-Bar camp. Ethan
thought he saw a glimmer of pity in the cattle king's eyes.
McKittrick was the kind of man who would respect courage
and commitment to one's duty. But he wouldn't let that
respect stand in the way of doing what he felt he had to
do. And as a Texas rancher he simply could not abide the

idea of a Kansas jury passing judgment on a Texas cowboy—especially one on his payroll.

"I wanted to get a look at you, Marshal," he said. "Some of the boys say you must be crazy to stand alone against us. But I can see you're not crazy. You're just one of those men who can't back down and then live with himself. I admire that. That's why I'm going to give you twenty-four hours to reconsider your position. Twenty-four hours, Marshal. If Tell and Clute aren't freed by then, my boys and I will be back. And next time we won't be doing any talking."

"If you or any of your boys come back into town and discharge your firearms," said Ethan, "I'll hold you personally responsible, McKittrick, and put you under arrest."

McKittrick chuckled. Then he touched the brim of his hat and turned his horse. The K-Bar drovers spared Ethan a few dark looks and then followed their boss back up the street the way they had come. It was apparent that they didn't want to wait twenty-four hours to settle things. But Ethan figured that was why McKittrick was boss and they weren't. The cattle king was no fool. He knew his men could take the Abilene marshal and free Jenkins, but it would have cost them dearly. Ethan thought he might have been able to account for four or five of the cowboys before they shot him down. And McKittrick cared about the men who rode for him. He didn't want to suffer those losses unless it was absolutely unavoidable. Next time he would come in hard and fast, and try to catch Ethan by surprise.

Quite apart from that, McKittrick was figuring that Tell Jenkins wasn't going anywhere, and twenty-four hours would give Ethan's nerves a chance to catch up with him.

He went back inside, racked the scattergun, and was pouring himself a cup of coffee from the pot atop the stove when G.W. Ransom showed up.

"When I was told the K-Bar crew was coming into town I figured I'd find you dead and the Jenkins boys sprung," admitted Ransom.

"I appreciate the vote of confidence."

"Look," said Ransom curtly, "I don't know what you're doing. Maybe it's about pride, or some code of honor that you live by. But I've got this town and the people who live in it to worry about. That's why I sent for some help. They'll be here tonight, on the westbound train."

"They?"

"Pinkerton agents. I hope you won't take offense, Marshal. I'd like for you to stay on. But this is one job that is just too big for you to handle all by yourself."

"Well, you'll do what you feel you have to do," said Ethan. "Coffee?"

Ransom was relieved. His impression was that Ethan was accepting the fact that the situation was going to be handled in a way that was not to his liking.

"No thanks. I have other business to attend to. Now that you know about the Pinkerton men, perhaps you should be at the depot when the train arrives, so that you can meet them."

"I'll be there."

The train was over two hours late. Even allowing for the railroad's customary inability to abide by anything remotely resembling a schedule, that was more tardy than usual. And it was certainly longer than G.W. Ransom and John White wanted to wait. So they repaired to the nearest saloon and paid the son of the telegrapher, whose office was located in the railroad depot, to come and fetch them when the train approached. For his part, Ethan returned to the jailhouse and waited to hear the steam whistle. When at last it came, he headed back to the depot, arriving there just as Ransom and White did. They were holding their hats down on their heads because, as was often the case, a stiff night wind was blowing across the prairie, pushing dust and tumbleweeds and whipping their long dusters around their legs. The mogul came chugging in, a great metal giant belching smoke, pulling the wood car and then several passenger cars, followed by a few freight cars. The conductor jumped off one of the passenger cars before the train had come to a complete stop and grimly approached Ransom and White, sparing Ethan a curious glance, his eyes lingering on the tin star attached to the breast of Ethan's frock coat.

"Howdy, Mr. Ransom," he said. "We had some trouble back down the line."

"What kind of trouble?"

"The killing kind."

"What happened?"

"There were some dead cows across the tracks, so we slowed the train—enough so's a wild bunch of Texans rode out of the night and jumped aboard and made us stop the train. They said they were on the hunt for a couple of Pinkerton men. Well, sir, they found what they were looking for. There was some shooting, and then the Texans rode away."

"I see," said Ransom bleakly. "And the Pinkerton men?"

The conductor tilted his head toward the freight cars at the end of the train. "We moved their bodies back there, so's not to inconvenience the other passengers."

Ransom looked at Ethan. "How the hell did they find out?"

Ethan shrugged and turned his attention back to the conductor. "How many riders would you say there were?"

"At least twenty. Probably more. Some stayed aboard their ponies and just kept circling the train."

Ethan nodded. "That means they were from more than one outfit. That it wasn't just the K-Bar crew."

"I thought you got the other cattlemen to agree not to get involved," said White.

"They agreed not to ride into Abilene and try to free Tell Jenkins. They didn't agree not to do anything else. The problem is that bringing Pinkerton men into this was certain to put a burr under a Texan's saddle. They worked for Abe Lincoln's Union during the late unpleasantness, and every Texan knows it. South of the Red River, Pinkerton is a bad word. Every Texas outfit around would gladly buy into hunting Pinkerton agents."

"So what do we do now?" asked Ransom, as though he had a very bad taste in his mouth.

"You tend to your business, which now includes giving two good men a decent burial. And let me tend to mine."

Fuming, White glowered at Ethan before turning to Ransom. "You aren't going to let him talk to you in that manner, are you, G.W.?"

Ransom sighed. "Yes, John, I reckon I am. So far he's still alive, Abilene is still standing, and Tell Jenkins is still in jail. Until any of that changes I suppose I'll just let the man do his job."

And with that, Ransom gave Ethan a curt nod and turned to the conductor. "I'll have some men come by shortly to pick up the bodies." Then he walked away, with a somewhat annoyed and bewildered John White tailing along behind.

Ethan took a long look at the train, thinking how easy it would be to hop aboard and head for points west. The fact that the Texans had found out about the imminent arrival of the Pinkerton men was one thing, a mystery that was yet to be solved. But there was nothing uncertain about the willingness of the Texans to do anything they had to do in order to free one of their own from a Kansas jail. Killing a pair of Pinkerton agents was no small matter, but they hadn't hesitated. And they wouldn't hesitate to gun down a town marshal either.

Spitting the wind-driven grit out of his mouth, Ethan turned and trudged back to the jailhouse.

CHAPTER SIX

They were right on time, arriving in Abilene shortly after noon. This time they didn't ride in together, but swept into town from all different directions, converging quickly on the jailhouse. McKittrick was one of the last to arrive on the scene, and when he got there his cowboys were already at work. Four of them had the windows covered, waiting for the barrel of a pistol or rifle to emerge through the shutter gun ports. Meanwhile, two others were working on the heavily timbered front door with axes. The last two were keeping an eye on the street and the nearby buildings, because McKittrick had warned them of the possibility that the good citizens of Abilene might decide to buy into the game. His cowboys were of the opinion that the townfolk didn't have the nerve, but McKittrick wasn't sure the inhabitants of the trail town should be dismissed so out of hand. But the street was empty, and apart from a few anxious faces framed in windows or doorways, one might have thought the town had suddenly become deserted.

"Marshal!" roared McKittrick. "I'll give you one chance to come out with your hands empty. You can walk away from this and stay alive."

There was no answer from inside the jailhouse.

McKittrick grimaced. The cowboys with the axes redoubled their efforts, and in a matter of minutes they had chopped a hole right in the middle of the door—a hole big enough for one to reach in and remove the bar that secured the door from the inside. McKittrick expected shooting from within, but there was nothing of the sort, and right then he got the first inkling that something might be very wrong. But before he could decide whether to urge caution upon his men, they were charging through the jailhouse door, brandishing their weapons, and he had no choice but to follow. The two men assigned to watch the street remained outside to continue doing so, and to take care of the others' horses.

The office was empty.

"He must have skedaddled," muttered one of the drovers.

"Yeah," rasped another. "He lost his nerve and headed for the tall timber, boss."

"Check the cells," said McKittrick, the hairs at the nape of his neck standing on end.

Two of the cowboys busted through the cell block door with fingers on triggers, ready to open up. But no shooting was required. The cells in the cell block were as empty as the office.

"They're not here, boss," called one of the cowboys.

McKittrick muttered a curse under his breath.

"McKittrick."

He whirled—and saw Ethan standing in the street in front of the jailhouse, a smoldering cheroot clenched in his teeth. The cattleman wondered what had happened to the two men assigned to watch the street. But he didn't have much time to wonder about it, because he recognized the item the marshal was holding in his left hand as a stick of dynamite—and even as McKittrick watched, his eyes widening, Ethan used the tip of the cheroot to light the long fuse dangling from one end of the dynamite stick.

"This is a thirty-second fuse, so listen tight," said Ethan. "Throw your guns out or I'm tossing this stick onto the porch. That will set off the box of dynamite located under the door. And that, in turn, will set off the box located directly below the cell block door. Thirty seconds from now there'll be nothing left of you boys or the jailhouse but a big hole in the ground. You've got ten seconds."

"Jesus," muttered McKittrick. "Lose the iron, boys!" He tossed his pistol through the door, and his men hastily followed suit. A veritable armory of weapons came flying out the door as the Texans rid themselves of rifles and sideguns. Still, Ethan waited until the last second to pluck the fuse and cap out of the stick of dynamite. The cap exploded as he tossed it away, and McKittrick wasn't the only man in the jailhouse who jumped at the detonation.

Drawing his Remington Army, Ethan entered the jailhouse and motioned for the Texans to file into the cell block. "Pick your cage, boys, the doors are all open. You're going to be my guests for a spell."

As his downcast men let themselves into their cells, McKittrick lingered in the office. "How long do you think you're gonna keep us locked up?" he asked coldly. There was no denying that Ethan Payne had gotten the better of him, and it was a hard pill to swallow for a such a prideful man.

"Until Tell Jenkins has his trial, or hell freezes over. Whichever comes first."

"And what about my herd?"

"That's not my problem, Mr. McKittrick. Now get into a cell."

An ashen McKittrick did as he was told. As soon as Ethan had them all securely locked in, he went back outside. The gambler, Clooney, still stood in the stark shade of the boardwalk, holding a shotgun unwaveringly at the two K-Bar cowboys who'd been assigned the task of watching the street. They were both scowling and looking sheepish at the same time, because there was no getting around the fact that they'd failed in the task set for them. Ethan and Clooney had gotten the drop on them without any trouble whatsoever.

"I've got it from here," Ethan told the gambler. "Thanks for your help."

Clooney shrugged. "Just protecting my wager," he replied, and grinned as he tossed the shotgun to the town marshal. "I've made a tidy sum today, thanks to you."

"Glad to hear it," replied Ethan. "Then you can buy me a drink later."

He escorted the two K-Bar cowboys into the jail and put them in a cell. McKittrick came to the door of his cell as Ethan was about to leave the cell block.

"Marshal, you've got just about my whole crew locked up in here. How long do you expect to keep us in these cages? I've got a herd of two thousand head out there with just three men to look after it, and Kansas chock full of old Jayhawkers and renegade Indians just itching to make off with some Texas beef."

"I'm sorry about that, McKittrick, but you should have thought about that before you rode in here with your boys to fill me full of lead."

The cattleman grimaced. "You're right—I shouldn't expect any mercy from you. But if I lose that herd, I'm finished."

Ethan nodded. "That would be a shame," he said, sincerely—and left the cell block.

He took the cell block keys with him as he departed the jailhouse and bent his steps in the direction of the Drover's Cottage. He didn't get far before G.W. Ransom intercepted him. People were beginning to emerge from hiding now, coming cautiously out onto the street, looking around as though they could scarcely believe that Abilene was still standing.

"What the hell happened?" asked Ransom, breathless from his run. "I was told McKittrick and his boys had showed up again. But then there wasn't any shooting—was there? I didn't hear anything. . . ."

"No, there wasn't any shooting, Mr. Ransom. The K-Bar outfit is safely tucked away in the jail."

"My God, man," said Ransom. "How did you manage that?"

The sound of boot heels hammering the warped and weathered boardwalk planking behind him caused Ethan to turn, and he saw the newspaperman, Eben Lewis, running to catch up with him.

"Marshal Payne! Is it over? You're still alive!"

Ethan laughed. "Don't sound so surprised."

"It's just that . . ." Lewis shook his head. "How did you do it?"

Ethan told them, just the bare bones, without elaboration, and with Ransom and Lewis hanging on every word. When he was done, Lewis was grinning from ear to ear.

"That's going to make a great story, Marshal."

"Nobody is going to believe it," said Ransom, astonished. "It's amazing. Tell me, Payne. Were you bluffing? Are there really two cases of dynamite under the jailhouse?"

"There are," said Payne. "I borrowed it from the Union Pacific. And as soon as I fetch the Jenkins bothers from the hotel, I'll get it back to the railroad."

"Well, I'll be damned," said Ransom. "I must confess, I underestimated you."

Ethan decided there was nothing to be gained by admitting to Ransom that he'd had no idea what to do about McKittrick until the night before, when he'd visited the depot to meet Ransom's Pinkerton men. It was then that he'd recalled the rumors floating around some of the Colorado goldfields he'd frequented before coming to Abilene that a railroad was thinking about trying to put a spur through the heart of the Rocky Mountains, and there'd been speculation as to how much dynamite they'd have to use to carve an iron road through the high country. Acquiring the dynamite from the UP had been a fairly simple matter; there'd been some at the depot, and all he'd had to do was explain to the stationmaster that he intended to use it on the very Texans who had held up the westbound train and executed the two Pinkerton agents.

"So do I get the exclusive on the story of your life, Marshal?" asked Lewis.

"Sure," said Ethan, without much enthusiasm. "When do you want to start?"

"As soon as we can. Right now would suit me."

"It wouldn't suit me, though. Tell you what. Come by the jailhouse after dinnertime, and we'll get started."

Once Lewis was gone, Ethan gave Ransom a nod and prepared to continue on his way. But Ransom grabbed his arm and pulled him closer, pitching his voice low so that no passersby could overhear what he had to say.

"So now that you've got McKittrick and most of his crew, what are you going to do with them?"

"Well, if you want my advice, you'll use all your influence to find some buyers for the K-Bar herd. Then, when McKittrick and his boys have their money, we can send them all home to Texas. Except for Tell Jenkins, of course."

"And you think they'd go home without Jenkins?"

"I think they could be persuaded, yes."

Ransom pursed his lips. He wasn't too certain of the wisdom behind Ethan's suggestion—setting the K-Bar cowboys loose seemed to him to be inviting more of the same kind of trouble—but he wasn't going to second-guess Abilene's new town marshal. Not this time.

"Then I'll see what I can do," he promised.

Ethan nodded and walked on. This time Ransom let him go. Watching the marshal walk away, Ransom decided he still wasn't quite sure what to think of Mr. Ethan Payne. Was he merely an opportunist, desperate enough to risk everything? Or was he a man of high integrity, the kind of man that any town should be proud to have as its enforcer of the law?

Only time would tell.

Word of the courage of Abilene's new marshal in standing up to the K-Bar outfit quickly spread, embellished at every telling until what Ethan Payne had done was guaranteed a place in the rich and varied lore of the Wild West. The facts were not that important, and it was a simple matter to sacrifice them on the altar of a good and entertaining story.

For his part, Ethan was pleasantly surprised to discover that the story Eben Lewis wrote about him for the St. Louis *Democrat* remained quite true to what he had told the newspaperman. And he'd been more or less candid, explaining how he had spurned the life of a poor Illinois farmer, lured by the fabled riches of the California goldfields, only to find that fortune eluded him. He spoke of how he had gone to work for the Eldorado Mining Company, but made no mention of the fact that Sir Edward Addison, the famous British engineer, had joined with a band of cutthroats—including his friend Gil Stark—in a scheme to hold up the Eldorado's gold shipments. He practiced this discretion out of concern for the feelings of Ellen Addison. Looking back on it now, he wasn't sure that he'd ever loved Ellen, though there could be no denying that he had lusted after her, but he was fairly certain that she had loved him, in her own unique way, and he owed her for the happiness that she had brought to an otherwise miserable sojourn in California.

He did tell Lewis about his run-in with the gang of cutthroats, though he left out any mention of Gil Stark, and made light of what the Eldorado Mining Company viewed as his heroics in recovering a shipment of gold. He did not discuss why he left the Eldorado's employ; again, that would have brought Ellen into it, and he would not do that. Once her father's complicity had come to light, she had chosen duty to him over love for Ethan, and when she was gone Ethan could find nothing to keep him in California. It was then that he'd taken a job with the Overland Stage Company, becoming a troubleshooter for Ben Holladay.

He left very little out of that chapter in the story of his life, apart from the fact that once again he'd run into his old friend Gil Stark, and once again Gil had been on the wrong side of the law—and yet again Ethan had let him go free when it had been his responsibility to bring Stark to justice. It wasn't that Ethan was trying to protect himself from a charge that he valued friendship over law and order, but rather that he chose to think about Gil Stark as little as possible. He readily explained to the newspaperman how it was that he'd lost his job over the killing of the station agent, Joe Cathcott, and why he'd had to do that deed.

And now here he was in Abilene, after some aimless years roaming from one Colorado gold camp to another, making a living, but not much of one, as a bouncer or wagon guard or hired gun. There was no established law in such places; the only law that could prevail under such circumstances was the law of the gun, and Ethan had discovered that the only currency he possessed was the reputation that preceded him.

When he was finished with his story, Ethan narrowed his eyes and gave Lewis a hard look. "Not what you'd expected, I see," he said, reading the young journalist's expression. "But it's the truth, and I'll expect you to print it, plain and unvarnished. I'm no hero, Mr. Lewis. Far from it."

Lewis had agreed, and his account in the *Democrat* would, indeed, turn out to be as plain and unvarnished as they came. The telling of the story, and seeing it in print, was cathartic for Ethan. He carried the burden of considerable guilt—guilt for having left Lilah Webster behind in Illinois; for letting Gil Stark go free not once but twice when by rights Gil should have paid for his sins; for giving in to his desires where Julie Cathcott was concerned, even while knowing in his heart that he was not going to make an honest woman of her; and for lingering just long enough to kill Joe Cathcott when he could have made tracks long before it became necessary to do so. Now the truth was out there—well, most of the truth anyway. He'd made his confession.

With that chore done, he went to the Lone Star and had Clooney buy him that drink.

"I want your promise that my name is left out of this business with the K-Bar," said the gambler.

"Why is that? I didn't know you were the modest type."

"It has nothing to do with modesty. It's just common sense. Look at it from my angle. I aimed a shotgun at a couple of Texas cowboys, and was all set to blow them to hell and gone. And all for the sake of getting one of their compañeros hanged. Now how do you think that will play south of the Red, Marshal?"

"I see what you mean."

Clooney nodded. "My life wouldn't be worth a plugged nickel. You, you've got that tin star to keep a lot of wild cowpunchers from trying to take you. But I'd be a prime target. Every Texan with a gun and a hankering to carve a notch in it would come gunning for me. No, sir. As far as I'm concerned, I wasn't anywhere around when you had your set-to with the K-Bar crew. And I've got a couple of witnesses who'll testify to that."

"You're smarter than I gave you credit for, Clooney."

"What did you tell that reporter from St. Louis?"

"I didn't mention your name. But somebody else might."

"Talk to him, then. You owe me that much, don't you think?"

Ethan nodded. "I owe you."

And he did talk to Lewis, and Clooney's name did not appear in the account that made the front page of the St. Louis *Democrat*. And it was this article that formed the basis for all the other journalistic renderings of the Abilene marshal's showdown with the K-Bar outfit that appeared in newspapers as geographically dispersed as the New York *Tribune* and the New Orleans *Picayune*.

Ransom came through, and in just a few days he'd found some buyers for the K-Bar herd. The transaction was undertaken in the cell block—Ethan wasn't going to let McKittrick and his boys out of jail until the time came for them to head for Texas. When it was done, he let the cattle king out and took him into the office and asked him bluntly if he was willing and able to head for home without Tell Jenkins.

McKittrick scowled. "Do I have a choice?"

"He's staying. You can, too. Or you can head for home. Those are your choices."

"I'm just curious about one thing, Marshal. Would you have tossed that stick of dynamite, and blown us all to hell?"

"Absolutely," drawled Ethan.

McKittrick nodded. "You're a hard man, and you drive a hard bargain. Yeah, I'm going home."

"What about your men?"

"They'll go, too, if I tell 'em to, and they won't make trouble."

"And Clute Jenkins? Will he go? If so, I'll set him free. But if he's just going to come gunning for me, I'll leave him to rot in jail."

"With Clute it's hard to say. I'll have a talk with him."

"You do that."

A couple of hours later McKittrick called Ethan into the cell block. "Clute says he'll go with us."

Ethan glanced at Tell Jenkins, who was sitting sullen and silent in one of the cells, and figured the Texan was having a hard time believing that his compañeros were about to leave him to die in Kansas—and without a shot being fired.

"Okay, then," said Ethan. "You'll be set loose first thing in the morning."

He was as good as his word. At daybreak he was back in the cell block, unlocking the cells and letting the cowboys file out. The handful of K-Bar riders who had not accompanied McKittrick into Abilene—and thus into the hoosegow—were out in the street, mounted on their cow ponies and holding the horses of their newly freed brethren. McKittrick and Clute Jenkins were the last ones out. Not a word passed between Clute and his brother. At the door, Ethan handed McKittrick a pair of panniers.

"They money for your herd's in here," said Ethan. "You're welcome to count it, if you want."

McKittrick shook his head. "No, I trust you."

"What about our guns?" asked Clute.

"Two miles due south of town, at Wentworth Springs, you'll find a wagon with all your artillery piled in the back."

Clute smiled coldly. "You don't leave nothing to chance, do you?"

"I try not to."

Clute stood there on the threshold, staring at Ethan, as though there was more he wanted to say—and do—but McKittrick stepped between them.

"Let's ride, Jenkins," said the cattleman gruffly.

Clute went to his horse. When McKittrick was mounted, he gave Ethan a curt nod and then wheeled his pony around. The K-Bar crew followed him down the street, their horses at the gallop.

Ethan watched them go, hoping it would be the last he ever saw of them—even while he had a strong hunch that Clute Jenkins had no intention of riding for Texas just yet.

He checked on Tell Jenkins, then took the scattergun out of the rack and locked up and headed across to the Alamo to get a cup of coffee. Once the barkeep had poured it for him, he took the cup to a corner table in the back of the nearly empty saloon and sat so that he could see the doors. A few minutes later, G.W. Ransom strolled in, looked around, spotted him, and crossed to join him at the table. Ethan was more or less expecting him; it seemed that every time something momentous happened, Ransom would show up shortly after the dust had cleared. Clearly he kept his ear to the ground where events important to Abilene were concerned. This morning he appeared to be in a good humor.

"So, I hear they're gone, Marshal," he said. "What a relief! I understand the circuit judge should arrive in town in the next few days, so we can proceed quickly with Tell Jenkins' trial." Belatedly, he noticed the scattergun laying on the table between them, and frowned. "Are you . . . expecting trouble?"

"Yeah, and I suggest you get down, Mr. Ransom, because it just walked through the door."

Ransom turned in his chair and recognized the man in the doorway, framed against a backdrop of bright morning daylight, as Clute Jenkins.

"Jesus," he muttered. "You let him go, too?"

Ethan didn't waste time answering, because Clute was scanning the dimly lit interior of the Alamo Saloon and had spotted him, and was coming forward, reaching for the pistol in the cross-draw holster on his hip. Rising, Ethan scooped the scattergun off the table. Clute drew the shooting iron and immediately began making smoke, and Ethan couldn't fail to notice that Ransom had frozen, so he kicked the man's chair over, sending him sprawling on the floor. Ethan realized that the scattergun was useless under the circumstances—the handful of men who were patronizing the Alamo this morning were bolting out the door behind Clute, and Ethan couldn't use the shotgun for fear of hitting an innocent bystander with a spray of buckshot. He tossed the scattergun aside and dived sideways as Clute filled the air around him with hot lead. Rolling, he overturned a table and stayed low behind it until Clute had expended all six rounds. In the momentary lull that followed, Ethan took a deep breath, drew his Remington Army, and got to his feet. Clute stood about fifteen feet away, reloading his thumb buster. Ethan drew a careful bead, aiming for a spot right above the cowboy's sternum.

"Drop the iron, Jenkins," he said.

"You go to hell," muttered Clute. He knew Ethan had the drop on him—and he didn't care.

"Don't make me kill you," said Ethan.

Clute grimly raised his pistol—and Ethan fired once. The Texan staggered backward, as though jerked violently by invisible strings. Ethan fired again, and the second bullet caught the man in the face as he went down. Clute Jenkins was dead before he hit the ground.

Eyes narrowed against the burning drift of powder smoke, Ethan drew a long breath and holstered the Remington. He gazed for a moment at the corpse of Clute Jenkins. It was amazing how many valid reasons a man could find to choose death over living. Clute had decided he did not want to go back to Texas and endure the shame of having left his brother to face Kansas justice. Ironically, by dying in an Abilene saloon, he would live for quite a long time in the collective memory of his fellow Texas cowboys, admired for having done the honorable thing, and dying by the cowboy code.

Ethan went over to help Ransom to his feet before moving on to the bar, where the apron was just now venturing a cautious look over the edge of the mahogany.

"Fred, I want you to make sure he gets a decent burial," said Ethan. "Never mind the expense of it—I'll pay whatever it takes."

"Sure thing, Marshal."

CHAPTER SEVEN

Tell Jenkins took the news of his brother's death calmly. Ethan thought it was at that moment that Jenkins became resigned to the truth—namely, that he was going to hang for shooting down Happy Jack Crawford. There were no surprises at his trial. It took but the better part of one day for a jury of twelve good and honest men to find the Texan guilty as charged, emboldened, perhaps, by the presence of their soon-to-be-legendary marshal in the courtroom. The judge sternly sentenced Jenkins to hang by the neck until he was dead—and may God have mercy on his soul. The scaffold was erected in a few days' time. Jenkins hardly said a word to Ethan during this entire period—not, at least, until the morning of the day he was destined to die. It was then, as he was about to be led on that long final walk to meet his Maker, that he smiled coldly at Ethan.

"Reckon I ain't gonna get a chance at you in this life," he murmured. "But me and my brother will be waitin' on you in hell, Marshal. We'll see each other again."

Ethan just nodded. He wasn't going to get into a senseless exchange of bold talk with a dead man. It did him no harm to let Tell Jenkins have his say.

Twenty minutes later, Happy Jack Crawford's killer paid his debt to society, and an hour after that was six feet under in Abilene's Boot Hill. The very next day it rained. Not much. Just a little. But you would have thought that God had sent manna down from heaven to feed a starving multitude; the local preachers proclaimed that the Almighty was rewarding his children for pursuing justice in Old Testament fashion, an eye for an eye. After all, Tell Jenkins was the Devil's minion, just like all Texans were, and he had paid the price that all the wicked were destined to pay. Not being much of a church-going man, Ethan did not hear any one of these sermons firsthand, but he heard tell of them—and just shook his head.

Some of the Abilene merchants were worried that the deaths of Clute and Tell Jenkins would spell doom for their town. Their leader, John Tyler White, found himself called upon to remind them that there had been no alternative; if McKittrick's cowboys had had their way and Tell Jenkins escaped justice, Abilene would have been labeled a lawless town and died a much-deserved death. White didn't much care for Ethan Payne personally, being suspicious, still, of the man's true motives for taking the job of Abilene's law bringer. But he couldn't deny that Payne had handled the Texans adroitly. They were a thin-skinned bunch, those Texans, always so concerned with their honor, always motivated more by prickly pride than cool reason. Thanks to Payne, it seemed unlikely that the Texans would boycott Abilene. The marshal had demonstrated a talent for diplomacy—not to mention plenty of grit—in visiting all the other Texas outfits prior to the inevitable showdown with the K-Bar crew. That had put Abilene and its new marshal firmly atop high moral ground, and most of the cowboys had conceded that if Clute and Tell Jenkins had ended up the Devil's guests in hell it was because they'd seemed dead set on getting there.

True, the season was nearly over, and it would be another eight months before anyone could say for sure whether the Texans were still all that interested in doing business here; the arrival of the herds beginning late next spring would tell that tale. But White was confident, and tried to impart that confidence among his less sanguine peers.

After the hanging of Tell Jenkins an aura of calm and reason descended on the town, and everybody seemed to go to extra lengths to be cordial to one another. Ethan had seen this phenomenon before; it tended to follow in the wake of a public execution. Human nature being what it was, though, he didn't really expect the peace and quiet to last for long. It helped that the season was almost over. The last of the Texas herds were coming up the trail now. There weren't that many Texas cowboys riding into town looking for something on which to spend their hard-earned wages. Those that did ride in appeared inclined to obey the law— even the new ordinance, proposed by the new marshal, that the town council had seen fit to rubber-stamp. Signs notifying visitors that the carrying of firearms was forbidden within the city limits were posted at all the principal points of entry. A good many inhabitants had braced themselves for a lot of resistance to this new regulation on the part of the Texans. But the trouble was minimal. When Ethan put drovers under arrest for failing to abide by the law, most of them went quietly to jail and obediently paid their fine. This was due primarily to Ethan's reputation as a fair-minded man who tried to deal squarely with cowboy, gambler, and merchant alike.

It didn't take long for Ethan to establish that his reign as Abilene's town marshal would be markedly different from Happy Jack Crawford's. Where Crawford had preferred to lean on the "bad element," Ethan practiced tolerance and gave wide latitude in almost every respect. Both the Texans and the transients—the gamblers and soiled doves—could agree that their situation was considerably improved. The latter group felt beholden to Ethan; word spread that he was responsible for the town council's lowering of the tax assessment that had previously made doing business in Abilene so expensive for them. Crawford's primary concern had been lining his own pockets, and his deputies had been willing participants in this endeavor.

Ethan wasn't all that interested in money. It was far more important to him that he keep his job, which would be a lot easier if he had all the factions in Abilene on his side. It wasn't going to be easy balancing the wishes of the Texans, the bad element, and the respectable folks, but from where Ethan was standing it sure was worth a try. Abilene was his anchor; without the job he would drift like tumbleweed. And he was sick and tired of doing that.

Ethan figured it was best to keep things simple, so he had just three principal rules. The gun ordinance had to be obeyed. Beating up a prostitute was strictly forbidden. And no one was to get killed. To help him enforce those rules, he finally hired two deputies. Ed Wilcox was an older man, husky and gray-haired, but despite his years he was still tough as nails, and he had plenty of law enforcement experience. Wilcox had been a town constable in St. Louis before going to work for the Union Pacific in a position not unlike the one Ethan had held with the Overland. He'd been a troubleshooter, and that meant he not only had to deal with situations that arose on the trains but also stepped in when problems arose among the work crews. Wilcox had enjoyed the job well enough, but he'd met an Abilene widow woman and fallen in love—something he had long sworn would never happen—and so he'd decided to give up the UP job, since it involved too much time away from his beloved, and came to Ethan looking for work. Ethan had taken to Ed right away. Wilcox was a straightforward, plain-spoken man—brave, responsible, and a veteran.

Johnny Rowe was brave, but there the similarities with Wilcox ended. Rowe was young, barely nineteen, and the only work experience he'd ever had was behind a plow. He'd come to Kansas with his family; his father had taken advantage of the Homestead Act of 1862 to acquire 160 acres in the great bend of the Arkansas River. But cholera had claimed his parents and Rowe had moved to Abilene, burdened with the responsibility of taking care of his younger sister. He'd found work doing odd jobs, construction work for the most part, before becoming a store clerk

for Fred Hanley at the Texas Mercantile. While sweeping
out the store one afternoon he had run afoul of a couple of
drunken cowboys; before Ethan could arrive the cowboys
had proceeded to use their quirts on Rowe and Rowe had
responded by taking up an axe handle and knocking them
both out cold. Ethan had offered Rowe a job, an offer readily accepted. Rowe had but one stipulation—he refused to
carry a pistol. "I'm probably the worst shot west of the
Mississippi," he told Ethan, "and no amount of practice will
make much improvement." So he opted, instead, for carrying a sawed-off axe handle—and any cowboy who was so
reckless as to make fun of him or his weapon of choice
quickly, and painfully, saw the error of his ways. Rowe
was a dark, slender youth, reserved and somewhat moody.
He reminded Ethan of his own younger days. Rowe also
demonstrated that he had a good head on his shoulders, and
could think clearly in a crisis. Best of all he had a well-
developed sense of right and wrong. His sole shortcoming
manifested itself only gradually: Rowe thought Ethan
Payne was the epitome of the perfect lawman and, try as
he might, Ethan had no luck in persuading him otherwise.

Eventually the season came to an end, and the first
bitter-cold gusts of wind came roaring in from the north,
heralding the approach of winter. The last of the herds came
up the trail, was sold, and then shipped off eastward by rail.
The Texas cowpunchers rode home. With the cowboys
gone many of the transients moved on to greener pastures.
Ethan looked forward to a nice, quiet winter. In a few
months the new cattle season would begin; when spring
came so would the first of the Texas cattle herds. Ethan
was confident that word would spread south of the Red
River that Abilene was a hospitable place for Texans, just
so long as they walked the line. Ransom told him that early
in the spring a delegation would head down the trail and
post circulars that touted Abilene's numerous amenities.
Representatives would also advertise in Texas newspapers
and take every opportunity to do some good old-fashioned
bolstering for Abilene's sake. Abilene was, after all, a busi-

ness, and you had to run it like one. Ethan understood. The way Ransom had handled the murders of the two Pinkerton agents had opened his eyes to the way things were. While the Union Pacific had been inclined to press the issue and hunt down the killers of those two men, Ransom had talked the railroad out of it, and had even made arrangements to make sure the families of the two men received a nice cash settlement.

Clooney didn't understand it, though. "I don't see the difference," he admitted to Ethan one evening over drinks, "between the killing of Happy Jack Crawford and the murders of those Pinkerton agents. Ransom was dead-set on seeing Tell Jenkins brought to justice. But where the Pinkertons were concerned he didn't seem to give a plugged nickel for justice."

"Well, for one thing, it didn't happen in Abilene."

"No, but the Pinkerton men were coming because Ransom asked for them. If you were Ransom, wouldn't that lay heavily on your conscience? Wouldn't you feel you owed it to those men to do everything in your power to bring their killers to justice?"

"But I'm not Ransom. And remember, it wasn't just one cowboy who killed those Pinkerton men. It was a whole gang of drovers. Trying to bring an entire outfit to justice would for certain start a full-scale war. And as every businessman knows, war has a negative impact on the bottom line. I don't know if Ransom has a conscience or not. But if he does he doesn't let it get in his way too often."

"You sound like you admire him."

"You sound like you don't."

"I don't trust any of those self-proclaimed, holier-than-thou town fathers," confessed the gambler.

"Well, try to keep your opinion to yourself. We'll all prosper if we can all just get along."

Clooney finished off his whiskey and smiled wryly. "A nice sentiment. But I'm afraid that one day you'll be forced to choose sides, Marshal. You'll have to decide whether to back the town council or the cowboys, or maybe even us—

the untouchables. And I don't have a clue what side you'll
choose."

During the off season Ethan and his deputies worked eight-
hour shifts. Wilcox and Rowe switched off on the
midnight-to-eight and the eight-to-four shifts, while Ethan
reserved the four-to-midnight leg for himself. That was
when trouble was most likely to occur, regardless of the
season, and he felt it was his duty as town marshal to take
on the brunt of that trouble. Without Texas cowboys to deal
with, most of the problems involved drifters and railroad
men who had too much to drink. Due to the special relationship Ransom and the other two fathers tried to maintain
with the Union Pacific, Ethan was expected to take it easy
on the latter, which he did. He also tended to go easy on
the drifters, keeping in mind that there but for the grace of
God went he.

When the Texas trade began rolling into Abilene again,
on the tail end of a long cold winter, Ethan and his deputies
switched to twelve-hour shifts. Wilcox and Rowe switched
off, working from six in the morning until six in the evening. That left Ethan and one deputy to work the night shift,
when the "Texas Side" of town was going full tilt. Ransom
urged Ethan to find another deputy so that he and his men
could take an occasional day off, but neither Ethan nor
Wilcox nor Rowe had anything else to do. "It's not like we
have any hobbies," Ethan told Ransom, "and Ed's the only
one with a family life to speak of. Even so, he says three
or four nights a week is about all he can take of that." In
lieu of a fourth man, Ethan persuaded Ransom to give Wilcox and Rowe a healthy pay raise. He wanted nothing more
for himself, however. He had no expenses to speak of. The
Drover's Cottage gave him a room for free, and he would
have gotten his food and drink gratis, as well, if he'd been
so inclined. The vast majority of his monthly wage was
deposited in the bank.

He had no preference when it came to which deputy he
worked with. Wilcox, the wily veteran, was better at sniff-

ing out potential trouble and keeping a lid on it; Rowe was the man you wanted watching your back when all hell was breaking loose. He was quick and aggressive and smart when fists started flying.

Ethan tried not to fall into any particular pattern while patrolling the streets. He let his ears and instincts guide him to the hot spots. Unlike some lawmen, he kept a low profile. Other town marshals were famous for making their rounds on horseback, keeping to the middle of the street; they believed a high profile on their part made would-be troublemakers think twice. They also argued that being on horseback allowed them to reach the trouble spots more quickly. But Ethan found that the possibility of his showing up anywhere at any given time without warning kept the rowdies on their toes. Besides, he felt too much like a target in the saddle of a tall horse roaming the streets. Instead he kept to the shadows, prowling the alleys and the boardwalks, instinctively avoiding open spaces and seldom silhouetting himself against lighted doors and windows.

On a warm night in late May, Ethan's prowling brought him to the corner of Texas and Cedar Streets. The Texas Side of Abilene was going great guns. The hitching posts were lined with cow ponies that wore more than a dozen different brands. Every gin joint and dance hall was doing a booming business. The boot heels of a hundred cowpokes whirling to the do-si-do resembled the thunder of stampeding herd, a steady undercurrent to the ebb and flow of boisterous voices, the tinkling of piano keeps, the jaded laughter of percentage girls, the clank of shot glasses, and the clatter of wheels of fortune. It was the pulse of Abilene, the music of making money, the only evidence necessary to demonstrate that Abilene was still the preferred destination of the Texas cattlemen. At least for this season.

Pausing in the indigo shadows of the main entrance to the Great Western Store, which advertised that it carried every single item a cowboy could ever want, Ethan fished the makings out of his long black frock coat and built a cigarette. From this vantage point he could see the length and breadth of the cowboy district. A pair of drovers came out of the Bull's Head Saloon, an establishment with an absentee owner in the person of that notorious Texas gunslinger, Ben Thompson. The two cowboys came stumbling through the batwings bellowing a boisterous rendition of a trail song, and making up enthusiasm for what they lacked in singing skills. As they turned down the boardwalk, a third man emerged from the mouth of an alley that ran between the Bull's Head and an adjacent clapboard structure. Ethan tensed reflexively. But the three men engaged in a moment of conversation. Then one of the cowboys laughed, and the pair of Texans moved on, the gut hooks strapped to their boots ringing on the warped planking of the boardwalk. The third man watched them go for a moment and then faded back into the alley.

Ethan was intrigued. There was something vaguely familiar about the third man, though at this distance, and in this light, he could not make out much about him. What was the man up to? Why was he lurking like a thief in the shadows? Ethan decided to find out. Pitching away the unsmoked quirly, he crossed the street and cut through to the trash-strewn alley that gave access to the rear of the Texas Street establishments. At the back corner of the Bull's Head he peered down the side alley where the man had been hiding. He was still there; Ethan could see him leaning against the saloon wall, his head turned toward Texas Street.

Considering his options, Ethan decided to just bide his time. He figured he could get up close without being spotted, but he wanted to identify the man before the man saw him. Ethan had to always keep in mind that he'd made a few enemies as an Overland troubleshooter, and to make matters worse he was now a Kansas town tamer with a reputation a lot of gunhawks he'd never met would be inclined to test. Besides, he had this gut hunch that he'd met the man before.

So he waited, and a few minutes later another erstwhile patron of the Bull's Head passed the mouth of the alley.

The man left the alley and placed himself in the cowboy's path. This put his back, more or less, to Ethan, and Ethan made his move, cat-footing down the alley. As he drew near, as yet undiscovered, he could make out some of the words exchanged by the two men.

"So what makes this one so special?" asked the cowboy who had just come out of the saloon. His voice was slurred and a little too loud from a surfeit of joy juice.

The other replied in hushed tones, and Ethan could not understand him.

"Two dollars!" exclaimed the cowboy. "I wouldn't pay eight bits for a poke even if she was the damned Queen of Sheba."

At that moment the cowboy's gaze shifted, and he saw Ethan for the first time. His eyes got wide and took a backward step. "Jesus Henry Christ," he muttered.

The other man turned—and Ethan recognized him.

It was Manolo, the youth who had once worked as a hostler at the Overland's Wolftrap Station, still thin as a reed, and his eyes still as dark as the Devil's heart. Manolo had stolen one of Ben Holladay's horses after getting into an altercation with Joe Cathcott. It had been Ethan's duty as Overland troubleshooter to get that horse back. But he hadn't even tried. Julie had liked Manolo, and for her sake Ethan had let him get away. A good many years had come and gone since last he'd seen Manolo. The Mexican wore a dark-green Chiquita and concho-studded trousers; he sported a pair of fancy silver spurs on his boots. A bandanna was tied in buccaneer fashion over his hair. Ethan looked for a knife. Manolo would never be without one. Sure enough, there was a bone-handled Bowie in a belt sheath. Startled, Manolo instinctively reached for it. But before the fifteen-inch blade could clear the sheath Ethan had a handful of Remington Army revolver.

"That would be a damned foolish thing to do," said Ethan quietly.

Manolo left the knife where it was and lifted his arms away from his body. His eyes glittered in an errant ray of moonlight, like polished obsidian in the darkness.

"I ain't done nothing, Marshal," declared the cowboy, suddenly stone cold sober. "I ain't heeled, neither. I was just walking along minding my own business when this feller stepped out and asked me if I wanted to spend some time with the prettiest lady in Abilene—"

"Keep walking, then," advised Ethan.

The cowboy didn't need to be told twice. He vanished like a bad dream.

Ethan carefully took the knife out of the sheath at Manolo's side, stuck it under his belt at the small of his back, and then holstered the Remington. He left the hammer thong off, however.

"The Overland horse," said Manolo, "I no have anymore."

"I'm not working for Ben Holladay anymore. If you think I'm interested in that horse-stealing stunt of yours, think again."

Manolo didn't look at all relieved, and he didn't volunteer any further information on his reason for lurking in an Abilene alley.

"So what are you doing here, Manolo? And how long have you been in town? Is what that Texan said the truth? Are you drumming up business for a calico queen?"

"We have only been here for one day," said the mestizo.

"We? Who's with you?"

Manolo looked away when he spoke the name. "Julie."

Ethan stared at him, certain that he hadn't heard right.

"I will take you to her," said Manolo. "If you want to see her."

The way he said it sounded like he thought Ethan would be a lot better off *not* seeing her, and Ethan figured he was probably right about that. But he couldn't resist.

"Lead the way," he said, wrestling with a strong premonition that Fate was in the process of dealing him a losing hand. It wasn't the first time, and it had gotten so that he could just about see it coming.

CHAPTER EIGHT

Manolo led the way, cutting through the alleys to the edge of town, and beyond. A hundred yards from the outskirts, across the dusty flats, stood a row of miserable shanties, structures that didn't look as though they could withstand a good strong gust of wind. These dwellings were occupied by women of ill repute. Soiled doves, calico queens, Mary Magdalenes, call them what you may. Neither Ethan nor his deputies patrolled there, and only ventured out when they received a report of a beating or a shooting. Ethan liked to think he had an understanding with the women of the Row, as it was called—they would stay out of Abilene and he would leave them alone.

Ethan's problem was that he simply did not want to believe that Manolo was being straight with him, that he was here with Julie and that Julie was in the Row, because if she really was then she'd become a whore, and to think of Julie as a whore was something Ethan didn't care to do. No, it simply couldn't be true. Halfway across the open ground, littered with trash and tumbleweeds, Ethan grabbed the mestizo by the arm and spun him around.

"What the hell are you up to, Manolo?"

"You want to see Julie? I take you to her."

"What is she doing in the Row?"

"What do you think? She sells herself."

"You lie!" Ethan gave Manolo a hard shove that sent the mestizo sprawling. Manolo was quick and agile—he sprang to his feet and tried to elude Ethan's grasp, but he wasn't *that* quick. Ethan shook him savagely, and then wrapped a hand around Manolo's throat. "You're a god-damn liar," he rasped through clenched teeth. "Julie would never do that, and you'd never let her. I don't know what kind of game you're playing here, but I don't like it."

Manolo's features bore no expression—his face was a stoic mask. There was no fear, no anger—nothing. He just stared blankly, returning Ethan's fierce gaze, and Ethan remembered now why he had never really felt comfortable around Manolo. He was one of the few people Ethan had never been able to read. Julie Cathcott had trusted him, even liked him, and for that reason Ethan had always given Manolo the benefit of the doubt. But that had been then. This was now.

"If you've got anything to say," he rasped, "you'd better hurry up and say it."

"I cannot stop her," said Manolo flatly, "so I try to help her."

Ethan grimly released the mestizo and gave him another shove. "Take me to her, then."

The Mexican went to one of the shanties and cautiously opened the door a crack to peer in. Ethan had no patience for whatever game Manolo was playing; he stepped up and threw the door open, pushing past the mestizo. By the feeble light of a tallow lamp, he saw someone, a woman, sprawled on a narrow bed with a stained and sagging mattress. He reached out to brush matted yellow hair away from the woman's face.

"My God," he breathed.

It *was* Julie.

She moved, moaning, turning over, and her blue eyes fluttered open briefly, then closed. Ethan realized that she was naked beneath a rancid-smelling blanket. Then he noticed the bottle of laudanum on a rickety table that, with the bed, constituted the sum total of the shanty's furnishings.

Ethan glowered at Manolo, who stood just inside the threshold. "How did this happen?" he asked. "How did she get like this?"

"After you kill her husband, she stayed on at Wolftrap," said Manolo. "When I heard Cathcott was dead I went back. By then she had started using the laudanum. I think it was to ease the pain of being lonely. She did not have to be alone. There were men who would have moved in with her. Maybe one or two might even have married her. But she did not want any of them. And then, when two Overland drivers fought over her with knives, *Señor* Holladay decided she was too much trouble to keep on."

"He let her go." Ethan shook his head. "That's one cold-hearted bastard."

"I go with her. The rumor was that you were in the Colorado gold camps. That is where we went. She was looking for you. One thing led to another, and she began to lay with men for money to pay for the laudanum. I tried to make her stop, but she told me to go away. I could not do that. So I stay with her, and try to make sure she does not lay with men who will beat her, or rob her. It is all I can do."

"Really." Ethan stared bleakly at Julie for a moment. This was his doing. There were no two ways about it. He should never have taken up with her. Because he had done so, and because he'd had to kill her jealous husband as a consequence, Julie had come to this.

A man appeared in the doorway. A quick glance told Ethan that he was a Texas drover, and a drunken one at that. The man leaned heavily against the door frame, fairly reeking of cheap whiskey, and tried to focus on Ethan. The latter's back was turned to him, and he didn't see the tin star on Ethan's shirt.

"Hey, mister," drawled the inebriated Texan, "if you're done ridin' her, I'd like to give it a whirl."

Ethan spun around and backhanded him, moving so

quickly that the cowboy didn't have a chance to defend himself. The blow staggered him, and his legs got tangled up together and he fell clumsily. The Row wasn't located inside the Abilene town limits, so the Texan was heeled; now, with murder glimmering in his eyes, he groped for the pistol at his side. Ethan stepped in and kicked it out of his hand as soon as the barrel of the hogleg cleared the holster. Reaching down, Ethan gathered two handfuls of the cowboy's shirt front and hauled the man to his feet, kneed him in the groin and then, as the drover jackknifed forward, felled him with a forearm across the back of his neck. Dazed, the Texan lay in the dust, writhing in pain and mumbling incoherently. Ethan started to turn away, but couldn't resist giving the cowboy a kick in the ribs for good measure. The drover rolled over, curled into a fetal ball, and puked up a stomach full of liquor.

Ethan noticed that several people—cowboys and working girls—had emerged from the shanties to see what the ruckus was all about. He held open the front of his frock coat so that everyone could get a good look at the star pinned to his shirt—and the Remington Army holstered on his hip—just in case there were people on the Row who didn't know him by sight.

"Go back inside and mind your own business," he said.

The onlookers wisely took his advice.

Going back inside the shanty, Ethan wrapped Julie in the blanket and carried her out and all the way to the Drover's Cottage. Manolo followed him that far, but didn't follow him into the hotel, and Ethan didn't invite him. The mestizo could fend for himself. Where he went and what happened to him was of no consequence to Ethan. The clerk at the desk stared at Ethan's burden, and looked like he was close to making some comment about the impropriety of bringing someone like Julie into an establishment like the Drover's. But there was something about the town marshal's expression that warned the clerk to keep his mouth shut. Taking her up to his room, Ethan put her in his bed and settled into a chair by the window, from which he could watch her. There he stayed through the night, sleeping not at all, seldom taking his eyes off her, and working his way through a whole host of might-have-beens and should-have-dones. It was a long and extremely unpleasant night. But by the looks of it, Julie Cathcott had suffered a good many of those, and all on his account.

When she came to, bright sunlight was slanting through the room's solitary window and seemed to drive daggers through her skull. She moaned and rolled away from the light, squeezing her eyes shut. Something cold and damp on her face made her open them again. Someone was bending over her, and she tried to focus on the face, but that wasn't easy to do because the room was tilting, and spinning a little to boot, so that she started to feel like she was going to throw up.

"Julie? Julie, it's me."

She recognized the voice, but for a moment failed to put a name to it. She couldn't remember much these days. That was the work of the laudanum. Not that she minded. What little she *could* remember simply convinced her that she was much better off forgetting. Her vision gradually cleared, and the sight of Ethan jogged her memory and elicited a gasp of surprise from her.

"It's okay, Julie," he said softly. "You're safe now."

"Where—where am I?"

"My room at the Drover's Cottage, in Abilene."

"Abilene . . ." Her voice faded, and then suddenly, violently, she leaned over the side of the bed and vomited. Ethan moved to sit beside her on the edge of the bed, brushing her disheveled yellow hair out of her face and telling her it would be all right, even though he didn't believe it, even though he knew that nothing was ever all right, at least not for very long. When she was done she lay back on the pillow, exhausted, looking pale and weak.

"Julie, I'm sorry," he said, his voice thick with emotion. "I shouldn't have left you. I'll make it up to you, somehow."

She reached out and touched his arm, her hand trembling, and he bent down to kiss her cheek and tasted the salt of her tears, and she whispered something that he could not hear. He bent closer, and heard one word. *Laudanum.* Racked with guilt, Ethan pulled away, told her he had to go out for a little while and urged her to get some sleep, and quickly left the room.

Clooney was sitting in a chair on the hotel veranda, the chair tilted back against the wall. A cigar was clenched in the gambler's teeth, and he was watching the activity in the stock pen across the way, as Texas longhorns were being herded onto slat-sided livestock cars hitched to a Union Pacific locomotive. Pale dust bled the summer sky of every trace of blue.

"Morning, Ethan," drawled Clooney. "Fine morning, too. But then, every morning I live to see is a fine morning, don't you think?"

"Could be," said Ethan, distracted. He paused to scan the empty lots around the Drover's Cottage, and the distant dusty town, squinting against the hurting brightness of the late morning sun. "What are you doing here? I thought you generally slept until noon."

Clooney smiled. "Generally. But I was hoping you'd have a few minutes, so we could talk."

Ethan gave him a hard, suspicious look. He had a feeling he knew what the gambler wanted to talk about, and it was a subject Ethan did not care, at the present time, to discuss with anyone. "Maybe later," he said brusquely, and left the veranda, bending his steps for the town.

The gambler caught up with him, fell into stride beside him. "Mind if I walk with you?"

"Would it make any difference if I *did* mind?"

Clooney shrugged. "Depends on how set you were on being alone."

Ethan sighed. "What do you want?"

"Just want to know what happened last night."

"You tell me."

"The whole town is talking. You damn near kicked a

cowboy to death and then you took a whore out of the shanty town and—"

"She's not a whore. And the next person who calls her that I *will* kick to death."

"Sorry, Ethan. I take it you know this woman."

"Yes, I know her," said Ethan bleakly. "And so do you. It's Julie Cathcott."

"The woman from Wolftrap Station? You're joking."

"I wish I was."

"Well, I'll be. How did she come to . . ." Clooney didn't finish the thought. For a moment he just walked along with Ethan and didn't say a word, which suited Ethan just fine. Finally, as they neared the edge of Abilene proper, Clooney cast a sidelong glance at the town marshal and said, "I don't know that you'll have any trouble from the Texans because of last night. But Ransom and White—now that's another story."

"I know."

"I'm not one to meddle in the affairs of others, usually, as you know," continued the gambler. "But in your case I make an exception." His smile was meant to disarm.

"Now why should I be so lucky," said Ethan dryly.

"Because I figure I'm better off with you being the town marshal then someone else—especially someone like Happy Jack Crawford."

Ethan nodded. He thought it possible that there was another reason—that Clooney wanted to be a friend, or felt that there was a bond of friendship that already existed between them. Ethan didn't agree, nor was he interested in having the gambler as a friend. It wasn't anything personal—he'd just learned that there was a high price to pay for having a friend, since a friend would sooner or later let you down, and that was a price Ethan was in no mood to pay. Still, he felt that there was more to Clooney's concern for his welfare than business, even though, if true, the gambler would never come right out and admit as much.

"Anyway," said Clooney, "if there's anything I can do, just let me know." And before Ethan had a chance to respond, the gambler veered off, heading for the Lone Star Saloon.

The Texas Side of Abilene was quiet after a typical night of excess, but the respectable side of town was bustling with activity. As Ethan negotiated the boardwalks, he got the distinct impression that the people were giving him longer, more speculative looks than usual, not to mention wider berths than was usually the case. Or maybe it was just his imagination. He knew how it must look to the upstanding citizens of the town—all the proper gentlemen and their proper ladies—to have their town marshal taken up with a trollop from the Row, installing her in his hotel room. And it wouldn't make any difference to them if they knew the whole story, if they were made aware of his history with Julie, and of what he owed her. They wouldn't care about that. And Ethan didn't care about them. He didn't care if they approved or not. He wasn't going to abandon Julie Cathcott again, no matter what the cost.

Entering a mercantile, he told the clerk he wanted to purchase a ready-made dress. He had no idea what kind of clothes Julie had come to Abilene with, but it was a safe bet that if she'd had any possessions with her in the shanty they were gone now, scavenged by the other denizens of the Row. A pair of ladies watched him as he picked a dress from the small selection available; they whispered behind their hands, intentionally indiscreet. It was all Ethan could do to refrain from telling them to mind their own business. The dress he chose was a plain, modest calico print that looked to him as though it would fit Julie perfectly. He knew her shape and size—after all, he'd spent many nights in her bed. It bothered him to think that an untold number of men had since lain with her. He tried to force that aspect of it out of his mind as he purchased the dress, along with a chemise, a pair of kid-and-cloth shoes, and a brush and mirror set. On his way out he tipped his hat to the ladies and gave them a cold smile.

As he started across the street he heard his name called out, and then a woman screamed, a scream of alarm, not of pain, and he whirled to see the Texas cowboy he'd roughed up last night on the Row shuffling stiffly out of an alley. The cowboy's face was swollen and bruised, and he moved like a man for whom even the slightest exertion was an intensely painful experience. Ethan figured he'd broken at least one or two of the man's ribs. The Texan had a pistol in hand. His features were twisted into a rictus of pure hate. Before Ethan could draw his Remington Army the cowboy raised his gun and fired. The range was long, over thirty feet, and there weren't many Texas cowpunchers who were very talented with the short gun; the bullet missed Ethan and struck a saddle horse tethered to a hitching rail that stood about a dozen paces behind the marshal. The animal screamed and fell, thrashing. Moving sideways, Ethan dropped his packages and drew the Remington and fired—he got the first shot off before the packages hit the ground. He was vaguely aware of the fact that people were scattering for cover up and down the street. But his attention was focused on the Texan, and even as the first bullet struck the cowboy in the shoulder and spun him around, Ethan was squeezing the trigger again, because there were no half measures for him; the cowboy had tried to kill him and now he was going to die, and Ethan wasn't going to take any foolish risks, like merely wounding his adversary. The second bullet slammed into the Texan's side and blew a hole in his belly. He dropped to his knees, sagged forward, then with one final supreme effort straightened and lifted his pistol. Ethan grimaced—and fired a third time, taking more careful aim, and putting the bullet right between the man's eyes. The cowboy's body slammed backward onto the hardpack of the blood-splattered street.

Taking a deep breath, Ethan lowered the Remington and approached the dead man, bending down to pluck the six-shooter from lifeless fingers, and taking a long look at his handiwork, wishing he'd at least known the man's name. He supposed he would learn it eventually—after all, this was a killing that would have repercussions. A killing that would change everything, perhaps undo all the hard work he had done to create an unspoken accord with the Texas cattlemen.

Several townsmen were venturing closer, among them Doc Fields and Tolliver, the cabinet maker who also made caskets for those destined for Boot Hill. They were both coming to see if there was work for them to do. Fields took one look at the cowboy and then turned to Tolliver. "He's all yours," he said, with a dismissive gesture, and walked away. Tolliver glanced at Ethan, an eyebrow raised, and Ethan knew what the man was thinking.

"Let his outfit pay for it," he said. "And if they don't, you can have his guns and whatever's in his pockets, as usual."

Tolliver nodded and, expressionless, sat on his heels beside the corpse and began to go through the man's pockets. It was common frontier practice for the casket-maker and undertaker to pay for their expenses in seeing to a person's mortal remains by confiscating the belongings of the dead.

Ethan picked up the things he had purchased at the mercantile and headed for the jail. He met Johnny Rowe halfway there.

"What happened?" asked Rowe. "I heard shooting."

"I had to kill a drover."

Rowe was shocked. Ever since he had pinned on the tin star and started working as Ethan Payne's deputy, he'd busted plenty of cowboy heads—but not a single Texan had been killed by Abilene's peace officers.

"How come?"

"It's a long story."

"Who was he? Who did he ride for?"

Ethan was ashamed to admit that he did not know the answer to either question. It was the least a man could do to know the identity of his victim.

"Well," said Rowe, looking at Ethan curiously, sensing that there was more to the story but knowing better than to press the issue, "I'll go see what I can find out."

Ethan nodded. "I'll hold down the fort. Besides, I expect Mr. Ransom will be coming to see me."

Rowe smiled ruefully. "I expect so."

The young deputy walked on and Ethan proceeded to the jail. Once there he poured some coffee from the pot atop the stove. The java was very strong and thick and lukewarm—the fire in the stove's belly had died down. Ethan drank it anyway. Then he sat behind the desk, put his feet up, and waited for Ransom. He didn't have to wait long. Ransom came in without knocking, his eyes like daggers.

"Damn it, Payne, what the hell do you think you're doing?"

"Defending myself."

"That kind of thing isn't supposed to happen on that side of town."

"I guess I should have asked him to step across the deadline before he drew on me," said Ethan dryly.

"And I'm guessing this has something to do with the woman in your hotel room."

Ethan felt his temper getting away from him. He was tired, having slept not at all the night before, and he'd just had to kill somebody. He wasn't in the best frame of mind, and he knew he wasn't going to be able to tolerate much of G.W. Ransom's holier-than-thou attitude.

"Look," he rasped, "you have every right to question me about the way I do my job. But my personal life is none of your affair. And I strongly advise you to stay out of my business."

Ransom snorted. "As long as you wear that badge you represent the town of Abilene, and its people. So when you start keeping a two-dollar whore in your hotel room—"

Ethan got up quickly, angrily, and as he swung his long legs off the desk he cleared it of the paper debris—wanted posters and old newspapers—that had cluttered it. The violence in his movements startled Ransom, who took a step back, and then recovered his composure and scowled, annoyed that he had shown fear—he, a man who had commanded soldiers in battle, and who had never flinched from danger. But there was something about Ethan Payne that scared any sensible man. There was that, and there was the indisputable fact that he was getting old, and it seemed that the less time you had left to you the more precious life became.

"You push a man too hard sometimes," said Ethan coldly.

Ransom nodded. "I won't deny that. But if you care about your future here, you'll heed my words."

"She's not a two-dollar whore."

"I'm told you took her from the Row. What was she doing there if she wasn't a prostitute?"

"She was there through no fault, and no choice, of her own. She was there because of me."

Ransom's eyes narrowed. "You know her?"

"I do. She's a good, decent woman who's fallen on hard times. Maybe you don't know anything about hard times, Mr. Ransom, but when you're in 'em you'd be surprised where you might end up."

"I've had my share," said Ransom, defensively. "I wasn't born with wealth, Marshal. I started out with nothing. I've worked hard to get where I am now."

"Some people work hard all their lives and never get anywhere. Never get an even break." Ethan was thinking first and foremost of Julie, who had labored long and hard to keep the Wolftrap Station going while her good-for-nothing husband lay about or took off yondering. But he realized that what he'd just said could also apply to his father; Abner Payne had not been a worthless drunk all his life. He'd worked diligently for years to make a go of his farm. But he'd sweated and bled for naught, and eventually his will to succeed, lacking nurture too long, wilted and died.

"People end up where they deserve to," said Ransom. "You land at the bottom, it's up to you whether you stay there or pick yourself up by your bootstraps and climb back up again."

Ethan shook his head. Only someone who had never been at the "bottom" would think the way Ransom thought.

"Sometimes you can't do it on your own," he replied. "Sometimes you need a helping hand. And I'm going to help her. Whether you like it or not."

"Fine. I can understand how you might want to help someone, especially someone you're acquainted with, someone from your past, who has fallen on hard times. That's admirable. But it's also futile. You can't help someone unless they're willing to help themselves. And while I do not know the women who work on the Row personally, I know enough about them to say with certitude that they have given up on themselves."

"I'm glad it's all so black and white for you, Ransom," said Ethan.

"How exactly do you propose to help this woman?"

"I'm not sure, yet."

"And while you figure that out, you put all the decent folk of Abilene at risk. Kill a Texas cowboy and you may have to deal with his whole outfit. You know that, Payne."

"I handled the situation with Tell Jenkins. I'll handle this. You don't need to worry."

"Obviously I do," murmured Ransom, on his way out the door.

CHAPTER NINE

When Ethan got back to the Drover's Cottage the clerk on duty at the desk handed him a telegram, which he said had just been delivered from the telegraph office. Ethan pocketed the telegram without giving it a glance. He had a lot on his mind. Twenty-four hours earlier he'd thought he was, if not exactly rolling in clover, certainly making some headway toward improving his lot in life. But all of a sudden everything had changed. He didn't feel sorry for himself. Self-pity was a waste of time. He'd learned that just watching his father. No, he could adjust to the new situation, and all of its ramifications. But his talk with Ransom—and the one with Clooney—had him wondering just what kind of ramifications there might be that he wasn't considering.

Most of all, though, he wanted to know what had happened to Julie that she had fallen so far from grace. He had thought of her often since leaving the employ of the Overland, and he'd wondered what had become of her. He'd hoped that a nice young man with a promising future had happened along and carried her off. If anyone deserved that, it was Julie Cathcott. The one thing he'd never in his wildest dreams imagined was that she would turn into a calico queen. There had to be more to it than what Manolo had told him.

And yet he wasn't sure if he should ask her. In the time they had spent together at Wolftrap Station, Julie had asked him about his past, and he'd been taciturn, telling her little, preferring not to dredge up old memories, set loose old ghosts. And she had understood his reticence for what it was, and respected his wishes. Surely, whatever had happened to her in years past had been dark and desperate, and something she would not wish to dwell on, and assuming that were so could he do any less for her than she had done for him?

She was in bed when he reached his room, sleeping fitfully. He opened up the trunk at the foot of the bed and took out a bottle of whiskey stashed within and then settled down in the chair by the window and swallowed a few doses of nerve medicine. It made him feel better, smoothed out the rough edges, and took the edge off the guilt he was feeling. It also made him drowsy; exhaustion caught up with him, and he drifted off into a light and troubled sleep, slumped in the chair, chin resting on chest.

He awoke with a start to see Julie sitting on the edge of the bed, looking at him from behind a veil of tousled hair the color of goldenrod. Her eyes were buried deep within darkened sockets, her lips were pale and cracked, her complexion like ash from a long-dead fire. She looked weak, brittle, almost lifeless. She had the counterpane pulled up around her shoulders to conceal her nakedness, but it was pulled up haphazardly, and her breasts were partially exposed, but she didn't even realize it, or if she realized it she didn't care. Ethan got up and pulled the counterpane tighter.

"Where's my medicine?" she asked, her voice a mere husk.

"I don't have any laudanum, Julie."

"I've got to have it. I can't live without it." The hysteria mounted swiftly, and she pushed him away, feeling trapped. "Get out of my way. You can't stop me!" She tried to get up, to walk to the door, but she took only one step before falling, and he was there to catch her. Even with his support she made no effort to stand, but rather hung there, dead weight in his arms. He sat down on the floor with his back to the bed's footboard and held her in his arms.

"Just let me go, Ethan," she whispered. "I'm begging you."

"I can't do that."

She mumbled something else that he could not make out, and then drifted into unconsciousness, and he sat there for a while, holding her close, finally getting up and laying her on the bed and covering her with sheet and counterpane, tucking her in snugly so that she would not roll out and hurt herself in her sleep.

There was a discreet tapping on the door. Ethan opened it to find the desk clerk standing in the hallway. The desk clerk tried to see past Ethan—like everyone else in Abilene he had heard the rumors about the marshal and the woman he'd brought out of the Row—but Ethan was too broad-beamed to allow it.

"What do you want?"

"There's a man downstairs. He won't go away. He says he wants to see you, or the woman."

"Mexican?"

The clerk nodded.

"Tell him he can come up—when he brings a doctor with him."

"Is . . . everything all right?"

"It will be." Ethan closed the door in the clerk's inquisitive face.

"The thing is," said the doctor after examining the unconscious Julie, "that if what this fellow says is true"—he gestured in the direction of Manolo, who stood in a corner of the room; the mestizo glanced at the physician and then returned his gaze to the frail form of the woman in the bed, where it had been fixed ever since his arrival in Ethan's hotel room—"then we can safely assume she is very much addicted to the opium. To abruptly withhold it from her entirely will be a severe shock to her system, one that I cannot in good conscience guarantee she will survive."

"So what are you saying?" asked Ethan. "That she can never be free of it?"

"She can be, but it will take a lot of work on your part, and suffering on hers. She must be withdrawn gradually from her reliance on the opium, you understand. It will take a firm commitment on your part, to help her through this."

"I'll help her through," murmured Ethan, gazing down at Julie. "I owe her that much."

The doctor nodded, searched his medical bag for a moment, and came up with a brown bottle. "Start with a spoonful three times a day. In a week's time reduce that to twice a day. A week later once a day. She will beg you for more. You must be firm. Do not let anything she says sway you. It is her only hope. If she is not weaned from this devil's milk then it will kill her, and sooner rather than later. She'll crave more and more of it, until one day she takes a dose that stops her heart."

"I understand," said Ethan. "You can count on me."

"*She's* counting on you, Marshal. That's the thing." The doctor closed up his bag. "I'll check back in about a week's time to see how she's doing."

Ethan walked him to the door. "Send me a bill, Doc. You know I'm good for it."

The craggy, white-haired sawbones smiled and nodded. "Yes, I know. We'll settle up later. Good day."

Ethan closed the door, turned to Manolo. "I could use your help," he said. "But I'm not sure I can trust you."

"I will do whatever is needed to help Miss Julie," said the mestizo.

"I don't question your dedication to her. But are you strong enough to resist her when she wants more of the laudanum than you're supposed to give?"

"You can trust me."

Ethan thought it over and, with some reluctance, handed Manolo the bottle. "I've got to go take care of some business," he said. "I should be back tonight. Never let her out of your sight. And do not let her out of this room. I'll have some food sent up from the restaurant across the street."

"It will be as you say," said Manolo.

Ethan gathered up his hat and gunbelt. He had the door open and was about to cross the threshold when he made a decision and gave Manolo another look—this one as hard as granite.

"If you fail me—and her—I'll kill you."

Manolo nodded. He knew Ethan Payne well enough to know that this was no idle threat.

Later that night Ethan remembered the telegram. He discovered it when he was searching the pockets of his frock coat for cigarette makings. As he opened the telegram the whole world suddenly faded. All the sights and sounds faded from his consciousness, so that he was aware of only one thing, the name on the telegram—*Lilah Webster*.

Dear Ethan stop I read about you in the newspaper stop until then I did not know if you were alive or dead stop even though I never heard from you I never gave up hope stop I still care about you stop if you get this at least let me know that you are well end

Stunned, Ethan stood at the window and stared out at the stockyards without really seeing them. In years past he had tried desperately to force Lilah Webster out of his mind—and out of his heart. The last time he had heard from her he'd been an Overland troubleshooter. In that letter she had informed him of her plans to marry another. He could still remember the words by heart, though long ago he had destroyed the letter, thinking that by destroying it he would also destroy the hold it had over him. *I wish things had turned out differently for us*, she had written. *I still think of you often, and care for you, and I hope you know that you will always be in my heart. I don't know when, exactly, I came to the realization that things were just not going to work out for us. I hope, as well, that you are happy wherever you are. God had other plans for us, and we must trust in His judgment, and be confident that His plans are superior to our own.*

Ethan had lost all faith in God's superior judgment, but he'd simply preferred to assume that in the years since that letter had reached him Lilah had lived a life of contentment and fulfillment. He assumed she was still married to—what was his name? Stephen, that was it—and the two of them probably even had children by now. She had no doubt learned how to put him out of her mind and get on with her life, and she would not have thought to wire him but for the fact that his name appeared in a newspaper article. Furthermore, she was only curious about his well-being for old times' sake, and nothing more.

Ethan glanced at Julie, who was sleeping soundly in the bed. That was the present, and perhaps even the future; the telegram represented the past that he was still trying to escape. He wadded the telegram up and tossed it aside.

Ethan figured the first order of business was to deal with any trouble that might be forthcoming from the outfit of the drover he'd killed. So he rode out to the cowboy camp, and he went alone, as was his custom. He told the outfit's big augur exactly what had happened, leaving nothing out and adding no embellishments. The big augur thought it over and decided the fact of the matter was that the altercation had been over a woman, nothing more nor less, and that made it a personal matter between Ethan and the dead man. The killing had been done fair and square—that is to say, face-to-face—and the confrontation had been instigated by the drover; this the rancher had already learned. The bottom line was that he had no quarrel with Abilene's marshal. More than that, he appreciated the fact that Abilene's marshal had taken it upon himself to pay for the funeral of the man he'd killed.

In the days to come Ethan worried most about Julie's physical condition. All the life seemed to have been sucked out of her. Her smiles, few and far between, were haunted by a deep and abiding sadness. Her composure was, at best, a fragile façade. At night her violent nightmares would rouse Ethan from his slumbers in the chair by the window, and he would shake her until she woke, and then sometimes hold her until she had fallen asleep again. Her craving for the laudanum was a terrible thing to behold. It drove her mad with longing. She begged him, cursed him, wailed and moaned and laughed hysterically. When he gave her a dose it seemed to quickly transform her into another person entirely—someone who was mellow and thoroughly contented. But the contentment was of short duration. As the effects of the opiate wore off she became ever more agitated. It was an exhausting, endless cycle.

Ethan went back to working the night shift, but when he was away from the hotel he made sure Manolo was always on hand to be certain that Julie did not try to run away. Or kill herself. At times she sank into such an abyss of black despair that he feared she might try to take her own life. His attempts to get her to talk to him, to tell him what had happened since last they'd seen each other, usually met with failure. She had but one thing on her mind, and that was how to get the next dose of laudanum as soon as possible. It was the only thing that really mattered to her. All he could do was wait—and hope. Hope that, in time, as he reduced her dosage, she would become more interested in . . . life.

It was a conversation that he had with Ed Wilcox that convinced him of the right thing to do where Julie was concerned. He arrived at the jail late in the afternoon to take over for Wilcox and begin his shift. As usual, Wilcox gave him a rundown on everything of note that had occurred during the previous eight hours, and that included one man arrested for public intoxication. When that chore was done, Wilcox usually picked up his hat and coat and bade Ethan farewell. But this time he hesitated, crushing the brim of his hat in his big, burly hands, clearly agonizing over how best to broach the subject that preoccupied him.

Ethan decided the deputy needed some prodding.

"Something's gnawing at you, Ed. Why don't you tell me what it is?"

Wilcox grimaced. "Ordinarily I'd mind my own business where you and that woman, Julie Cathcott, are concerned. Thing is, it's becoming my business now."

"How do you figure?" Ethan tried to mask his annoyance, but his words were clipped.

"Before she came along you were sitting pretty, Ethan. Just about everybody in Abilene thought you were doing a damned fine job as town marshal. But now there are a lot of folks out there who are talking bad about you. Saying that they don't want your kind wearing the marshal's badge." Wilcox shook his head. "It's plumb amazing how people can change so quick-like. How they can turn on you without warning."

"Well, until they turn town marshal into an elective office, we don't have to worry about what they think."

Wilcox peered at him. "You know, when I heard all about how you got the drop on McKittrick and them K-Bar cowboys, I figured you had to be one of the smartest of God's critters. But what you just said is one of the dumbest things I ever heard. It's not just the townfolk, Ethan. It's the railroad men and drovers and the drifters. Keeping them on the straight and narrow isn't all about tin stars and shooting irons. It's about what you and I and everyone else who wears a star stands for. Do we stand for right? Or wrong? If you stand for right they're less likely to test you. If you're wrong they'll figure you're no better than they are, and have no place telling them what they can or cannot do. I don't know if that makes much sense. I'm not good with words. . . ."

"It makes sense," said Ethan. "But you don't know the whole story about me and Julie."

"No, I don't. But the whole story doesn't matter near as much as the appearance of it."

Ethan sighed, settled back in his chair and moodily stared at the clutter on the desk in front of him. Wilcox stood there, waiting warily for the chewing out he figured was forthcoming. Ethan, though, had no desire to chastise his deputy. He knew that Ed was saying these things because Wilcox liked him. It wasn't that Ed worried about losing his job, but he was concerned about Ethan keeping his. Ethan couldn't lash out at someone who had his best interests at heart, even if what he had to say was unpalatable.

"I guess you're right, Ed," said Ethan. "I know it matters what people think. I've made the job more dangerous for all of us by what I've done. It's up to me to set it right. And there's only one way to do that."

Wilcox breathed an immense sigh of relief. He figured Ethan was going to give the woman some money and put her on the next train out of town. All he knew about the woman was that the marshal had been acquainted with her in the past, and there was some talk about how Ethan Payne had killed a man over her, but Wilcox didn't know any of the details, and he didn't know anyone who did, because the marshal had been tight-lipped about his history with Julie Cathcott.

"If there's anything I can do to help, just ask," said Wilcox.

"I'm going to marry her, Ed."

It took a moment to sink in. Wilcox was flabbergasted. "You've got to be kidding."

"Nope." Ethan fixed a steely eye on his deputy. "You don't have a problem with that, do you, Ed?"

Wilcox wanted to point out that marrying the prostitute wasn't going to improve the situation one bit. Yet he distinctly heard the challenge in Ethan's query, and thought better of stating an objection to the marshal's plan.

Ethan stood up and went to the stove and poured himself some coffee. "I hope this won't cause you a problem, Ed," he said flatly. "You're a fine deputy, and I'd hate to lose you."

That was about as plain an ultimatum as Wilcox had ever received. Either he kept his opinions to himself from here on in or he could find another job. The only thing that kept him from telling Ethan what he could do with that ultimatum was his loyalty to Abilene's town marshal. That loyalty was being tested, but it remained more or less intact.

"I'll stand with you," he said.

"Good. Don't worry so much, Ed. Any trouble that comes from this, I can handle it."

"Sure," said Wilcox, and he could only hope he sounded confident.

CHAPTER TEN

His name was Renny, and he was a gun for hire whose reputation reached from the Bloody Border with Mexico to the Absaroka country. But he didn't look like much more than a down-at-heels drifter. A gaunt man, without an ounce of fat on him, he was of medium height, with brown hair and brown eyes, and a three-day stubble of beard on his cheeks. His clothes were dusty and ordinary. His headgear was a beat-up, sweat-stained campaign hat. The pistol at his side was a Colt residing in a plain, worn holster, and the saddle under him was a run-of-the-mill hull lacking any embellishments. The horse the saddle was strapped to was a lanky sorrel with one stocking and no brand; the cayuse didn't look like much, but Renny knew it had plenty of bottom. All in all, both horse and rider looked as unremarkable—and durable—as the rolling prairie that stretched seemingly without end in every direction. In fact the only thing that broke the monotony of the prairie was the train sitting on the tracks that lay east-to-west across the grasslands. The train consisted of a dark-red locomotive, a coal car, a green passenger car, and a caboose. Renny had seen the plume of black smoke rising from the mogul's diamond-shaped stack many miles back. Now he was close enough to see that two horses were tethered to the back of the train, and two people were standing on the front platform of the passenger car. One was a man, and by his attire Renny took him to be a member of the train's crew. The other person was a woman, tall and trim in a tight-waisted blue serge skirt and short jacket, with a pale yellow chemise beneath the latter. Her raven-black hair was tied in a ponytail, and hung long and straight down her back. The hair, the strong cheekbones, and the dark brown eyes that looked almost black gave Renny reason to think she had Indian blood in her. She had white blood in her, too—that accounted for her angular features, especially the delicately sculptured nose, and the height. Like many half-breed women, she was pretty.

Renny scanned the train as he rode near, wary as always when approaching a situation with so many unknowns. The windows of the passenger car were covered with brocaded curtains. There was a young man covered with soot who shoveled coal into the mogul's firebox. There was no movement in or around the caboose. The man who stood with the raven-haired woman pulled something from the pocket of his overalls—a movement that drew Renny's attention. It was a timepiece, and he checked it before showing it to the woman, apparently at her request, because the first thing she said as Renny checked his horse beside the passenger car was: "You're late, Mr. Renny."

"Am I too late? If so, I'll just turn around and go back where I come from."

"No," she said. "Not too late."

"Then why waste time talking about it?"

"Mr. Marston doesn't like to be kept waiting. Besides, this is UP track, and there is a westbound train due in a little over an hour."

"Like I said, why waste time, then?"

She allowed herself a taut smile—just the faintest curling up of one side of her mouth. Her gaze, he noticed, was very direct, and he liked that.

"Come inside, Mr. Renny. Ben, take Mr. Renny's horse to the back of the train."

Renny dismounted, handed the reins to the man named Ben, and hesitated, watching the man lead the sorrel toward the back of the caboose where the other two horses were tethered.

"Don't worry, Mr. Renny," she said. "We don't have designs on your horse."

"It's just that I like to do things for myself."

"You should let others do for you every now and then," she said, and this time her smile was broader, and saucy, and she turned with a flare of one finely curved hip to open the door to the passenger car and step inside. He went in after her.

It was like walking into the palace of a maharajah. After crossing days of endless prairie, the sheer opulence of the car's interior made Renny stop in his tracks and gape at his surroundings. The elegant furniture was upholstered in shiny black horsehair and gold velveteen. The walls were covered with a maroon brocade. The damask curtains were the same shade as the walls. Oils of lush, misty landscapes and a voluptuous nude portrait hung on the walls in ornate gilt frames. Gas wall lamps reflected off polished brass fixtures. Crystal decanters gleamed on a rich mahogany sideboard.

There were three men in the car. Two sat facing each other on opposite sofas. The one on Renny's left was young, hardly more than a kid—Renny doubted that he'd yet found shaving necessary. He was duded up in black concho-studded trousers and a short black jacket adorned with fancy beadwork, and there was a black sombrero on the sofa beside him. His pearl-handled pistols were lodged in cross-draw holsters. In spite of his outfit he wasn't from south of the border; he had pale, freckled skin, unruly carrot-red hair and a lazy blue eye. The man on Renny's right was tall, angular, with long flowing locks the color of ripened wheat, a bushy mustache concealing his mouth, and dark, hooded eyes. He was clad in a dusty frock coat and trousers of black broadcloth and wore big Chihuahuan spurs on his boots. Renny couldn't see any guns, but something told him the man was heeled, and knew how to use whatever artillery he had secreted on his person.

"Ah, this must be Mr. Renny," said the third man. He was seated in a wheelchair, clad in an impeccable red smoking jacket. He had the soft, pale face of a poet, an unruly mop of walnut-brown hair with a streak of white running right through it, and a faint accent Renny pegged as British. "So glad you could make it. Perhaps our guest would care for a drink to wash down the dust of a long trail, Elyse. Just name your poison, Mr. Renny."

Renny briefly scanned the sideboard. "I'll settle for anything that has a kick."

With that cat-like smile still on her lips, the woman went to the sideboard and poured him a drink, and while she performed this amenity, Renny returned his attention to the man with the long yellow hair, and gave him a curt nod.

"Howdy, Killough."

The man returned the nod. "Hello, Renny. How're life down Texas way?"

"Same as always. Short and brutal."

Gentleman Jim Killough chuckled, a deep, rumbling sound. "That's what I know. It would've been plenty short for me had I stuck around Fort Worth any longer than I did."

"They were real disappointed in not getting a chance to hang you," said Renny. "One of the three men you shot dead around that poker table was the son of a very powerful man. I'm surprised he didn't send a few bounty men after you."

"Oh, he did." Killough smirked beneath the thick mustache. "I sent two of 'em back to him in pine boxes, ready for planting. After that I just left 'em where they lay. It was getting too damned expensive to ship 'em home."

"I wasn't aware that the two of you were acquainted," said the man in the wheelchair.

"We know each other," said Killough. "But we aren't what you'd call friends. You might say we show each other some professional courtesy. And that's about all."

"Well then, Mr. Renny, allow me to introduce myself, and my other guest. I am Ash Marston. And this is Willie Creed, who has made quite a name for himself down around Tucson and Yuma."

Renny peered at Creed. "I've heard of him," he told Marston. "I've heard he likes to backshoot people."

Creed stiffened, his features hardening with anger. Killough's low, soft chuckle came again. "You haven't changed, Renny. As tactful as a bull in heat."

"I never backshot nobody," muttered Creed, sulky.

"That's not what I've heard," said Renny.

"There are a few rumors floating around about me that aren't true," said Killough. "And about you, too, Renny, I'd wager."

"I can't deny that," said Renny. Elyse approached him with a shot glass two-thirds full of an amber liquid. He accepted the glass, sniffed it, and then took a sip. It was bourbon, a smooth liquid flame sliding down his throat and exploding in his belly.

"Now, gentlemen," said Marston, his voice like silk wrapped around steel. "I did not invite the three of you here to fight among yourselves."

"I'm past ready to find out why you *did* invite us," said Killough.

"But before you do that," said Renny, "I'll take the five hundred dollars you said you'd pay me just to come here."

"Certainly." Marston nodded to Elyse. She moved to a desk tucked away in a corner of the passenger car and, opening a drawer, took out a canvas money sack, which she dangled in front of Renny, smiling coyly.

"Five hundred dollars in gold double eagles, Mr. Renny," she said. "I believe that was the price of getting you here. There's a lot more where that came from, by the way."

"Absolutely," concurred Marston. "Ten thousand dollars, in fact. That's the bounty I'm offering to one and all of you for the death of one Ethan Payne."

"I know that name," said Killough. "He used to troubleshoot for the Overland Mail. Seem to recall hearing that he's a lawman now."

"In Abilene," said Renny. "There's a lot of talk about him down in Texas. He outfoxed the whole K-Bar outfit when they rode in to bust one of their own out of the Abilene hoosegow. Rigged the whole jail up with dynamite and threatened to blow them all to kingdom come if they didn't shed their iron."

"I've met Ethan Payne," said Willie Creed.

The others looked at him.

Creed nodded. "When I was eleven years old I got a job as a hostler at the Ten Fork Station of the Overland. Payne was the troubleshooter for that section. They say he killed a stationmaster after sleeping with the man's wife. That's why he got hog-legged."

"I didn't know you worked for the Overland," said Marston, with a glance at Elyse. "And I thought I'd found out all there is to know about the three of you."

Creed grinned. "Willie Creed ain't my real name. I changed it not long after I stole a bunch of Overland stock. The beginning of my life of crime, you might say. That was after Payne left Ben Holladay's employ, of course. I wouldn't have chanced it long as he was troubleshooter, on account of he's the last man I'd want on my trail. The man they sent after me wasn't near as good as he thought he was. I killed him. My first killing, too. Lot easier than I thought it would be."

"Sounds to me like you're afraid of this man Payne," said Killough.

Creed's eyes narrowed. "I ain't afraid of no man."

"There's a difference between fear and respect, Killough," said Renny.

"Yeah," said Creed, appreciating Renny's advocacy. "I respect him but I ain't afraid of him."

"Mr. Renny is right," said Marston. "And he's right about Payne being town marshal of Abilene."

"Why do you want him dead?" asked Killough.

"Does that matter? Kill him, Mr. Killough, and you're ten thousand dollars richer."

Gentleman Jim chuckled. "I kill a peace officer and I become one of the most wanted men in the West. If I'm going to be on the run for the rest of my life I want to know why."

Marston pursed his lips. "Very well," he said, and his voice took on a harsh edge. "I want Ethan Payne dead because nearly twenty years ago he sentenced me to a lifetime in this chair."

"He crippled you?" asked Creed.

"I don't like that word, and I'll thank you to refrain from using it again. I first met Payne on a riverboat bound for New Orleans. He and a friend of his were headed for the goldfields of California. During the journey downriver, I entered into a partnership with his friend. We robbed several of the well-to-do passengers of their valuables. We were preparing to make good our escape one night when Payne interfered. We struggled, and he threw me overboard. I was swept away by the current and very nearly drowned, but I was caught up in debris that had been trapped by a sandbar. For a moment I thought Lady Luck was smiling down on me. And then, out of the darkness, the trunk of a tree was hurled against me by the force of the river. The impact snapped my spine. I don't remember much of what happened after that. I'm told that I was fortunate to have been spotted the next morning by the crew of a keelboat passing nearby. They fished me out of the river and took me downriver to the next town, leaving me there in the care of the local physician. There wasn't anything he could do for me, of course. My body was dead from the waist down."

"And you blame Payne for that?" asked Killough. "Sounds like to me you just had a run of bad luck that night."

Marston glowered at him. "If you're not interested in making ten thousand dollars, Mr. Killough, you're free to take your five-hundred-dollar fee and leave."

Killough raised a hand. "No, I'll stick around for a while and hear the rest of the story. It's not like I have pressing business elsewhere." He ruefully examined the bottom of his empty shot glass. "I wouldn't turn down another drink, either."

Elyse sashayed forward and plucked the glass from his fingers. "Allow me," she said.

Killough smirked. "Why, yes, ma'am. I'd allow you to do just about anything." He watched Elyse walk to the sideboard, then glanced at Marston. "Not trying to move in on your territory or anything, Marston."

Watching both Marston and Elyse, Renny thought it likely that their relationship was not strictly business. He could only assume that what attracted a woman like Elyse to a man like Marston was money. He couldn't imagine it being anything else.

Marston chose to ignore Killough's comment. "It's revenge I want, gentlemen. Revenge is what kept me alive. Eventually I realized that while my body was broken, I could still rely on my mind. And I have used my mind to become a wealthy man. It took many years, and I worked very diligently to get where I am today." He made a gesture to indicate the opulent passenger car in which they sat. "And I did it for one reason, and one reason only. To be able to afford my vengeance. That's why I asked the three of you here. The West is full of killers. There are gun artists galore. But I narrowed it down to you three gentlemen."

He paused because Elyse had returned to Killough with the shot glass refilled. Gentleman Jim accepted it with a nod and made a point of watching the woman's hips sway as she walked to the front of the passenger car—even though he was aware of Marston's scrutiny.

Marston turned his attention to Willie Creed. "While I was not aware that you began your life of crime as a horse thief, Mr. Creed, I do know that you made your reputation with the gun in the Pecos River range war in New Mexico several years ago. Ethan Payne wouldn't be the first peace officer you've killed. There was that Santa Rosa sheriff;

most accounts claim you slipped into his house while he
was sleeping, put a gun to his head, and woke him up so
that he could beg for his life before you pulled the trigger."

"He was in the employ of Big John Cafferty, and he
lynched three of my friends. He wasn't no lawman."

"The state of New Mexico disagrees with you, apparently. That's why they have a five-thousand-dollar reward
posted, dead or alive, with your name on it."

Willie Creed shrugged. "That's okay. I didn't much care
for New Mexico anyway."

"Since then you've spent most of your time along the
border, getting into frequent scrapes with assorted *pistole-
ros* and bounty men. No one's quite sure how many you've
put in their graves. Estimates range from a dozen to fifty."

"I ain't counting," said Creed.

"You must be pretty fast, kid," said Killough.

"Faster than you, old man."

Killough smiled. Renny knew this only because the
man's mustache moved. "That's probably true," drawled
Gentleman Jim. "But fast ain't everything. You might put
two or three bullets in me before I got off a shot. But I'd
get that shot off, and the one would be all I'd need to curl
your toes."

"James Edward Killough," said Marston. "You have two
weaknesses, they say. Women and cards. They are the reason you were cashiered out of the Confederate Army and
spent much of the war in an Atlanta prison. You escaped
when Sherman marched through, and made your way west.
You've accounted for fifteen men, all of them in fair fights,
either irate husbands or men you've cheated at the poker
table who come for you with gun in hand."

Killough raised his glass to Marston. "What else is worth
dying for?"

"Your problem is that you're persona non grata in Texas,
California, Colorado—that's just to name a few places
where they've got a bullet with your name on it. You are
running out of places to go, Mr. Killough. Ten thousand

dollars would expand your horizons substantially, I would think."

"I'm always open to new possibilities," acknowledged Killough, and Renny expected him to glance again at Elyse, giving his comment a double meaning. But Gentleman Jim didn't take his eyes off Marston, which meant he had more tact than Renny had given him credit for.

Marston turned his attention finally to Renny. "And then there's you, Mr. Renny. Your early years are shrouded in mystery. My most reliable sources say that your parents were pioneers on the Texas frontier, and were slain by Comanches. That the Indians took you captive as a young child and raised you up as one of their own. Others say that isn't so, that there were a John and Martha Renny who were killed by Comanche raiders in 1848, but that all their children were killed, as well. I'm also told but cannot confirm that you were once a Texas Ranger, only to be dishonorably discharged from that service due to criminal activities. You've hired your gun out to the highest bidder in a number of range and railroad wars. Your victims number between twenty-five and one hundred, depending on who you talk to. And you've spent the last eighteen months rotting in a Chihuahuan jail on a charge of murder."

"It wasn't murder," said Renny. "I've never murdered, anyway. If I kill a man, it's in a fair fight. But he was the brother of the alcalde's wife. That's why they threw me in the jail. I was about to break out of there when you bought my way out, Mr. Marston."

"Wait a minute," said Killough. "You bought Renny out of some stinking Mexican jail and paid him five hundred dollars besides? I think we've been short-changed, Willie, what do you think?"

Renny wasn't sure if Gentleman Jim was kidding or not. With Killough you never really knew. That was one of the traits that made him so dangerous. Gentleman Jim could give you a big smile, buy you a drink, pat you on the back—and then put a bullet in your gut in the blink of an eye. When he'd been down in Texas, Killough had acted like he was in some sort of competition with Renny, saying how he was deadlier with a thumb buster and had sent more sinners to meet their Maker than Renny had. It was like he'd been issuing a challenge, trying to provoke Renny into a confrontation so that they could settle, once and for all, who was better. But Renny never accepted such challenges, if he could avoid doing so. And then Gentleman Jim had been forced to flee the Lone Star State in a big hurry just to save his hide. But it seemed the intervening years had not changed the man; he still hated to see Renny get more consideration than he'd gotten.

"I dunno," said Willie, confused. "Reckon it depends on how much it cost to spring him."

"Not much," said Marston wrily. "It was Mexico, after all."

"I just don't see why you bothered bringing Renny up here at all," said Killough. "No offense, pard," he told Renny. "In fact, I don't see why you sent for Willie boy, either, Marston. I can do this job with my eyes closed. I'm the only one you needed."

"I want to make *sure* Payne dies," rasped Marston. "The three of you can work in concert, if you like—though, from what I know of you, I doubt that's a real possibility. Or you each can try to be the first one to call Payne out, or draw straws. I don't care. The only thing I care about— well, you know what it is. Surely one of you can get the job done. I'm leaving nothing to chance."

"How do we collect the ten thousand?" asked Creed.

"Elyse will go to Abilene, check into a hotel there. When Payne is dead, she will send me a telegram confirming that fact. When she receives my approval, she will see to it that you collect your payment."

"Why should we trust you?" asked Willie Creed. "Once I kill Payne I'll be on the run, and you could just decide not to pay up."

"Elyse is my guarantee. She is worth a great deal more than ten thousand dollars to me."

Creed looked at her and grinned. "Yeah. I can see how she would be."

"I wouldn't worry so much if I were you, Willie boy," said Killough. "Seeing as how you won't be collecting the payment anyway."

"We'll see about that," sneered Creed.

"I take that to mean that the two of you agree to the terms. What about you, Mr. Renny? You haven't said much. Are you in or out?"

"I reckon I'm in."

"Splendid," said Marston, rubbing his hands together. "Then our business is concluded, gentlemen. Thank you for coming. Elyse will show you out."

Willie Creed was the first one on his feet and out of the car. By the time Renny and Killough reached the front platform, Creed was already at the rear of the train, mounting his pony. A moment later he galloped by, bidding them farewell with a piercing rebel yell and leaving them in the drifting dust kicked up by his horse's hooves.

"Some people are just in a hurry to die," observed Killough, shaking his head. "Care to ride with me, Renny? We can talk about old times."

"I'd just as soon forget old times," replied Renny.

Killough smiled. He looked at Elyse, who stood with them on the platform, and touched the brim of his hat. "I will look forward to seeing a lot more of you ma'am, once we reconvene in Abilene."

"I can't wait," she said, in a way that left Renny wondering if she was sincere.

Killough stepped down off the platform and headed for the back of the train and his horse. Renny started to leave the platform, too, but Elyse stopped him with a hand on his arm.

"I'll be in Abilene when you arrive," she told him. "At the Drovers' Cottage, under the name of Elyse Smith."

He nodded, and left the platform. A dry western wind carried the strong aroma of sunburnt grass, but he couldn't get her fragrance out of his mind. Why had she provided him with that last morsel of information? Was it an invitation? One thing was certain—there was a lot more to Elyse than met the eye. Of course, what met the eye was beguiling enough.

Killough was mounted; he checked his horse alongside Renny. "Don't get in my way, amigo," advised Gentleman Jim. "For ten thousand dollars I'll gladly kill *two* men."

Renny watched him ride away. Killough looked like a dandy, and Creed was still a kid, but he knew better than to underestimate either one of them. Thanks to Marston, and his twisted desire for vengeance, death was riding to Abilene. As for himself, Renny figured it was more curiosity than anything else that had prompted him to go along with Marston's scheme. He wanted to see how this would play out. And he wanted to find out more about the woman, Elyse. The ten thousand dollars—and whether Ethan Payne lived or died—wasn't all that important to him. He was just along for the ride.

As he rode away from the private train, he noticed that Elyse still stood on the passenger car's platform, shading her eyes, watching him go.

CHAPTER ELEVEN

On the day he was supposed to be married, Ethan Payne knocked on the door to Julie's room and got no answer. He knocked again, and a third time. She was supposed to be there, waiting for him to come and fetch her, so that they could go together to stand before the justice of the peace. Had she run away? Ethan doubted it. She would know that he'd come after her, that he'd catch her and bring her back. She knew him well enough to know that. Alarmed, he tried the door. It was unlocked, and he entered the room. She sat in a chair by the window, wearing the new dress he had bought her for this occasion, and she was gazing out at the stockyard, filled with Texas cattle bound for eastern slaughterhouses. She didn't turn her head to see who had come through the door.

"Julie," he said softly. "It's time."

"Don't go through with this, Ethan."

He went to the bed, hat in hand, and sat on the edge of it, a vantage point from which he could better see her face. She looked much better than she had a month ago, when he had found her in the shanty on the Row, consumed by her addiction to laudanum. Two weeks ago she had begun to take some notice of her surroundings, and to eat as though she had an appetite. Her cheeks were no longer gaunt. Her color had returned. She had beaten the addiction, and no longer begged for the opiate, or cursed him for withholding it from her. Many days had passed since she'd exhibited any signs of delirium. Still, she was much changed from the vibrant young woman he had known at Wolftrap Station. A deep and abiding sadness haunted her eyes and the corners of her mouth, which seemed to have forgotten how to smile. There was no joy of life within her, just a weariness that invaded every move she made, every word she spoke, every breath she took. Ethan had come to realize that getting her past the addiction to laudanum—saving her life—had merely been the first step in a long recovery. Somehow he had to help her recapture the will to live. He could only hope that this would return to her in time. Time, they said, was the great healer. Time could heal everything. He was committed to giving her as much time as she needed. It was a debt he owed.

"You used to want me to ask you to marry me," he said, trying to sound light-hearted. "What changed your mind?"

"That was in another lifetime."

"It's not too late. The way I see it, there's more to both of us ending up here in Abilene at the same time than mere coincidence."

"Or it could be just more of your bad luck," she said, and this time she looked at him and managed a wan smile, looking as though she felt sorry for him.

"Not bad luck at all. It's a chance for me to do the right thing for a change. Jesus, Julie. If you only knew how many times I made the *wrong* turn. One of those times was when I left you there at Wolftrap. When I couldn't bring myself to make a commitment to you—the commitment I knew you hoped I would make. See, back then, I was living in the past. But I'm not doing that anymore."

"Aren't you?" she asked gently.

"We have a second chance now, Julie. Both of us. Unless . . . unless this is about your husband. Maybe you can't stomach marrying the man who killed him."

"I never blamed you for that. If anything, it was his fault.

He had to try you." She shook her head. "Foolish pride. No, it isn't about *him* at all."

Ethan slid off the edge of the bed, down to one knee in front of her, and took her hands, which were folded in her lap, and placed them between his own. "Then what's the problem?"

She gazed earnestly into his eyes. "Me. I'm the problem, Ethan. Don't you understand? I'm a two-dollar whore."

He rose, taking her by the shoulders and lifting her to her feet, a little roughly, and she gasped in surprise. "No," he snapped. "No, you're not. Not any longer."

The rough handling sparked some anger in her. "I always will be, to some. You think just because I spend most of my time up here in this room that I don't know what people are saying? Not about me, but about you."

"You're mistaken if you think I care. And if anyone calls you a whore in my presence it'll be the last thing they do."

"You see? That's just what I'm talking about. Your job is dangerous enough. I'll just make it more dangerous."

"Then I'll quit."

"And do what?"

"I don't know. I'll find something."

"This is all you have. You can't quit."

"I'll have you. And you're more important to me than any job. I let you get away once, Julie. Just like I let everything else get away. I'm not going to let that happen again."

"Let go of me," she whispered fiercely, squirming in his grasp. He complied, and she turned her back on him, looking out the window again.

"At least you're honest," she murmured. "At least you're not doing this because you love me. That would make it hurt all the worse."

Ethan shook his head, exasperated. "Of course I love you. I loved you at Wolftrap. I just . . . I just couldn't tell you."

"I know. Because of the girl in Illinois."

"I should have told you about her at the start. I'd made

her a promise, and I thought at the time that I could still keep it."

"Were you keeping it when you shared my bed, Ethan?" There was a faint hint of reproach in her voice. "I'm sorry. That wasn't fair. You needed me and I needed you. At least you never made me any promises."

Ethan didn't say anything. Her words cut deeply, but he suffered in silence, feeling that he deserved the wounds.

Julie sighed. "I'll marry you, Ethan."

He had hoped for a little enthusiasm. It sounded as though she was agreeing against her better judgment. Or perhaps because she had nothing to lose, or because she was trying to make the best of a bad situation. But he would take what he could get, and hinge his hopes on some future day when Julie might realize that she'd made the right decision.

They were met downstairs by the gambler, Clooney, who, executing a gallant bow, handed Julie a bouquet of wildflowers.

"You're up a little early, aren't you?" asked Ethan.

Clooney grinned. "Just call me an incurable romantic, but I wouldn't miss an occasion like this. Miss, I have to say you're the prettiest bride I think I've ever laid eyes on. You're a lucky man, Payne."

"Yes, I know." Glancing at Julie, he could see that in spite of her frame of mind she was flattered, and she accepted the flowers with a heartfelt thanks. He made a mental note to swing by the Lone Star at his earliest convenience and buy Clooney a drink. He appreciated the gambler's presence, and knew why he was here. Clooney represented the rest of Abilene's "bad element," and they were showing their support for the town marshal. Ethan found it ironic that of all the cliques in Abilene—the Texans, the respectable folk, and the group Clooney represented—it was only the latter that he could rely on.

Johnny Rowe was waiting for them in front of the house used by the justice of the peace as both office and residence. The deputy looked uncomfortable in a suit coat; his brawny farmer's shoulders threatened to pop the seams. He quit tugging on his collar as Ethan and the others approached, digging in a coat pocket to produce a small box.

"I got the ring, boss," he said.

Ethan nodded. "Then I reckon we're all set." He took a quick look along the street. Abilene was quiet. He knew that somewhere Ed Wilcox was on patrol. Glancing at Julie, Ethan wondered—not for the first time—if he was doing the right thing. She stood there, watching him, looking so fragile in the hot Kansas sun, her yellow hair whipped by the ceaseless prairie wind. He unstrapped his gunbelt and handed it to Clooney, since Rowe was going to be part of the ceremony as his best man. Extending his arm to Julie, he gave her a smile he hoped looked confident. She hooked her arm under his and they went inside together, followed by Rowe and Clooney.

A moment later, Willie Creed rode around a nearby corner on a tired and lathered horse. He sat the saddle with his shoulders slumped and his hat brim pulled down low over his eyes, like a rider wrapped up in his own private world of misery after a long trail. But beneath the hat brim, his eyes were alert, sweeping the street, missing nothing— and searching for one thing in particular: a tin star.

After the ceremony, they emerged from the office of the justice of the peace to find a buggy harnessed to a big black mare waiting for them. Ethan paid the boy waiting with the buggy and sent him on his way back to the livery. Then he helped Julie up into the conveyance before turning to Rowe.

"Think you and Ed can handle things for a couple of days?"

"Why sure, boss. Don't worry about a thing."

"Everything will be the same when you get back," said Clooney.

Ethan nodded. He understood. Clooney was assuring him that if Rowe and Wilcox needed help, they'd get it. Of course, he wasn't giving that assurance in so many words, since Rowe was standing right there.

Ethan climbed into the buggy beside Julie and took up the reins. It was then that Clooney remembered, and stepped forward to hand the marshal his gunbelt. "Don't expect you'll need this, but you never know. Might come across a rattler, or some other varmint."

Ethan laid the gunbelt on the seat between him and his bride and whipped up the mare.

He drove north out of town, and where the road forked he took the turn to Plunkett's Mill. This lane ran along a creek lined with cottonwoods. Julie didn't say a word. She gazed at the countryside, and occasionally smelled the flowers she still clutched in a hand. Ethan left her alone with her thoughts. She had hardly ventured out of his hotel room in a month's time, and this had to be something of a treat for her.

Four miles from the fork in the road, he pulled off the lane, across a wooden bridge that spanned the creek, and up to a small sod house built into the slope of a grassy hillock.

She looked at him. "Who lives here?"

"Well, if you like it, we do."

"Ethan—are you serious?"

He nodded, smiling at her astonishment. "It's up to you, though. Take a look around. If you say yes, then all I've got to do is sign a piece of paper at the bank when we get back to town."

As though in a daze, she slowly got out of the buggy and took a long look around. The sod house faced the creek, and was shaded by several big cottonwoods. Beyond the creek, she could see the wagon trace that had brought them here from the road, twisting like twin serpents across a grassy vale. He waited until her eyes had drunk their fill of this scene and she had turned to the house itself before catching up with her.

"Now, it's not much," he hastened to add.

Standing at the threshold, she looked inside for a moment, and he waited behind her, holding his breath, until she turned and smiled warmly at him and said, "I love it."

"Beats living in that hotel, anyway, right?"

She put her arms around his neck, and for the first time since he'd found her again she looked happy. His heart quickened.

"Depending on the time of year, I'll have to work nights sometimes."

She shook her head. "I spent many a night alone at Wolftrap. I can take care of myself. If only Manolo were still around. . . ."

Ethan nodded, and kept to himself the fact that he was personally relieved that the mestizo had disappeared two weeks ago. It had happened right when Ethan had let his intentions of marrying Julie be known. He figured that hadn't been welcome news where Manolo was concerned. Ethan had often wondered whether Manolo's feelings for Julie had extended beyond friendship; he knew that for her that was all there was. Apparently the same could not be said for the mestizo. So he was glad that the mysterious young man was gone.

"I know a man in town who has a dog—it's part wolf, in fact—that he's looking to give away," said Ethan. "You keep that animal chained up out here, no one will be able to get within a hundred yards of the place without you knowing about it."

"I'm not worried, but if it will make you feel better . . ." She turned and went inside to take a closer look around.

Ethan followed her, paused just inside the door to watch her explore her new home. There were two rooms with an adjoining door, a single window in each room and a puncheon floor throughout. The walls, roof, and floor were sound. There were few furnishings, and all of it rough-hewn—a table with two benches in the first room, a bed, a small table, and a rocking chair with a couple of back slats missing in the other. When she saw the bed, Julie stopped moving. Ethan could tell that her body tensed, and somehow he knew exactly what she was thinking. He thought that was odd—before, it had been Julie who so often seemed able to read his mind.

"It doesn't matter," he said.

"What?" His voice startled her. "What doesn't matter?"

"What you . . . used to do to survive."

"When we first met I'd only been with one other man. My husband. And that . . . that wasn't very often. But now. Now I feel so . . ." She shook her head. "I don't even know how many there were. Most of the time I wasn't even aware of what was happening."

Desperately wanting to change the subject, sensing that Julie's happiness was slipping away, Ethan threw an idle look around the room and saw the fireplace. "I'd better go see if I can find something to burn. This time of year the nights can get pretty cool."

He hurried outside. The sod house had been uninhabited for nearly a year, according to the president of the bank, and there was some deadwood accumulated under the cottonwoods. Ethan proceeded to collect armloads, depositing the firewood against the front wall of the house, near the front door. When he'd gathered up all that he could find, he sat on his heels with his back to the wall and built a smoke, still reluctant to go inside, afraid of the mood Julie would be in, and at a loss what to do next. Before he was finished with the cigarette, she emerged from the house. Giving him a tremulous smile, she walked down to the creek. Ethan watched her, thinking she had just gone down for a closer look, and was surprised when she shed the dress he had bought her. Mesmerized, he didn't move—scarcely dared breathe—as she knelt down in the shallows of the creek and washed herself, her hair gleaming like spun gold in the sunlight, her skin milky white like alabaster. She did not look over at him, and he wondered if she was self-conscious; after all, they knew each other intimately, but much time had passed since those idyllic days at Wolftrap Station. At least they seemed idyllic to him now; at the time he'd been troubled by thoughts of Lilah, and of how he was breaking his promise to her, and not for the first time—there had been his relationship with Ellen Addison in California. Ethan shook his head, silently cursing himself. He needed to stop dwelling on the past; he had a chance now to make a future for himself, but to do that he had to exorcise all the old ghosts. Looking at Julie, kneeling in the creek in the speckled shade of the dusty cottonwoods, he committed himself to her happiness. In his opinion he hadn't accomplished very many positive things in his life, but it was never too late to start.

Julie left the creek, her pale, slender body glistening in the sunlight. She put the dress back on and returned to the house and stood before him, extending a hand. He flicked away the cigarette that had died between his fingers and rose, taking her hand and let her lead him inside, into the bedroom, where she wrapped her arms around his neck and kissed him tentatively. Bathing in the creek had been like a ritual, a cleansing, and it was up to him to accept her, which he did without hesitation. He was able to take everything that had happened to her between this moment and the day he had last seen her, at Wolftrap, and treat it all as though it had never happened. And he could only hope that she could do the same.

CHAPTER TWELVE

Johnny Rowe couldn't wait to get out of the ill-fitting suit coat and back into his everyday clothes. After that he went to Hargreave's mercantile and lingered there for most of the afternoon, shooting the breeze with some of the men who came in to sit around the cold potbelly stove and drink coffee and trade tall tales. He scared up a checker game with Hargreave himself. The store owner's curiosity got the better of him, and he broached the subject that Rowe had fervently hoped no one would bring up.

"I hear tell the marshal went ahead and did it," said Hargreave. "Married that woman, I mean. That true, Johnny? Were you there?"

Rowe fired a disapproving look across the checker board at Hargreave. "He asked me to be his best man and I was proud to stand for him."

Hargreave shook his head. "There's nothing like a woman to be the undoing of a man."

"You're living proof, Bob," said one of the other men, speaking over a corncob pipe stuck between his teeth. "You've been undone for—what's it been?—nigh on twenty years."

Everyone laughed, including Hargreave—with the exception of Rowe, who held a steady gaze on the store owner.

"You don't have to approve of what the marshal done," he said gravely. "But I'd advise you not to be careless when you talk about Mrs. Payne from now on."

Hargreave held up his hands. "Don't get your hackles up, Johnny. It don't make me no never mind if the marshal wants to take a wife. And I doubt any man in town is fool enough to speak bad of her in his presence, or yours. But the womenfolk—now that's another matter. I've overheard my wife and some of her friends talking, and I'm telling you it'll be a cold day in hell before they ever accept Mrs. Payne into what you might call Abilene's polite society."

Johnny Rowe smiled faintly. "I don't think that really matters to either one of them, Bob. Your wife and all the other old biddies in town can be as holier-than-thou as they want to. But what gets me is that their town is a whole lot safer place to live, thanks to the marshal. I don't think anyone can deny that." He glanced at the other men, who dutifully shook their heads. "I mean, there's only been one killing in more than two months. And that's some kind of record for this town, from what I've heard."

"Yeah," said Hargreave wryly. "Of course, that one killing was the cowboy Marshal Payne gunned down."

"In self-defense."

"Step on a Texan's pride the way the marshal did with that man and you're asking for it."

"So I guess you'd rather have Happy Jack Crawford back," said Rowe, jumping three of Hargreave's checkers.

Scowling at the board, Hargreave grunted. "Not saying that at all. Payne has done a good job. All I'm saying is, if he's thinking about joining the ranks of the respectable folk around here, then marrying a prostitute is a funny way of going about it." He hesitantly made his move on the board.

Rowe shrugged. "And we'd all be better off if we started minding our own business." He jumped four more of Hargreave's checkers, clearing the board. The storekeeper groaned.

"How much do I owe you now, Johnny?"

"One hundred and twelve dollars, Bob."

"I wish you'd go ahead and take it out in merchandise so's we could start even again."

"Nah," said the deputy. "I figure I'll just keeping beating you at checkers until my marker's so big I can trade it in for a half interest in the whole shebang."

Hargreave leaned forward. "You're a hard worker, Johnny. Come work for me for a year or two and I'll give you a part interest in the store."

Rowe shook his head. "I'm partial to the job I've got now. Some might think it's gotten pretty dull, with so little trouble breaking out of late. But that suits me just fine. I don't mind that I got one of the safest jobs around now, thanks to Marshal Payne."

"Well, it won't always be safe," warned Hargreave. "I've seen it before. A town tamer comes along, cracks skulls, sheds blood, and generally raises all kinds of hell in the process of bringing law and order. And then, when the town is tamed, he becomes a liability rather than an asset. And he has to be gotten rid of. If he goes peaceably then that's all well and good. But such men don't usually like to be thrown out with the garbage. One day Abilene will be too civilized for the likes of Ethan Payne. And somehow I doubt he'll go quietly. And if he doesn't, he'll have to be gotten rid of."

Rowe just sat back in his chair and stared at Hargreave.

"I know you're loyal to the man," said Hargreave, almost apologetically. "But I like you, Johnny. You're a good boy and I'd hate to see you come to a bad end just because you've hitched your wagon to the wrong horse. If you know what I mean."

Rowe stood up, a grim expression on his face, and checked the clock on the wall. "I better be getting over to the restaurant for my dinner. See you boys later."

"Bye, Johnny."

"Take care of yerself, Johnny boy."

The shadows cast by the false front buildings on the west side of the main thoroughfare were stretching across the rutted hardpack of the street as Johnny Rowe left the mercantile. He walked south two blocks and entered Kelso's Restaurant, where he usually ate supper before going on the night shift. As usual Mr. Kelso was doing the cooking and Mrs. Kelso, a plump, red-faced, and perpetually cheerful matron, waited tables. She asked him if he wanted the usual and he said yes. After giving her husband the order she brought Rowe a glass of milk and, tilting her head to one side, hands planted on her broad hips, asked him if anything was the matter. Rowe had to smile; Mrs. Kelso fussed over him like she was his mother, and she knew him well enough to know when he was bothered by something. He assured her that he was fine, and she gave him a look that made it plain she didn't believe a word of it, but she didn't press the issue and left him alone with his thoughts. While he waited for his steak and potatoes, Rowe pondered Hargreave's predictions about how Ethan Payne's stint as Abilene's lawman would end. Much as he hated to admit it, he figured the storekeeper was probably right on at least a couple of counts—that sooner or later Abilene would decide that Payne's brand of lawbringing was too rough for the town, and that he would not go quietly. And then what would happen? Rowe didn't particularly want to speculate beyond that point.

When his grub came he ate it all, with gusto—there wasn't much of anything that could rob Johnny Rowe of his appetite. Having grown up on a farm, he'd learned to eat whether he was hungry or not, because you could be certain there was plenty of hard work ahead of you before you'd be able to sit down to your next meal. He finished off the steak—a good, solid pound of meat—the potatoes, and his milk, and debated Mrs. Kelso's offer of a slice of cream pie before telling her he'd probably drop in later that evening and have dessert. She promised to save him a piece and, as always, told him to be careful while he paid his bill and left the eatery.

He went next to the jail. Ed Wilcox showed up a few minutes later to find Rowe cooking up a fresh batch of coffee. Wilcox noticed that Rowe's weapon of choice, the sawn-off axe handle, lay across a stack of wanted posters on the desk.

"Anything going on out there, Ed?" asked Rowe.

"Nothing to speak of. It's been real quiet all day. *Too* quiet, almost."

Rowe laughed. "How can it be *too* quiet?"

"You know what I mean. Like how it goes deathly still right before a big storm hits. That kind of too quiet."

"You're a superstitious old codger, Ed," kidded Rowe. "I remember when that black cat strolled right in here one day and jumped on top of the desk. You shot up out of that chair like somebody had built a fire in your pants."

"Maybe I am that way. But it could be the reason I've lived so long."

Johnny Rowe laughed at that. "You've lived this long 'cause you're too ornery to die, Ed."

Ed Wilcox shrugged. "You just be careful out there. Like I said, it's *too* quiet. I'm telling you, Johnny, you ought to carry a gun with you. Take that sawed off ten-guage up there in the rack."

Rowe adamantly shook his head. "I start carrying a gun, I'm more likely to be shot at. That's just how it works. Those Texans may be wilder than Comanches, but they believe in fair play. They're not likely to resort to gunplay if they see I'm not heeled."

Wilcox shrugged. "Suit yourself. I'll be back at daybreak."

Rowe waved him out of the office. He waited around until the boy from Kelso's arrived with two plates of food, one for each of the prisoners in the cellblock. He checked the wanted posters. About once a week a new bunch of "papers" came in on the westbound train from Kansas City. It paid to familiarize oneself with the fugitives described

on the posters. You never knew when one might wander
into town, though they generally swung a wide loop around
Abilene. That was because of Ethan Payne's reputation—
and, in Rowe's opinion, was just one more reason why the
townfolk ought to count their blessings where he was concerned, instead of being so judgmental about his choice of
brides. But it had been Rowe's experience that to expect
clear thinking from people was akin to expecting milk from
a bull—it just wasn't going to happen.

Having spent nearly an hour in the office, Rowe rose
from behind the desk, picked up the axe handle, and ventured out onto the boardwalk. The sun had set—the last
remnants of daylight streaked the western sky, and the first
stars were glittering overhead. It was time to make his
rounds.

Clooney was a fixture at the Lone Star. Hardly a night
passed that he wasn't at his table over in the corner, dealing
poker and taking money from the men foolish enough to
try their luck against him. Although he seemed oblivious
to everything except the game, the fact was that very little
happened in the saloon that escaped his attention. He always sat with his back to the wall, facing the doors, so he
could watch the comings and goings. The Lone Star was
one of Abilene's most popular watering holes; during the
cattle season it was usually filled with customers, most of
them Texas drovers. They flocked to the bar for whiskey,
flirted with the percentage girls, and, if they had wages
burning holes in their pockets, threw their money away at
the faro table or the wheel of fortune, or in the poker game
presided over by Clooney. If the Lone Star happened to be
their first stop upon arrival in Abilene, they checked their
guns at the mahogany; a big sign behind the bar advised
them that a town ordinance required them to do so. On this
particular night Clooney was curious to see whether the
absence of Ethan Payne would result in some laxness on
the part of the Texans in their obedience to the law. Payne's
wedding had been mentioned in the local newspaper, and

while it had been a small and private affair, that didn't mean that the word wouldn't spread quickly through the ranks of the cowpunchers. They'd figure that, tonight at least, the famous town tamer wouldn't be on duty, and being the reckless souls that they were, at least some of them might feel inclined to test the mettle of the deputies. That was just the nature of these Texans, mused Clooney—always pushing authority to the limit.

As the evening progressed, however, he was pleased to note that everyone was more or less behaving themselves, and nothing appeared to be out of the ordinary. Johnny Rowe dropped in while making his rounds, and none of the Texans tested him, so he moved on. About a half hour later a man with long yellow hair, dressed in a frock coat and gold vest, strolled into the saloon. His arrival made Clooney freeze in mid-deal. He knew this man. He also knew that trouble followed Gentleman Jim Killough about as closely as the shadow cast by his long, lanky frame.

"Hey, you gonna deal or not?" asked one of the three men at the table. He sounded cross, but Clooney didn't take offense. He'd taken just about all of the cowboy's hard-earned money during the past hour.

"Sure," he said, and finished distributing the pasteboards. Even though Killough's presence distracted him, he was able to win the hand. The cowboy who had urged him to get on with the deal threw his cards down in disgust and quit the game, as broke as when he'd headed up the trail from Texas. Clooney handed the deck to the man on his left. "I'll be sitting this one out, gents," he said pleasantly, and got up to go to the bar. That was where Killough had parked himself; the drovers had made plenty of room for him without his even having to ask. There was something about Gentleman Jim that prompted sensible men to do that.

As Clooney came up beside him, Killough was watching the barkeep pour whiskey into a shotglass. He didn't look at Clooney, but Clooney didn't take offense; he figured that

Gentleman Jim had already seen him at the table, and knew who it was that stood beside him.

"Looks to me like a quality place," remarked Gentleman Jim. "I reckon they wouldn't water down the who-hit-john, now would they?"

The barkeep looked up at Killough, as poker-faced as could be, then glanced at Clooney, who shook his head. The bartender gave the slightest of shrugs and moved on down the bar to pour for someone else.

"Don't worry," said Clooney. "It's the real thing."

Killough took a sip of the whiskey, nodded in satisfaction, and then knocked it back, emptying the glass. "That hit the spot. Buy you a drink?"

"I'm buying," said Clooney. He put some hard money on the bar, knowing that the apron would work his way back along the bar in short order. In the meantime he fished a cheroot out of a pocket, bit off the tip, flicked a sulfur match to life with a thumbnail, and lit the smoke. "Long time no see, Jim. Last time was Carson City, as I recall, back in sixty-six."

"Sixty-seven," corrected Killough.

"You got into a scrape there—over a woman, if memory serves—and had to leave in a hurry."

Gentleman Jim stroked his luxurious mustache and chuckled. "The story of my life. I stay anywhere longer than a few days I seem to end up neck-deep in hot water."

"I would try to stay out of hot water in Abilene, Jim," advised Clooney.

"I never look for trouble." Killough glanced over at Clooney's table in the corner. "Looks like you've got a sweet arrangement here."

"I'm doing okay."

The apron returned; seeing the money on the bar, he refilled Killough's glass and poured a drink for Clooney. Killough waited until he had moved on before speaking.

"I take it your warning is on account of the local law. I hear he's a hard man, this Ethan Payne."

"You heard right."

"How well do you know him?" This time Killough just sipped the whiskey, relishing the blossom of heat in his belly.

"I consider him a friend," said Clooney frankly.

"If he's a friend then you need to tell him to watch his back. I happen to know that a feller by the name of Willie Creed is coming to Abilene to kill him. I don't know if you've heard of Creed, but he's a backshooter."

"I've heard the name. Don't know anything about him." Clooney peered sidelong at Killough. "What I'm wondering is, how do *you* know about him?"

"I heard him bragging about it in a watering hole up in Ellsworth. He'd had a little too much to drink, and he was telling anybody who'd listen how many men he'd killed, and how he was going to add another notch on his gun for Marshal Payne. Seems he's being paid ten thousand dollars to do the deed."

Clooney stared at Killough. "Ten thousand dollars! Now who would pay that kind of money to have Payne killed?"

Gentleman Jim shrugged. "I didn't ask. I try to mind my own business these days."

"Then why are you telling me about this?"

"Because you said the marshal was a friend."

Clooney puffed on his cheroot a moment, peering at Killough through the pungent blue smoke that hung thickly in the air between them. "No offense, Jim, but I've never known you to do anything unless you figured there was something in it for you."

Killough laughed and clapped Clooney on the back. "Well, of course! You put in a good word for me with your friend the marshal. I might want to stay here in Abilene for a spell, and it pays to be on good terms with the local law. That's a lesson I should have learned from you a long time ago."

Clooney started to tell Gentleman Jim Killough that he wasn't Ethan Payne's friend because he sought some advantage as a result of the friendship. But he realized that Killough wouldn't believe him. It was likely that everyone thought the same thing, even Payne himself. And Clooney couldn't even say why he cared that this was so.

"Is Creed here now?"

Killough shrugged again. "Can't say. I just rode into town myself."

"What does he look like?"

"You can't miss him. Scrawny kid who dresses up like a bandolero, all in black."

Clooney threw a quick but thorough look around the Lone Star to confirm that no one fitting that description was present. "If he's in Abilene looking for the marshal he's out of luck."

"Payne's not here?"

Clooney shook his head. He was debating whether he ought to ride out to the place Payne had bought and warn the marshal about Creed. He'd never been out that way, but Payne had told him where it was. He decided that tomorrow would be soon enough. Barging in on the man's wedding night would be in bad taste—and it wasn't necessary; if Creed *was* in Abilene tonight he wouldn't find what he was looking for, and nobody was going to tell him where to find his target. As far as Clooney knew, only he and the marshal's deputies were aware of how or where to find Payne.

"So where is he?" asked Killough.

"Out of town for a few days. Thanks for the information, Jim. I'll be sure to tell the marshal what you did. Oh, and you better check any hideouts you're carrying. You can't go around Abilene heeled. It's against the law."

Aware that Killough was watching him without really seeming to, Clooney went back to his table and got back into the poker game, resolved to tell Johnny Rowe what Gentleman Jim had told him as soon as the deputy's rounds brought him back to the Lone Star.

But Johnny Rowe never made it back to the Lone Star Saloon. He was nearly finished making his rounds, and was on his way back to the jailhouse, when someone stepped from the black shadows of an alleyway that he had just passed and said, "Hey, lawman."

Rowe turned. The man standing ten feet from him was hardly more than a boy, all duded up like a Mexican dandy, with black chaqueta, black trousers sporting conchos, and a black sombrero with a silver band. He wondered if maybe this was a Texas drover who had gone a little overboard buying new duds with the three months' worth of wages he'd been paid at trail's end. But then he noticed the matching pair of pearl-handled pistols in the fancy cross-draw holsters, and Rowe forgot all about how silly the young man looked.

"This must be your first time in Abilene," said Rowe, frowning. "There's a new town ordinance. You've got to check your guns. You can't go around heeled." He extended his left hand—the axe handle was gripped in his right. "Give the rig to me and you can come pick it up at the marshal's office when you're on your way out of town."

Willie Creed grinned at him. "You Marshal Ethan Payne?"

"No. I'm his deputy."

"Where is Payne?"

"He's not around."

The grin disappeared, replaced by a petulant scowl. "Well, damn. Just my luck."

"Hand over those pistols, mister," said Rowe sternly. "Or get out of town."

Creed shrugged. "If you say so." He reached down and pulled the pistols out of their holsters, holding them out to Rowe, butt first. Rowe relaxed. For a minute he'd thought this one was going to be one of those hard-nosed cowboys who bucked authority at every opportunity and damn the consequences. He snugged the sawed-off axe handle under his belt and reached for the pistols. But before he could touch them, Creed twirled the guns around, and Rowe found himself facing the business ends of a pair of .45-caliber smoke makers. Creed fired the pistols simultaneously. At point-blank range, the impact of the bullets crashing into Johnny Rowe's chest lifted him up off his feet and slammed him down hard. Rowe tried frantically to suck air into his lungs, but his lungs didn't seem to be working any longer. His boot heels beat a frantic tattoo on the weathered planks of the boardwalk as he fought to hold on to life—a fight he lost a few agonizing seconds later.

Creed twirled the pistols back into the holsters and looked impassively at the dead man. "I reckon the marshal will be around, now," he murmured, and, with a furtive scan of the street, he disappeared back into the shadows of the alley from whence he had come.

CHAPTER THIRTEEN

Ethan Payne was up at first light, leaving Julie sleeping peacefully, dressing quietly so as not to wake her. In the other room he built a fire to dispel some of the night cold that lingered in the sod house. Then he took up an empty bucket and stepped outside, heading down to the creek to fetch some water. Just as he sat on his heels in the shallows something caused him to look up and glance to the west, where the wagon trace meandered down through a grassy vale between the hills. Two men on horseback were coming along the trace. He couldn't identify them at this distance in the uncertain light, so he walked back to the sod house and retrieved his pistol, and was waiting just outside the door as Clooney and Ed Wilcox rode up. Their long faces warned him that the news they were bearing wasn't good.

"Morning, Ed, Clooney," he said, putting the pistol under his belt. "What brings you out this way so early in the morning?"

"Ed wanted to ride out last night," said Clooney. "But I talked him out of it."

"Johnny's been killed," said Wilcox bleakly. "Happened last night."

Ethan felt as though someone had hit him in the mid-section, knocking all the wind out of him. It took him a minute to recover from the shock of the news.

"How did it happen? Who did it?"

"Well," said Ed, with a sidelong glance at Clooney. "Nobody actually saw the shooting. Several people heard it, though. They all agree two shots were fired. And Johnny . . . Johnny was hit twice in the chest."

"Nobody saw it, that's true," said Clooney, swinging down out of the saddle and checking the cinch. "But we have a pretty good idea who did the deed. A kid by the name of Willie Creed. A gunslinger."

Ethan nodded bleakly. "I've heard of him. What makes you think he did it?"

"An old acquaintance of mine showed up last night," said Clooney, and proceeded to tell Ethan all the salient details of his conversation with Gentleman Jim Killough at the bar in the Lone Star.

"So let's say Killough is telling the truth," said Ethan. "If Creed is after me, why did he kill Johnny?"

"To bring you back," said Clooney. "To get you within killing distance."

Ethan nodded. That made sense. From what he'd heard of Willie Creed, the man was bloody-minded enough to do what Clooney was suggesting. And that made Ethan feel even more responsible for Johnny's death than he already did.

"Okay," he said grimly. "Where's Creed now?"

Wilcox shook his head morosely. "Have no idea, Ethan. Can't find him. But I deputized six good men, and they're still combing through Abilene looking for the son of a bitch."

"I'll be ready in ten minutes," said Ethan. "Ed, you'll ride back with me. Clooney, do me a favor and stay here with Julie. I'll send someone out to spell you. But no matter what happens, or what she says, I don't want her to come back to Abilene. If Creed will kill Johnny Rowe just to get to me, her life is in danger simply because she's my wife."

Clooney nodded. "You can count on me."

"Now wait just a doggone minute," said Wilcox, exasperated. "No offense, Ethan, but you must be crazy. If what Clooney's friend said is true, then you going back to Abilene is just playing right into Creed's hands."

"Last time I checked," said Ethan curtly, "I was still the town marshal. My deputy has been killed. What would you have me do, Ed? Go find a hole to crawl into and hide?"

"I'm not saying that. All I'm saying is, give me twenty-four hours. I'll deputize more men if I have to, but I'll find this Creed feller, and I'll either put him behind bars or six feet under."

"No," said Ethan flatly.

"I told you he'd say no," Clooney remarked to Ed Wilcox.

Ethan wasn't inclined to waste any more time talking. He went to the corral where the horse had spent the night and harnessed the animal to the buggy. Then he went inside the sod house, praying that Julie still slept. But she was awake, sitting up in bed with the counterpane pulled up to conceal her nakedness. The expression on her face alerted Ethan to the fact that she knew something was wrong, that the honeymoon was over, and that her husband was about to go into harm's way. She'd always had the knack. It seemed she could take one look at him and know the truth.

"Who is that outside?" she asked. She'd heard Clooney and Ed Wilcox talking while Ethan had been hitching horse to buggy.

"Clooney and Ed," he replied. "They rode out to tell me that Johnny Rowe was shot last night."

"Oh, my God," she breathed. "Will he be all right?"

"No." That was all he had to say. She understood.

"Who did it?"

Ethan wondered whether he should tell her everything—and decided that, indeed, he should be completely honest with her. That was what she would want, and more than that, it was what she deserved. He hadn't always been truthful during their Wolftrap days, and she'd been well aware of that fact. Besides, he needed to give her the credit she deserved, and assume she could handle the truth. Julie was resilient; one of the things he admired most about her back during his time with the Overland was the way she ran the station regardless of the hardships or perils that this entailed.

"A man named Creed. He shot Rowe to get me to come into Abilene. You see, it's me he's after. Rumor has it that someone paid him ten thousand dollars to kill me."

"Who would do such a thing?" she asked, breathlessly.

"That'll be the first thing I ask Creed when I see him," replied Ethan grimly. "Clooney is going to stay here with you for a spell. I don't want you to come to Abilene until it's safe. And I'll send for you then."

"And what happens if you get killed, Ethan? What do I do then?"

He didn't have an answer for her. He'd worked hard to create a situation where she could feel happy again, could even entertain hopes and dreams for the future. But that wasn't enough, he realized now. Because that situation could go up in smoke in an instant. And she would always have to live with that fear. Ethan wasn't sure if Julie loved him—at most he could only hope that someday she would—but she depended on him. He was all she had. She didn't even have Manolo, now that Ethan had chased the mestizo off. What would she do if something happened to him? Where would she go? Would she have to return to the profession from which he had rescued her? And if she did that would she also resort once again to laudanum to dull the pain? These were very real possibilities, but Ethan couldn't let any of that happen. Somehow he had to make sure that, no matter what happened to him, Julie would never have to worry about the future. How precisely he would do that remained a mystery.

"I'll be back soon," he said, not knowing what else to say, and hurried out of the sod house.

That afternoon Ed Wilcox found Ethan in the back room of the undertaker's place. In the middle of the small, windowless room was a casket laid across a pair of sawhorses.

Johnny Rowe lay in the casket, his hands folded peacefully across his chest. Ethan sat on one of several chairs along the walls. The other chairs were unoccupied; the marshal was the only living soul in the room. Wilcox crossed to stand near Ethan's chair and waited until the latter turned his attention away from the casket and looked up.

"We've searched high and low for Creed," said Wilcox. "Can't find the bastard. He must have lit out."

"There are plenty of places in Abilene for a rat to hide," said Ethan. "But don't worry about it, Ed. I don't have to find him. That's the thing. He'll find me."

"I'd rather find him first," said Wilcox. He glanced at the casket. "Damn that hardheaded kid." Ethan knew he meant Johnny Rowe. "I kept telling him he needed to go heeled, but he wouldn't listen. And now look at him."

"It probably wouldn't have made any difference," sighed Ethan. "Creed is a cold-blooded killer. Johnny wasn't."

"Well, I've got three good men outside, Ethan. They're armed to the teeth, and determined to watch your back until that vermin Creed's been dealt with."

Ethan shook his head. "No."

Wilcox sighed, exasperated. "Last thing I said to Johnny was that he was hardheaded as a mule. Same applies to you. There's a cold-blooded killer out there somewhere, gunning for you. And you won't let me help you."

Ethan looked at him, his face devoid of emotion. "You can't help me. If you surround me with armed guards, this man Creed will just bide his time. He'll wait until the time is right. I don't want to wait that long, Ed. I want to get it over with. And the only way to get Creed out into the open is to give him a target."

"I don't like that plan," confessed Wilcox. "You're good, Ethan. You've got plenty of nerve and you know how to walk 'em down. But nobody can dodge a bullet in the back. I've been doing some asking around. There are some in this town who've heard of Willie Creed. More than one has said he's a backshooter."

"I'll handle it, Ed. I don't want anyone else to get killed."

Wilcox grimaced. "That's it, isn't it? That's what's bothering you. You feel like Johnny here got killed on your account. That somehow it's your fault that he's laid out in that box."

Agitated, Ethan got up quickly and moved to the back door. He opened it and stood there, framed against the afternoon sunlight with his back to the deputy. One of Ed's guards was patrolling the alley. He gave Ethan a curt nod. The mere fact that the marshal was standing there where someone could conceivably take a shot at him made Wilcox as nervous as a long-tailed cat in a room full of rocking chairs. He knew that Ethan was probably right—a bodyguard tagging along behind wasn't going to solve anything. Willie Creed wasn't a fool. He wouldn't come out of hiding and tangle with three or four men with rifles. No, he'd wait until Ethan was alone. It would be better to get it over with, one way or the other. Sure beat waiting for days, weeks, maybe even months, expecting a killer to jump around every corner with guns blazing.

"He *did* die on my account," said Ethan hoarsely. "There's no two ways around it." He turned back to face Wilcox. "Let me tell you what you can do if you want to help. Get those men out there to help you watch over my wife. I reckon this Creed fellow is enough of a bastard to go after her if he thought it would smoke me out."

"Okay," said Wilcox, deciding that he might as well give up trying to keep Ethan alive. The least he could do for the marshal would be to see to it that his bride came to no harm. "That way at least you'll have somebody to mourn over your grave."

Ethan had to smile. He knew Wilcox was just being ornery, that the man was fundamentally unequipped to admit that he cared.

"At least she would," he replied. "I know you wouldn't, you cuss."

Wilcox took one last look at Johnny Rowe. Then, shak-

ing his head morosely, he left the back room through the
door into the alley. He made a curt gesture for the man on
guard to follow him. Ethan watched the two disappear
around the corner before going back to his chair. He wanted
to sit with Johnny a little while longer. He left the door
open—it would have suited him just fine if Willie Creed
came strolling in to try him here and now. He'd killed before, but he'd never relished doing it. Now, though, for the
first time in his life, he was in a killing mood.

Ed Wilcox rode out to the sod house where he knew Ethan
Payne had left his bride, accompanied by two of the men
he had deputized, and who had volunteered to help the town
marshal in the only way he would allow them to—watching
over the new Mrs. Payne.

When they arrived at their destination, Julie ran out to
meet them. Wilcox felt a surge of pity for her when he saw
the look of terror on her face—he realized she was fully
expecting him to inform her of her husband's death. He
figured that terror would not leave her until she heard that
Willie Creed was dead, and maybe not even then. He
quickly assured her that Ethan was well, and that he had
sent them out to protect her. She breathed a sigh of relief
at the welcome news he had brought her and invited them
inside, apologizing for the barren condition of the house
and the cupboard as they filed over the threshold. Mrs. Wilcox was nothing if not thoughtful—when she'd heard
where Ed was going she loaded him down with coffee and
flour and sugar and beans and a loaf of bread she had baked
that morning. She was a kind-hearted soul, which was one
of the reasons Ed loved her, and she was also determined
to set an example for the rest of the women in Abilene
where Julie Payne was concerned. *Judge not, lest ye be
judged* were words she tried to live by, and thought others
would do well to abide by, too.

Julie was stunned by the gifts, and stammered a thank
you.

"Think nothing of it, ma'am," said Wilcox, hat rolled

up in his hands. "I reckon these boys can go scare up some game, too. That should be enough to get you by, at least for a few days."

"I'll make us all some coffee," she said.

"Not for me," said Wilcox. "I have to get right back to town." He glanced at Clooney, who, as was his custom, was leaning against a wall in the background, looking like he didn't have a care in the world and was indifferent to the goings-on, even while he watched every move and listened intently to every word. "You going to ride in with me, then? To tell you the truth, I don't cotton to your kind, but the marshal thinks you're sound enough to depend on, so I guess that's good enough for me."

Clooney smiled. "Thanks, Deputy. I'll sleep better tonight knowing I'm fit company for you."

Wilcox grimaced, and headed for the door. But Julie stopped him, a hand resting on his arm.

"Ethan is going after the man who killed Johnny Rowe by himself, isn't he?"

"Well, I wouldn't exactly call it 'going after,' ma'am. He's kinda waiting on this Creed feller to come to him."

"Will you watch his back, Mr. Wilcox? Don't do it for me, but for him. I'm supposing that the two of you are friends. And I figure you don't think much of me."

"Now, I . . ."

"No. It's all right. I understand. But you will do it for him, won't you?"

"I'll try," said Wilcox grimly. He wanted to add that he couldn't promise anything, as he didn't want to be put in a position where he had to return to face Julie knowing she was a widow, and explain why he had failed to keep his promise. But he opted not to say more on that score, as it would tend merely to add to her anxiety.

"Thank you," she said. "I'm just afraid that . . . that even if Creed fails, there will be others. Since it seems someone wants Ethan dead badly enough to pay ten thousand dollars to see it done."

Wilcox shrugged. He'd been thinking the same thing—

how even if they got Creed before he got to Ethan Payne there would be others coming down the pike to try their hand. Ten thousand dollars was a fortune for most men in the West. More than the biggest reward he'd ever seen posted, and more than most long riders could net in a dozen stage holdups. He knew plenty of hard cases who would slit their own mother's throat for half that much money. So Creed would just be the first. And he was sorry that Julie Payne had thought about this, too, since it meant she understood that as long as that ten-thousand-dollar price was on her husband's head she would never be able to rest easy. The only way to put an end to the whole business was to find out who had put that money up—and do away with him.

"Try not to fret," he said, almost wincing at how lame his words sounded.

"I just keep wondering who it could be," she murmured. "Your husband is a good man."

She smiled wanly. "He doesn't think so, you know."

"But he is. A good man is one who stands up for the right. And that's what Ethan Payne does. Such a man will make plenty of enemies in this country, as it's chock full of those who've chosen wrong over right as a way of life."

She nodded, and he watched her, admiringly, as she pulled herself together and presented him with a calm and dry-eyed demeanor that had to be a struggle for her to maintain.

"I better get going," he said, eager to get away from the sod house—or, more particularly, away from Julie Payne. It was no picnic being around a woman in such distress, knowing that there was very little you could do to ease her mind other than to utter assurances with a confidence you had to manufacture.

As he and Clooney rode away from the sod house, he reflected on what Mrs. Payne had said about him not liking her. It was true that he had thought poorly of her, since her presence in Abilene had led Ethan Payne, a man he respected and admired, to make a decision that would likely have unpleasant consequences. Now he felt guilty for having judged a woman he'd never even met. Because now that he'd met Julie Payne, he couldn't help but like her. There were a lot of women who would not be able to stand up as well as she to the pressure of this situation. Others would bemoan their fate, or curse their bad luck, focusing on their own misery to the exclusion of all else. But Julie's first concern was for her husband, not for herself. She had sought help for him rather than sympathy for herself.

"She's a good woman," remarked Clooney, after they had ridden about a mile in silence.

The comment startled Wilcox; it was as though the gambler had read his mind. "What do you know about good women?" he asked. Even though the cardsharp was Ethan's friend, he did not trust men of the Clooney's ilk.

Clooney grinned. "Now that you mention it, not much. I mean, I have very little personal experience where good women are concerned. But I do know one when I see one. And that woman back there *is* one."

"Yeah," said Wilcox gruffly. "I reckon that's true. I should have come to the wedding."

Clooney decided to leave the deputy alone to wallow in his guilt, and they rode the rest of the way into Abilene without a word passing between them.

CHAPTER FOURTEEN

As usual, Clooney was at his table in the corner of the Lone Star Saloon that night. But he was sufficiently distracted so that after a couple of hours he was just barely breaking even. He had always prided himself on his ability to concentrate on the game no matter what was happening around him, and regardless of how troubled he might be by other things that there were going on in his life. Tonight, though, he kept an eye on the door; before they'd parted company, Ed Wilcox had told him that Ethan Payne was going to be making his rounds tonight, working alone in hopes of flushing Willie Creed out into the open. It was a desperately risky strategy, but it was just the kind of thing Payne would do. Clooney also watched out for Gentleman Jim Killough. The more he thought about Killough, and speculated on why Gentleman Jim had gone to the trouble of coming to Abilene with advance warning about Creed's intentions, the less comfortable he felt.

It was Killough who showed up first. On his way to the bar he glanced at Clooney's table and nodded to the gambler. He ordered a drink, flirted with a pretty percentage girl, and then meandered over to the table to lean against the wall and watch the game. His presence made Clooney and the other players nervous; the only difference was that

Clooney gave no indication of this while the others did not mask their annoyance. When the hand had been played, one of the cowboys got up and left. Killough asked for an invite to sit in, and Clooney provided it. After one more hand the other two players departed as well, one with the comment that he wasn't foolish enough to sit in a game with *two* cardsharps. That left Clooney alone with Killough, and the former realized that this was precisely what the latter had hoped for. Ordinarily Killough's interference in his work would have angered Clooney, but tonight he was more interested in finding out what Gentleman Jim's game was than playing his own.

"Heard what happened to that deputy," said Killough, shaking his head. "That Willie Creed is a bad piece of work. He must have known it wasn't Ethan Payne. If he didn't, he's bound to know it by now. Have you heard anything?"

"Not much. I know the marshal is back in town. So it will all be over for Mr. Creed soon enough."

Killough smirked. "You have a real high opinion of Payne, don't you?"

"He's the one I'd put my money on."

Gentleman Jim pondered this testimonial, sipping his whiskey, after which he wiped his luxuriant mustache. "He's that good, is he?"

Clooney shrugged. "He's no quick-draw gun artist, of course. But in a scrape there are few tougher."

"Maybe that's so, face to face. But remember, Willie Creed is a notorious backshooter."

"All I can say is, he'd better make the first shot count. Because he probably won't get off a second. And then, whoever is offering all that money for the marshal's hide would have to find somebody else to do his dirty work for him. Have any idea who that might be?"

Killough looked at him sharply. "Why are you asking me?"

Clooney started shuffling the pasteboards. "Oh, I don't know. It's just that you always seem to have your ear to the ground. You usually know what's going on, more than most."

"Well," said Killough, playing along. "He might send a whole passel of killers all at once. The only problem with that is you'd be hard pressed to find a bunch of professional guns who could work together without going at each other."

"That's true. Maybe the marshal won't kill Creed right off. Maybe he'll get him to talk. That way we'd find out who was behind all of this, wouldn't we?"

"He won't take Creed alive," said Killough, with more confidence than he actually felt. It hadn't occurred to him that Creed might not be killed. And if he wasn't, he probably would spill the beans about Marston and the meeting on the private train out in the middle of nowhere. And that meant he'd like as not mention the name of Gentleman Jim Killough. Killough cursed silently. He had made up his mind to betray Creed to Clooney in hopes that word would reach Ethan Payne, so that the marshal would be ready for the kid and, killing him, would eliminate some of the competition. Because Killough wanted that ten thousand dollars. And, too, he'd figured that after killing Creed the marshal might lower his guard. Killough had thought this was a smarter way of going about things than trying to kill Willie Creed himself. But now he was starting to wonder. Obviously he hadn't thought the whole business through, or considered all the possible outcomes.

"How about a quick hand or two of five card stud, Jim," said Clooney amiably.

"No, I don't think so." Poker was the last thing on Killough's mind.

"You're not afraid of me, are you?" Clooney took the sting out of those words with a crooked smile. "You used to be pretty good with cards. You still make a living as a gambler, don't you? Or do you ply some other trade?"

Gentleman Jim Killough looked Clooney straight in the eye and drawled, "What are you saying, friend?"

Clooney looked as innocent as a babe in arms. "Just

wondering why you won't play a hand of poker, Jim. That's all."

"I've got to get going," said Killough, finishing off his drink and rising quickly.

"By the way," said Clooney idly, as though it were really an afterthought, "I told Payne about you."

"Told him what?" rasped Killough.

"Just that you were trying to warn him about Willie Creed. He was pretty preoccupied, on account of his deputy and friend just being shot down, but I'm sure he's grateful for your help."

"It was nothing. See you around, Clooney."

"See you, Jim."

Still shuffling the cards, Clooney watched Gentleman Jim Killough leave the Lone Star like a man on a mission. Now, more than ever, he suspected that there was more to Killough, and what he was doing, than met the eye. Whatever it was, he wouldn't find out about it sitting here. He put down the cards, put his winnings in his hat, and got up and stopped off at the bar to tell one of the bartenders that he was stepping outside for a few minutes, handing him the hat. The employees of the Lone Star knew to keep his table clear if he ever left it. And they would take good care of his money. Clooney was well liked by all the others who worked in the saloon; he was generous when it came to tipping them for looking out for his interests, buying them drinks and even, on one occasion, supplying a small loan, no questions asked.

Once outside, Clooney lit up a Mexican cheroot and, while pretending to be focused on putting match flame to the cigar's tip, scanned the night-shrouded street. There was plenty going on on the Texas Side of Abilene this evening. Cowboys were going in and out of watering holes and dance halls, the tie rails were lined with horses. Light blazed from dozens of windows, along with the sounds of the Texas Side in full swing—the laughter of women, the shouting of men, the thunder of boot heels on a dance floor, the tinny tinkling of a piano from over there and the shriek of a fiddle over there—coming from all points of the compass. Even so, it wasn't all that hard locating Gentleman Jim Killough even at night, in a crowded street—a tall man dressed to the nines, with long yellow hair to his shoulders. Clooney saw him a block away at the intersection of two streets, standing in front of another saloon talking to a girl in satin and feathers, obviously a calico queen trying to drum up some business. Abilene's marshal didn't tolerate soiled doves accosting men on the street—they were supposed to stay on the Row, or in one of the town's several bordellos. Clooney took another quick scan of the street, wondering where Ethan Payne was. Then he started walking toward the intersection where Killough stood, keeping to the deeper shadows of the boardwalk.

He'd taken only a dozen steps when he saw Ethan, coming around the corner ahead of him, turning in his direction. Clooney stopped, glanced at Killough. The calico queen was facing in the right direction to see Payne, and she hastily turned away from Killough and walked into the saloon. Her reaction caused Killough to turn and survey the street. Ethan was only thirty paces away, and Gentleman Jim saw the badge pinned to the black frock coat worn by the marshal. Ethan, though, was unaware of Killough. His attention was homed in on a trio of cowboys emerging from a dance hall, one of them cutting loose with a drunken Rebel yell, and all three with a bad case of the staggers. When they saw the marshal coming toward them the cowboys straightened up and quieted down in a hurry. Confirming that they were not heeled, Ethan gave them a nod and walked on by. They parted like the Red Sea to let him pass.

By this time Clooney had faded into the nearest alley, and he was deep in the shadows with his back pressed against a wall, concealed behind some empty and carelessly stacked crates, as Ethan passed the mouth of the alley not much more than spitting distance away. The marshal glanced down the alley, but he didn't see the gambler, and moved on. Clooney waited. A moment later he saw Killough, across the street, sticking close to the buildings, moving in the same direction as Ethan. Clooney had no doubt that he was shadowing the marshal. The gambler waited for a moment before emerging from the alley and following Ethan. Killough was ahead of him, on the other side of the street—if Gentleman Jim happened to look back, perhaps to see if anyone was tailing the marshal, he would see that Clooney was doing just that. But Killough didn't look back. He was keeping his eyes on Ethan.

When the marshal reached the Lone Star he stepped into the saloon. Clooney stopped and once more sidled into a convenient alley. Once Ethan was inside, Killough crossed the street. For a moment Clooney thought he was going into the Lone Star as well, but instead Gentleman Jim waited at the corner of the building, unaware that Clooney was in hiding not thirty paces down the street from him. The gambler couldn't figure out what Killough was up to. He had to assume that Gentleman Jim was armed. Was he waiting, then, for Ethan to emerge from the saloon, intent on shooting him as he did so? Clooney reached into the pocket of his coat, closed his hand around the over-and-under derringer he kept there. He was violating the town ordinance forbidding the carrying of guns, but he never sat down to a poker game unarmed. He made up his mind that if Killough made a suspicious move when Ethan came out of the Lone Star he would rush forward and fire both barrels into Gentleman Jim, without hesitation or remorse.

But when Ethan came outside, Killough just stepped back out of the light slanting through the Lone Star's plate glass window. The marshal paused, scanned the street, saw Killough, gave him a quick once-over, and then turned to continue up the street. Killough waited a moment before following. Clooney fell in thirty paces behind Gentleman Jim. Maybe, mused the gambler, Killough was biding his time, waiting for a more secluded spot to make his move. Or maybe he had no designs on the marshal's life—maybe he had taken it upon himself to watch Ethan's back, in case Willie Creed showed up. In Clooney's opinion, that would be wholly out of character for Gentleman Jim, who struck him as a man who would never stick his neck out unless there was an something in it for him. But he had to concede that he might have misjudged Killough altogether.

They were two blocks up the street from the Lone Star when it happened. Clooney had just left the boardwalk and was walking in the street, because his view of Ethan was sometimes blocked by Killough's tall, lanky frame, when he saw a shadow move at the mouth of an alley right after the marshal passed by. What occurred next took only seconds, and yet from Clooney's perspective everyone was moving in slow motion, and he saw it all quite clearly. The shadow turned out to be a man clad in black, wearing a sombrero—even in the darkness the shape of the sombrero was quite distinctive. He had his back to Killough and Clooney, looking after the unsuspecting Ethan, and Clooney realized that this had to be Willie Creed, and that he was about to spring an ambush. But before Clooney could react Killough leaped forward, and in the same instant the man Clooney assumed was Creed whirled, sensing that someone was behind him even before he heard a sound. Clooney shouted a warning intended for Ethan a heartbeat before muzzle flash lit up the night. Clooney heard two gunshots and saw Killough going down, giving him a clearer view of Creed, who was spinning around to face Ethan, bringing his matched set of pistols to bear on the marshal. But Killough had distracted him just long enough—Ethan had his gun drawn, and when Creed turned on him the marshal fired without hesitation. Falling backward, Creed triggered one of his pistols, and Ethan fired again—for a few seconds the crashing of gun thunder filled the street. Clooney had the derringer in his hand, but there was no need for that, not anymore. Willie Creed lay on his back on the boardwalk; the gunslinger lifted his head and stared at Ethan, who stood over him, and tried to raise one of his pistols, straining to do so, as though the gun was as heavy as an anvil. Ethan kicked the gun away and Creed made a wheezing sound, arching his back, and died.

Clooney realized he needed to breathe and sucked air

into his lungs, lowering the derringer. Ethan Payne looked at him, and then they both looked at Killough, who was lying on his side in the dust of the street, clutching at his right thigh. Hearing shouts behind him, Clooney glanced over a shoulder to see men running up from every direction, curious to know what all the shooting signified.

"What the hell are you doing here?" Ethan asked him.

"Following him," said Clooney, nodding at Killough.

"And who is he?"

"Gentleman Jim Killough. The man who told me about Willie Creed's plans."

Ethan looked again at Killough, and Clooney couldn't decipher his expression. The marshal scanned the faces of the crowd that was gathering, then said, "One of you go fetch the doctor. We've got a wounded man here." He holstered his Remington Army and sat on his heels next to Killough. "I guess I owe you my thanks. Hadn't been for you he might have plugged me."

"Don't mention it," hissed Gentleman Jim through teeth clenched against excruciating pain.

"Wondering one thing, though," continued Ethan. "Why do you care so much whether I live or die?"

"I'm asking myself the same question. I need to learn how to mind my own business."

Ethan took off his belt and applied it as a tourniquet on Killough's leg, above the wound, to slow the bleeding. A moment later Doc Fields arrived, huffing and puffing after a long run. He took one look at Killough and ordered four of the men in the crowd to carry the wounded man back to his office. As the four picked Killough up and carted him off, the sawbones glanced at Ethan.

"How bad are you hit, Marshal?"

Clooney was startled; he hadn't realized that Ethan had been shot.

Ethan shook his head. "It's just a flesh wound. Nothing, really."

"Is that right." Doc Fields lifted Ethan's frock coat, and Clooney saw that the marshal's shirt was soaked with blood. "Come to my office, and I'll sew you up."

"Sure." Ethan took a few steps, and then his knees seemed to give out on him. But Clooney was there, expecting something like that to happen; the gambler wrapped Ethan's arm around his shoulders and gave him the support he needed to make it the rest of the way to the doctor's place.

When Renny knocked on the hotel room door, she opened it right away as though she'd been expecting him, and she smiled warmly when she saw who it was. Renny was surprised to find that a wave of relief passed over him when he set eyes on Elyse Smith. Several days had passed since their first meeting on Marston's private train. Since then, Renny had taken his time riding to Abilene and, upon arrival, had chosen to spend a day and a night out on the prairie, debating whether or not to continue on into town or head back to Texas. He was inclined, in some respects, to do the latter, as he had no abiding interest in doing Marston's dirty work for him. Ten thousand dollars was a temptation, but Renny had learned there were a lot of things more important than money. Like freedom. After eighteen months in a Mexican jail, he had no desire to be a guest at a crossbar hotel anytime soon, and killing a lawman was as sure a way as any to earn a one-way ticket to jail, where they'd let you rot until time came to hang you. Renny was pretty certain he'd be a lot better off just going home to Texas and finding some legitimate line of work. Not that he intended to hang up his guns. Nor did he even consider wearing a badge. But there were plenty of propertied men who needed their possessions protected from the lawless element—which was a pretty large element in the Lone Star state. And if you worked for a big augur you were pretty much protected from legal repercussions if you had to shoot someone.

So Renny was all set to turn his horse southward and make for the Red River. Except there was one problem. He wanted to see Elyse again. He wasn't exactly sure why. It wasn't as though he had any sort of chance with her. They came from two different worlds. He wouldn't fit into hers any more than she would fit into his. And yet there was something about her that interested him, intrigued him in a way that no other woman ever had. And Renny had met plenty of women, most of them hardy pioneer stock or women of the night. Elyse was different from any of them—she had a peculiar combination of refinement and danger attached to her. Renny knew somehow that she could ride like a man and shoot like a gunslinger. And she could probably also make sense of an opera, which had recently become all the rage in the West—and which Renny couldn't make heads nor tails of. He certainly didn't expect her to be as interested in him as he was in her, which was why her obvious delight at seeing him again caught the gunfighter off guard.

"Come in," she said in a conspiratorial whisper, and grabbed his arm to pull him across the threshold into her room. Then she stuck her head out and quickly scanned the hallway before closing the door and turning the key. She turned and, leaning against the door, gave him another bright smile—the kind of smile that could magically turn everything in the world to rights.

"I was beginning to wonder what had happened to you," she said. "Wondered if maybe you had changed your mind and gone home."

"I thought about it."

She moved to a table on which stood a silver flask. She put a silver-plated hideout pistol down on the table—it was the first Renny was aware that she'd even had a gun on her person—before picking up the flask and holding it out to Renny.

"It's brandy," she said. "Cognac, actually. Not your drink, I suspect, but it will cut the dust. That is, if you don't mind drinking after me."

Renny grinned and took the flask and had a swig. The cognac was like sugary flame as it rolled down his throat, making him gasp.

"I almost did change my mind," he said. "I don't cotton to the idea of spending the rest of my life in jail, or playing host to a necktie party. That eighteen months I spent in a Mexican hellhole gave me plenty of time to think about things."

"What things?" She seemed genuinely interested in what he had to say, and Renny appreciated that. In his younger years he'd been a real loner, not needing anyone or anything, willing to strike out on his own and dependant on no one. In recent years, though, he'd experienced loneliness. And he didn't care for the experience, not one bit. Most people, though, could take one look at him and know him for what he was, and when they knew that they tended to give him a wide berth. It was the path he had chosen for himself, and so he didn't complain, but that didn't mean he had to like it. Elyse, on the other hand, wasn't afraid of him. Nor was she repulsed by the man he was; she did not judge him, as so many others did.

He took another swig of the cognac, then put the flask down on the table. "Well," he said, moving to the window to look out at the nearby stockyards, "about what's really important in life. I got to thinking that it was real easy to kill people—a lot easier than trying to live with them. And I was thinking about how the kind of work I did meant I couldn't have what a lot of other men had. Things like a family. A place to call home. Somewhere where nobody can run me out because they don't like my type." He grinned at her, suddenly embarrassed. "I reckon I'm boring you."

"Not at all."

"Anyway, I've killed more men than I care to remember. Problem is, I do remember. I remember them all. They're always with me. I've got enough ghosts to deal with. Enough sins to answer for. I don't want any more. So I'm not particularly interested in earning Mr. Marston's money. The way I see it, if he wants Ethan Payne dead so bad, let him do it himself. I understand the desire for vengeance. But what good is it if someone else does it for you?"

"You have to be a man to do that," said Elyse.

Renny looked at her sharply. Was that contempt for Marston that he detected in her voice? She moved to the table and picked up the flask and had a drink.

"How is it that you're with Marston, anyway?" asked Renny, daring to voice a question that had been bothering him ever since the moment he'd arrived at Marston's private train.

"That's a long story," she said curtly, "and one I don't like to tell." She glanced at him, and relented slightly. "Maybe later. So, if you didn't come to earn the ten-thousand-dollar bounty on the marshal's head, why *did* you come?"

Renny couldn't bring himself to admit the truth. "Curiosity, mostly."

"Curious about . . . me?" she asked, with exaggerated coyness.

"About how this whole thing plays out."

"It's already been set in motion. Willie Creed was killed last night by Marshal Payne."

"No kidding. And what about Jim Killough?"

"Word has it that he tried to warn the marshal about Creed. He was at the shooting last night, apparently trying to stop Creed. He got shot for his troubles."

"Is he going to pull through?"

"That's what I've heard."

Renny paced to a corner of the room and back again, mulling over the news. A slow smile creased his face. "He's a clever son of a gun. You've got to give him that."

"Because warning the marshal was his way of getting rid of Creed."

"That's right. One thing is certain—if Jim Killough does something it's because he thinks he'll profit from doing it, one way or another."

"He gets rid of Creed, and that's one less man to compete with for the ten thousand dollars."

"And at the same time, if he plays his cards right, he

earns the marshal's trust. That way, he can pick his time and place to strike."

"But," said Elyse, "he's still got to get rid of you, somehow."

Renny nodded. "Right. I wonder how he plans to do that. Should be interesting."

"You could get rid of him first," she suggested.

"Pick a fight with him? Call him out?"

"Don't you think you could best him?"

Renny thought it over. "They say he's fast. I've never been particularly fast."

"And yet you've survived . . . how many gunfights?"

"It's not like you read in those penny dreadfuls, miss. The ones that have become so popular back east, or so I've heard. You don't have two men squaring off in the middle of the street at high noon. In all my days I've never seen a fight like that. It might happen in a street. Or in an alley. Or in a place of business. And you end up with a couple of pilgrims shooting fast and hunting for cover at the same time. More often than not they don't hit each other. In fact, an innocent bystander is just as likely to get killed in a gunfight as the principals."

"You haven't answered my question. How have you survived?"

"Because I take my time. I don't worry about all the lead flying my way. If a bullet has my name on it, so be it. I just focus on hitting my mark."

"I see." Elyse took another sip from the flask, then walked across the room to Renny—*sashayed* would be a better term to describe how she moved—to offer him another drink. He shook his head, paying the flask precious little attention, captured instead by her flawless skin and ruby red lips, slightly parted, and her dark brown eyes that in this light looked black and shiny, like polished obsidian. It took his breath away just for her to be standing so near.

"Well," she said, softly, "I must confess, I'd hate to see you get killed, Mr. Renny."

"Not 'mister.' Just call me Renny."

"And you'll call me Elyse. Do we have a deal?" She stuck out a hand.

He smiled and took her hand and shook it. "Deal." She seemed reluctant to remove her hand from his.

"I told myself I wouldn't play favorites," she said. "But the truth is I was hoping you would be the one to earn the ten thousand dollars. Now I discover that you have no intention of trying to take Marshal Payne."

"Nope. I have no plans in that department. Like I said, I'm just here because . . . because I'm curious." He still couldn't bring himself to tell her the truth—that the only reason he was in Abilene was to see her again.

She seemed to make her mind up about something. "Are you free for dinner?"

"Why, sure." He'd been trying to work up the nerve to ask her. She did it so effortlessly, as though she hadn't agonized over it for even a second. But then, he doubted that Elyse Smith, or whatever her name really was, had ever had to worry about rejection.

"Good. Give me an hour to freshen up and change. I'll meet you downstairs in the lobby."

"Okay." He started for the hotel room door.

"And if it won't bore you too much, I'll tell you the story of my life," she said. "Including how I came to work with Mr. Marston. And what I intend to do about it."

He left the Drover's Cottage and headed into town, intent on finding a saloon where he could get a drink or two, and speculating on what Elyse had meant by her last remark.

CHAPTER FIFTEEN

"I was born in New Orleans," Elyse said, sitting across the table from him in Kelso's Restaurant. Renny tried to ignore the envious looks thrown his way by the mostly male clientele of the place. How he could blame them for being envious of him? Elyse was easily the prettiest woman in town, if not on the entire frontier. She looked particularly fetching in a maroon dress of taffeta and lace that accentuated her narrow waist, full breasts, and flaring hips. Pearls graced her elegant neck, and Renny figured they'd been a gift from Marston. That made *him* jealous, although he reminded himself that he had no right or reason to feel jealousy. Her long, lustrous black hair, shining richly in the light from the lamps on the restaurant walls, was piled up on top of her head and held there with long pins. "My mother," she continued, "was the quadroon mistress of a very wealthy businessman."

That explained her coloring, mused Renny. She had Negro blood in her. It just intrigued him all the more.

"She was not in love with him, however. Her heart belonged to a young doctor. But he was very poor, being inclined to serve the poor of the city without expectation of payment for services rendered. He could not maintain her in the lifestyle to which she was accustomed, and she, having grown up in the worst sort of poverty, refused to return to living hand to mouth. And so she found herself in a deliciously ironic situation: mistress to a man who slipped away from his wife whenever he could, while in turn she slipped away from him to be with the man she loved when she was able to do so. I hope I'm not boring you, Renny."

"Not at all." Their dinner lay before them, scarcely touched. Renny wasn't hungry, and she didn't seem at all interested in food, either. They'd been served by a plump woman who wore a black armband. When Renny had asked her about it she'd replied that she wore the armband to demonstrate her grief for the passing of a fine young man, the deputy named Johnny Rowe, and when she spoke the name Renny saw tears welling up in her eyes. He felt truly sorry for her—and glad that Willie Creed was dead. Of course then he reminded himself that he wasn't much better than Willie Creed.

"One day my mother went to visit the young doctor, and discovered that he had a patient. This patient was a man who had been found in the river by a keelboat crew, and carried down to New Orleans. The keelboat men thought he was so badly injured that he would die long before they reached the city, but somehow he hung on to life. When they arrived they took him to the doctor because they knew he would do what he could for the injured man, even though the injured man clearly had no money to pay for medical treatment.

"That injured man was Marston."

"Yes. The doctor nursed Marston back to health. Later on, when Marston began to meet with some success in his business ventures, he remained in contact with the doctor. That's how I met Marston. One day my mother couldn't make her assignation with the doctor, and she sent me to deliver that message. Marston was at the doctor's home. We were introduced, and that was all; I thought no more about him until the day he arrived at my mother's door asking for permission to court me. He was quite the gen-

tleman, and my mother was very taken with him, despite
the fact that he was crippled. She encouraged me to see
him, which I did, out of respect for her. He was obviously
very taken with me, and I was just as obviously disinter-
ested in him, but he didn't let that deter him. I didn't realize
it at first, but learned not long after I started seeing Marston,
that my mother was ill. Terminally ill. She was concerned
about my future. The man who kept her was under no ob-
ligation to take care of me. If anything, I would be an
embarrassment to him, and she actually feared for my
safety if my well-being depended on him. Then I understood why she was so eager for me to find a man like
Marston.

"And then I learned his terrible secret. He could not
make love to a woman. He confessed this to me on the
same day that he asked me to marry him. He said he understood that I was a healthy young woman, that I had
desires that he could not slake, and that we could make
some sort of arrangement. He asked only that I never leave
him."

"So the two of you are married," said Renny, his heart
sinking.

"No. I told him I could not marry someone I didn't love.
But we did make an arrangement. He would pay me to stay
with him. Occasionally I might even pose as his wife. The
sum he offered was one I could not refuse. But you see,
with Marston, money is no option. He wanted me around.
He wanted to own me. And it didn't really matter to him
how that was accomplished, or what it cost."

"I see," said Renny. The full tragedy of Elyse's story
struck him then. Because of the circumstances of her birth
she had been denied a normal, happy existence. No self-
respecting gentleman in New Orleans would marry someone from her background. They might vie to keep her as a
mistress, but that would be all. He could understand why
she'd accepted Marston's arrangement. Even though it
meant she would have to stay with a man she had no feelings for, at least she didn't have to go to bed with him, to

boot. That was at least some small improvement over her mother's situation.

"My mother died a few weeks later. That's when I accepted Marston's offer. He was as good as his word. He made sure I had the best of everything at my disposal. In addition, he paid New Orleans' finest pistol shot and master swordsman to teach me their arts. I already knew English and French—Marston had me tutored in Spanish and German until I was fluent in both languages. He even sent me, for two years, to a college for women in Maryland. I am who I am today because of him."

"So you *do* have feelings for him, after all. At least gratitude."

"No," she said bluntly. "In fact, I despise him. I am his prisoner. I have stolen for him. I have seduced men to further his business interests. I have even killed for him. I don't like the person I have become."

"Then why don't you leave him? Start all over?"

She gave him a wry look. "Start all over. How easily you said that. But especially a man in your line of work should know how difficult that can be. I tried to get away from him, once. I went as far away as I could, as quickly as I was able. I thought I had escaped him. But then two men came. They beat me. They raped me. They abused me for days. I thought they were going to kill me. But they didn't. The last thing one of them said to me was that Marston had sent them, and that if I didn't go back to him they would come find me again. And next time would be worse." She laughed softly, bitterly. "Worse? I guess they meant the next time I'd end up dead. But in the condition I was in at the time, I wasn't sure that being dead was worse."

"So you went back."

Elyse nodded. "And the strange thing is, Marston acted like nothing had ever happened. Like I had never been gone. He never, ever made mention of my leaving, or of his sending those two men after me."

Renny didn't say anything. He realized at that moment,

with a certainty as strong as any he'd ever experienced, that he was going to have to kill Ash Marston. So he would have one more sin to atone for. One more ghost to haunt him. But in this case it would be worth it. Marston was truly evil, as wicked a man as any he'd ever heard of, and he'd heard of—and met—plenty of bad hombres.

They finished their meal in silence. Elyse seemed very subdued, and it wasn't until they had left Kelso's that she worked up the nerve to ask him what had been foremost on her mind since she'd told her story.

"You think less of me now, don't you?" she asked. "Now that I've told you all about myself."

"That's not true."

"I can't blame it all on Marston, I know. I bear some responsibility for the position in which I find myself. I did agree to his proposal of my own free will. It's true, I didn't know what I was getting myself into, but . . ."

"But nothing. It's not your fault. None of it."

She smiled gratefully at him, and, being very ladylike, did not argue with him. They walked side by side to the Drover's Cottage. He pulled up short at the veranda and thanked her for going to dinner with him. He wanted to tell her that it had been the most pleasant evening he could remember ever having, but feared that might sound too sappy.

Elyse stepped close to him, took his hand between hers. "I don't want you to think I'm a loose woman, Renny. But I don't want you to go. I . . . want you to stay with me tonight."

Renny was speechless with desire. But then there wasn't really anything he needed to say. All he needed to do was follow her inside and up the stairs and down the hallway to her room. And that's exactly what he did. Even though he knew, somehow, where all of this was going to lead. He would not be able to simply walk away from Elyse. And that meant, ultimately, he would have to deal with Mr. Ash Marston, one way or another. He had no illusions about that. Marston might be crippled, but he was still a very powerful man. Was Elyse worth the risk? Following her into the hotel and up the stairs, Renny was quite certain that she was.

Ethan had been lucky—the bullet that had struck him in the side, right below the ribcage, had passed completely through without smashing bone or damaging an organ. All Doc Fields had to do was stop the bleeding, which he did by dousing the wound with alcohol, cauterizing the entry and exit wounds with the blade of a sterilized knife heated by a flame, and then sewing them up. Intensely agonizing though it was, Ethan managed to endure all of this without passing out, and with only a few doses of whiskey to blunt the pain. But he was so weakened by the ordeal that he could hardly move, and remained the rest of the night and most of the next day on a blood-stained table in the doctor's back room.

After treating Ethan, Doc Fields went into the front room where Killough was laid out on another table, and proceeded to work on his leg. This patient was out cold, which made the sawbones' job a little easier. Ethan listened to Fields muttering occasionally to his young assistant, but he couldn't tell what Killough's prognosis was. He finally drifted off into an exhausted sleep.

When he awoke, he found himself on a narrow cot in a corner of the back room. Julie was there, with Ed Wilcox standing behind her, looking if anything more worried than she, and wringing his hat in his hands. Julie smiled as Ethan opened his eyes, and it was a pleasure to see that first thing. She was trying very hard to remain composed, but he knew her well enough to see beyond the façade and to appreciate how tough it was for her.

"What are you doing here?" he asked, still groggy from several hours of deep sleep.

"I brought her, boss," said Wilcox. "I figured it was safe enough, now that Creed's dead. And I thought it might do you some good to see her."

"It does," said Ethan.

"The doctor says you'll be fine," she told him, taking his hand between hers and squeezing it.

"I'll be right as rain before you know it." Ethan thought it might be a good idea to prove it, so he tried to sit up. The pain returned with a vengeance—so intense that it made him gasp. It felt like someone was cutting him open right across the midsection with a dull knife.

"Don't be foolish," she chided him gently, pushing him back down as he strained to defeat the pain and his physical weakness. "You must give yourself time to heal, Ethan."

"She's right," said Wilcox. "You don't need to worry about a thing for a while, boss. I'll keep on a couple of the boys I deputized to help me watch over things while you're recoverin'."

Ethan nodded. "How's Killough?"

"Doc says he'll pull through. Keep his leg, too. But he won't be doing the do-si-do anytime soon, I can tell you."

"If it weren't for him, Creed might have gotten me."

"Yeah, I know. Clooney told me all about what happened."

"Clooney. Yes, that's right. He was there, too."

"He was keeping an eye on Killough. So you were covered six ways to Sunday. But still the bastard—excuse me, ma'am—Creed managed to put a hole in you. A few inches to one side and you'd have been gutshot."

"Only one problem," muttered Ethan. "We didn't find out who hired Creed to kill me."

"You can worry about that later," said Julie sternly. "For now you have to concentrate on getting well."

Ethan smiled at her. "Yes, ma'am."

"Ed, you should leave. He needs his rest."

"I'm gone," said Wilcox, and hurried out.

"I'm going to speak to the doctor," Julie told her husband. "I'll be right in the other room if you need anything."

"I'm fine."

"No, you're not fine. You were nearly killed. Why did I have to fall in love with a man who risks his life every day? Why couldn't you have been a banker, or a doctor?"

"Well, Doc Fields is available. He's been widowed for years now, I hear."

She had to smile. "You're awful," she said. "If you weren't hurt, I'd hurt you."

Ethan started to laugh, but the pain cut through him again, and he decided not to. But he gave her a wolfish grin as she turned and left the room.

In a matter of minutes Ethan was asleep again.

When he woke next it was dark outside—there was a window in the wall directly across the room from him. A taper flickered on the table by the bed, lending uncertain light to the interior of the room, enough for him to see Julie curled up asleep in a big chair over in the corner. The door to the front room was closed. He listened hard for a few minutes, wondering if Doc Fields was still up and about. But he couldn't hear a thing. He had no idea what time it was. All he knew was that he had a raging thirst. Then he saw the glass of water on the table. He knew this was Julie's doing, that she had thoughtfully left it within reach in case he woke with a thirst. He reached out, lifted his head enough to put the rim of the glass to his lips, and drank. Then he put the glass back on the table and just lay there a moment, watching Julie as she slept, and thinking how lucky he was—far luckier than he had any right to be—to have gotten a second chance with her. The day he'd found her in that squalid shack on the Row, his luck had changed. He was certain of that now. There were times when he still thought about Lilah Webster—and Ellen Addison too—but they were only vaguely bittersweet memories now, not guilt-edged daggers stabbing at his heart. He had Julie to thank for that. For her sake he'd finally been able to put those ghosts to rest.

As content as he could ever remember being—and he thought that a little odd since he was laid up with a fresh bullet hole in his side—Ethan Payne went back to sleep.

* * *

Renny woke in the early morning hours with Elyse asleep beside him, her warm, smooth body pressed up against his beneath the linen sheet. Moving slowly, carefully, so as not to awaken her, he raised the sheet and swung his legs off the bed and stood slowly, wincing as the wooden slats beneath the mattress creaked as his weight was removed. Elyse moaned, stirred, turned over, but she did not open her eyes. Renny watched her a moment, telling himself, and not for the first time, that if he was smart he would just walk away. He'd made love to her, and it had been quite an experience. But now he had to think of her the way he thought about all of the other women he had known, which is to say not at all, and be on his way without regret. Yet he knew he wasn't going to do that. Not this time. Not with this woman. A friend had once told him that when a man fell in love with a woman he was as good as dead, that he might as well put a pistol to his head and pull the trigger, as that would save him a great deal of misery. That friend had talked about the black widow spider; the female of the species ate the male after breeding, and in his opinion human females did much the same thing. Renny had never given it much thought. He'd always assumed that he would never fall in love, would never marry and have a family. After all, he was a gunslinger, and that meant he was poor material for the making of a family man. So he'd been content with satisfying his sexual yearnings with the occasional señorita or border town tramp, with no strings attached. But with Elyse it just couldn't be that way.

He moved to the window of the hotel room and looked out at the distant town of Abilene. Most of the buildings were dark, even on the Texas Side, where the nightly festivities had wound down some time ago. He could have closely estimated the time if the stars had been visible, but the night sky was overcast. Opening the window—again, doing it slowly, cautiously, so as not to make any noise that might disturb Elyse in her slumbers—he took a deep breath of fresh air, and smelled rain. He wondered how Gentleman Jim Killough was doing. All Elyse had been able to tell him was that Killough had been shot last night. Renny decided he didn't much care whether Killough lived or died, or whether, if he lived, he would be able to kill Abilene's marshal and collect his ten thousand dollars. Because Renny realized that he was no longer a player in that game—if he had ever been one.

A sound made him turn his head, and he saw that Elyse was awake, on her feet, and coming toward him. Though the night was very dark, and the room darker still, he could still make her out sufficiently to admire what he saw. She came up behind him and slipped her arms under his, clasping her hands together against his chest, pressing her firm breasts against his back, and resting her head on his shoulder.

"It's cool tonight," she whispered. "Keep me warm."

"Rain's coming," he said, and shut the window, pulling the curtains closed.

"Why are you awake? Can't sleep?"

"Just thinking."

"About what?"

He smiled wryly. "What do you think?"

"Well, I hope you're thinking about me," she said, and nibbled playfully on his shoulder.

"I am. About you—and me."

She lifted her head, looking at his profile with an earnest expression on her face. "Let's not think about tomorrow, Renny."

"I can't help thinking about it. You can't stay with Marston, Elyse. Not now. I want you to stay with me."

"I know." She was silent for a moment, thinking. "I have the ten thousand dollars Marston promised to whichever one of you killed Payne. We can take that money and run away together. Although he makes sure I have everything I want, he doesn't give me any money. I don't have access to his bank accounts. I don't have a dollar to my name, really. So that ten thousand is all I can get my hands on. But it should be enough, shouldn't it?"

"Enough to keep us alive until the men he sends to kill

me, or both of us, start showing up," said Renny. "He'll pay ten thousand to see Ethan Payne dead, there's no telling how much he would pay to get you back, Elyse. I know I'd pay a king's ransom, if I had it."

"What a sweet thing to say."

"A man like Marston is jealous of what he has. And of all the things he has, he'll be most jealous of you. I can't blame him for that."

"I know," she murmured. "It has to do with his . . . condition. He feels like he's not half a man only because he can keep me around. But if he loses me he loses whatever self-esteem he has. I figured that much out that time I ran away and he had me brought back. But this time I'll be with you. And you won't let them take me back, will you?"

She sounded almost like a little girl, he thought, pleading with an adult to protect her from a monster.

"The men he'll send will be just like me. I may beat one of them, or maybe six of them, but sooner or later . . ."

He didn't have to finish. She understood what he meant, and she knew it was true.

"Then what will we do?" she asked with a sigh.

He turned to face her, held her close, kissed her on the lips. He knew the answer. It was the only solution to their problem. But he didn't feel as though it was necessary to spell it out for her. She was smart, she would figure it out, if she hadn't already.

"Right now we'll go back to bed," he said.

She smiled, a salacious curve of her full, moist lips. "I like the way you . . . think, Mr. Renny."

"Why, thank you, ma'am."

She dragged him back to bed.

CHAPTER SIXTEEN

After spending two nights and the better part of two days in the back room of Doc Fields' formaldehyde-scented office, Ethan was finally paroled into the custody of his wife, for which he was eternally grateful. The walls had begun to close in on him. The sawbones advised him to get at least two or three weeks of bedrest, and he suggested to Julie that, wherever she intended to move Ethan, it should be close by. Julie had made up her mind to transfer her husband to the Drovers' Cottage, to the room he had rented for her, but Ethan was having no part of that. He wanted to go out to the sod house on the road to Plunkett's Mill, away from Abilene, away from everyone. Ransom had come to see him, as had White, and Clooney, and a dozen other well-wishers, most of them from the so-called "bad element" of the Texas Side, from a saloon keeper to a bartender to a couple of Clooney's fellow cardsharps. A Texas cattle baron by the name of Caulfield dropped in to wish him a speedy recovery, and to assure him that he spoke for all the outfits. Ethan was grateful for their concern, but he just wanted to be left alone. Left alone with Julie, that is. It was extremely tiring trying to hide the pain, and constantly assuring visitors that he would soon be his old self. Ethan was one of those men who did not like to be fussed over. Like a wild animal, when he was hurt he wanted to crawl off into a hole and be left alone until the healing process had run its course.

"Now, you make sure to check the wound daily," Doc Fields instructed Julie. "And change the dressings at least once a day for the first week or so. Keep an eye out for infection. That's the one thing we really have to worry about. If he starts running a fever, get him back in here pronto." He turned to Ethan. "As for you, you stay off your feet, or I'll have you right back in this room, strapped to that cot, if necessary."

"Yes, sir!" said Ethan dryly. "How's Killough?"

"He'll live. And walk again, too. I'd say you both were damned lucky. In his case, the bullet hit about two inches above the knee. Nicked the bone, but missed the kneecap, which is what made all the difference."

"Can I see him?"

"No. I had him moved to my house. My assistant is keeping an eye on him. It'll be a while before he's up and about."

"Okay. What about my bill?"

"Paid."

"By who?"

"The businessmen on the Texas Side. They're paying Mr. Killough's bill, as well. I hear it was your friend Clooney's idea."

"I see." Ethan figured White would be bending Ransom's ear when he heard about that. As the representative of all the "respectable" businesses in Abilene, White had long been of the unshakeable opinion that the town marshal was snugly in the pocket of the men and women who owned the bucket-of-blood saloons, dance halls, and brothels on the Texas Side. This would merely confirm his suspicions. Though White had not said as much to his face, Ethan was sure the man wanted him gone. But now that he was married, and had a responsibility to someone other than himself, Ethan was more determined than ever to hold onto his job. And if John Tyler White didn't like it he could go

to hell. Of course, Ethan would have preferred to pay his
own bill. But he wasn't going to play the ungrateful wretch
and insist that Doc Fields give Clooney's associates their
money back.

As soon as they'd left the doctor's office—Ethan had to
pause and lean heavily against a wall about twenty paces
along the boardwalks—he told Julie that he didn't want to
go to the Drover's Cottage.

"I don't want to trade one small room for another. I'd
rather go out to the house, where I can sit out in the shade
of the cottonwoods, down by the creek."

"That sounds wonderful, Ethan, but I doubt you could
make the trip."

"I can make it," he assured her. He had no illusions
about how painful the journey to the sod house would be,
but some things were worth a high cost.

Julie wasn't convinced, but she could tell that Ethan
wanted this badly, so she nodded her acquiescence. Then
she bade him sit on a bench out front of a general store,
and told him she would go fetch a buggy. That suited
Ethan, as every step he'd taken had sent jolts of pain
through his body. So he sat there and nodded to the passersby who spoke to him. Belatedly, he realized that the
undertaker's place was almost directly across the street, and
there behind a plate glass window was the corpse of Willie
Creed, lying in his coffin, which had been propped up so
that anyone who wanted to could stop in the street and
gawk at the notorious dead man. It was a macabre scene;
as Ethan watched, a couple of women passed the window
and, glimpsing the corpse, covered their eyes and hurried
on. A moment later three boys wandered by and pretended
to get into a gunfight with the dead man, shooting at them
with their forefingers, thumbs raised, and then running off
when a man came by and told them to quit their shenani-
gans. Creed was all dressed up in his black bandolero
clothes; the sombrero had been pinned to his shirtfront,
right below his hands, which were neatly folded over his
chest. Ethan found himself wondering what had transpired

in Creed's past that had brought him to such a bad end. And so soon—it struck him that the man he had killed the other night was hardly more than a boy. His wayward course through life would no doubt be the subject of the preacher's sermon this Sunday coming up; his end would be touted as the comeuppance deserved by one who had been led astray by the Devil's blandishments. But Ethan figured it was just a matter of Willie Creed being dealt a poor hand. Some people were just snakebit where life was concerned, and it wasn't really a matter of choice. One thing would lead to another, and even if your intentions were good, you could wind up on the wrong side of the line.

Sitting there, staring across the broad, dusty street at the man he had killed, Ethan wondered for the hundredth time who had hired Willie Creed to hunt him down and kill him. He'd racked his brain trying to figure that one out. He'd made some enemies, but none had the resources to offer a ten-thousand-dollar bounty for his head. At least none that he knew of. He'd thought of McKittrick, the Texas cattle king he'd humiliated last year, the employer of the Jenkins brothers, both of whom were six feet under thanks to Abilene's new marshal. But he didn't think hiring a gunslinger to do his work for him was McKittrick's style. He'd even speculated on whether John Tyler White could have been the man behind Creed. White probably had the wherewithal to pay that reward, but, as much as he disliked Ethan Payne, he didn't seem to be the type who would resort to such underhanded tactics. The fact remained that as long as there was someone out there who wanted him dead that badly, Ethan couldn't rest easy. Not that he was all that worried about his own welfare. But he was worried about Julie. She was in danger, too.

She arrived with the buggy, and he climbed into the conveyance without assistance. She took up the reins and drove out of town. She handled the horse well; while working at the Wolftrap Station she'd learned how to handle harness stock. So all Ethan had to do was try to control the pain. They only had to go a few miles, but they were the longest miles he'd ever had to endure. By the time they reached the sod house he was soaked with sweat and pale as a ghost, and she had to help him out of the buggy and inside. He silently cursed himself for being so weak. Stretching out on the bed with a groan, he lay there until the pain had subsided. Julie brought him some broth, and though he had no appetite, he dutifully ate it all. Then he went to sleep. There wasn't much else to do. Only time would restore him.

When he awoke the day was waning, and with Julie's help he got up, went outside, walked down to the creek, and sat down with his back to one of the cottonwoods so he could watch the sunset. She sat beside him and together in silence they enjoyed the serenity of the moment—the whisper of the ever-present prairie wind in the branches overhead, the song of meadowlarks in the tall grass, the gurgling of the nearby creek, and somewhere far off the yip-yip-yip of a coyote.

"This isn't fair to you," he said finally.

"What? What isn't fair?"

"Don't get me wrong. I'm glad you're here. But it isn't fair, this situation I've put you in. The day after we're married I have to leave you, and you have to sit here and wait and wonder when and if I'll come back, knowing that a hard case like Creed is gunning for me."

"I'm not complaining."

He looked at her. "You never have. Even at Wolftrap, where God knows you had plenty to complain about, you never did."

She sighed. "So what are you saying, Ethan? That you regret having married me?"

"No. I'll never regret that. I'm just apologizing, I guess."

"I won't lie to you. I'd rather you weren't doing what you do. I wish you would take that tin star off your coat. I wish you never had to resort to your guns again."

"What would I do?"

"I won't even make a suggestion. Because if you can't

think of something else you'd like to do on your own, then my doing so won't make a bit of difference."

He was silent for a moment, lost in thought, and she left him alone.

"Earlier today I was thinking that I'd hold on to this job no matter what, and in spite of the fact that there are some in Abilene who want to see me gone. I'd do that because I want to take care of you, to be able to afford to get you the things you want, so that you never have to work your fingers to the bone like you did when you were on the Overland line."

"I never minded hard work."

"I know. And neither do I. Since it's what you want, I'll give up the star."

"Really? You mean it, Ethan?"

He nodded gravely. "But there's some unfinished business I have to attend to first. I have to find out who offered Willie Creed that ten thousand dollars. Because I can't hang up my guns until that business is resolved. It doesn't matter what I do or where I go, that will always be hanging over our heads, and I'll always have to be looking over my shoulder—and worrying about you getting caught in the crossfire."

She leaned over and kissed him on the cheek and he took the opportunity to breathe deeply the fragrance of her long yellow hair. "I'm going to hold you to it, Ethan Payne," she said softly.

He smiled, trying to look more confident than he felt. It was the right thing to do, this he knew. And for her he would do anything. But it didn't make him feel any better about the future, because he didn't have the slightest idea what kind of work he might be able to find. Farming was out of the question; he'd left Illinois in the first place because he didn't want to be a dirt-poor plow pusher all his life. He didn't know the first thing about raising cattle. While working for the Eldorado Mine in California he'd learned a good deal about freighting, but that kind of job would take him away from Julie for long periods of time.

The fact remained, sorry as it was, that he'd bought himself
a reputation early on as a handy man with a gun. It had
started with those outlaws he'd tracked down and killed in
California, the ones who had stolen the Eldorado gold shipment that he'd been charged with protecting. That incident
had led directly to his being offered the job of Overland
troubleshooter. And he'd made a name for himself working
for the Stagecoach King, Ben Holladay. In the gold fields
of Colorado the only job of any consequence he'd found
was as a gun guard for mine shipments. Once a man started
living by the gun it was damned hard to make a living any
other way. People figured that was all you were good for.
Ethan was inclined to think they were right, too. He'd never
doubted that he could handle a job like being a trail town
lawman. But he had grave doubts about his ability to succeed at much of anything else.

They sat there under the cottonwood until the sun had
dropped below the horizon and the last shreds of daylight
had bled out of the sky. Only then did they go back inside.
Ethan sat at the table and watched her while she cooked up
some bean soup and biscuits. It felt good to be sitting under
one's own roof, keeping company with a woman you were
proud to call your own. For nearly twenty years he'd never
had a place to call his own, and his soul was weary of the
yondering. If it meant making Julie happy, and keeping this
contented feeling of belonging, then he would do whatever
it took.

Later that night he came suddenly awake, unsure at first
of what had roused him. Julie lay beside him—she had
wanted to give him the bed due to his condition, but he'd
insisted that she share it with him—and she was sleeping
soundly. He lay quite still for a moment, and then heard
the whicker of the horse out at the corral. Something had
alarmed the animal. There was something—or someone—
out there that shouldn't be. Stifling a groan, Ethan got out
of bed and took his gun from its rig, which lay coiled on
a ladderback chair nearby. Clad only in his under riggings,
he moved to the room's only window and peered out

through a narrow gap between the closed curtains, fashioned long ago from a burlap sack. After dark storm clouds had rolled in, threatening rain, which meant it was darker than usual, and he could scarcely see anything but the dark shapes of the cottonwood trees.

The horse whickered again, louder this time. Peering as hard as he could into the darkness, he could make out the animal's shape. It was pacing back and forth along the edge of the corral. Without a doubt there was something in the night that the horse didn't like. Ethan moved, cat-footed, into the other room. He opened the front door a bit and peered through the crack; this time he thought he saw another moving shadow, down beneath the trees. His first instinct was to venture out and solve the mystery. It could be a panther, or a wolf, or a horse thief. There hadn't been Indian problems in this area for years, but that didn't mean there weren't still some renegade Kiowas who occasionally made trouble. But Ethan knew he had to think about Julie first. He wasn't in any shape to tangle with a predator of either the two-legged or four-legged variety, and if he lost, if he got himself killed, then he'd be leaving Julie defenseless. No, he had to be pragmatic; much as he might want to investigate, the wiser course was to remain in the sod house. So he closed the door and barred it, took up a position at the window, and kept watch. The horse issued no further alarms. Ethan watched for an hour. That was about as long as he could bear to stand; the pain from his wound was excruciating. So he made his way back to bed. But he didn't go back to sleep. He lay there, beside Julie, pistol in hand and resting on his chest, and listened to the night until dawn came.

That morning, he didn't tell Julie anything about the night before. He got dressed and emerged from the bedroom in time to see her pick up the water bucket, intent on heading down to the creek to fetch some water for coffee, and he told her he wanted to come along. She advised against it. He wasn't strong enough yet. He assured her that he was. There was no way he could let her go out there alone. Julie relented, and together they walked down to the creek. She didn't notice that his pistol was snugged under his belt, in the small of his back. A light, misty rain was falling. The horse in the corral seemed okay. Ethan scanned the horizon. Nothing out of the ordinary. He began to search the ground. A chill ran down his spine when he saw the tracks in the dirt. A man, wearing boots, had come from the creek, moving toward the corral, then turned around and retraced his steps. While Julie filled the bucket with water, Ethan stood on the bank of the creek and looked for tracks on the other side. He didn't see any, but there were some freshly broken reeds yonder. Again he scanned the rim of the surrounding high ground. The hairs at the nape of his neck were standing on end. He didn't see anyone, yet he felt as though he was being watched. Maybe it was just his imagination. Still, a man with a ten-thousand-dollar bounty on his head could be forgiven for imagining such things. Could it be that Willie Creed's replacement was in the vicinity?

"Is something the matter, Ethan?"

He looked at her. She'd finished filling the bucket and was standing there, watching him curiously. He had been so engrossed in surveying the surrounding countryside that he hadn't even noticed.

"No, nothing at all," he said, and smiled, hoping that the smile didn't look forced. He could see no point in telling her what he knew, and what he suspected. That would only alarm her, and what would that accomplish?

They went back inside. She brewed some coffee and then started on some biscuits. She told him that one day soon they would have to invite Ed Wilcox and his wife out for dinner, in return for the kindness they had shown in supplying her with some provisions while he'd gone into Abilene to flush Creed out of hiding. Ethan wasn't listening. She brought him a cup of steaming coffee, strong and black the way he liked, and sat down at the table across from him with an earnest expression on her lovely face.

"Okay," she said. "Tell me."

He pretended he didn't know what she meant. "Tell you what?"

She sighed. "I've always been able to tell when something is bothering you. And now something is bothering you."

Ethan smiled. "That's true—you always were able to read me pretty well."

"So? I'm waiting."

He drew a long breath. "It's probably nothing. We had a visitor last night."

"A visitor?"

"I never saw him. He was sneaking around the corral. I did spot his tracks this morning. Probably just a horse thief."

She thought about that for a moment, and he watched her closely, knowing that she was smart enough to speculate along the same lines as he had.

"Or it could be someone else hoping to collect that ten-thousand-dollar reward."

"I was wrong to want to come out here. I think we should go back to town."

"It's me you're worried about. But you don't need to, Ethan. I can take care of myself. Lord knows I did at Wolf-trap, being by myself most of the time."

"I know. But I don't want anything to happen to you."

"We won't be any safer in Abilene than we are here."

"I wish I'd gotten that wolf-dog I told you about. But with everything that's happened, I just didn't think of it."

"Then why don't we go in a few days, when you're feeling stronger?" asked Julie. "If it would make you feel better, let's go get the dog."

He nodded. "Good idea. But let's go today. Right now."

"Ethan, you're in no shape to—"

He reached across and put his hand over hers. "You'd be surprised what I'm in shape for," he said, grinning.

Julie blushed. "Really, now. Tell you what. You prove to me that you're in shape for *that*, and I'll consider driving you into town today."

He laughed. "You're on."

CHAPTER SEVENTEEN

A week after the killing of Willie Creed, Clooney paid a visit to Gentleman Jim Killough, who was still housed at Doc Fields' place. He couldn't even guess what condition Killough might be in, but he was mildly surprised to see the man on Fields' front porch clad only in an old nightshirt, with a week-old stubble of beard on his face, and his long yellow locks lying tangled on his shoulders. He looked pale and haggard. All in all, it was quite a different picture from the way Gentleman Jim usually looked. There was a thick dressing on his leg—so thick, in fact, that it prevented him from bending the knee, so that he had to sit with the leg fully extended.

"How are you, Jim?" asked Clooney pleasantly. "I brought you a present." He held up a bottle of whiskey.

Killough's eyes lit up. His features were animated with joy. "I feel a damned sight better, of a sudden," he declared, reaching for the bottle. Uncorking it with his teeth, he spit the cork to one side, took a long draught, and came up gasping. "Now, that's the kind of medicine I've been needing. Some real, honest-to-God, hundred-proof painkiller." He peered at Clooney. "I better drink this up right now. Otherwise, the doc might find out about it. And that old buzzard would get real mad at you, Clooney."

"If you need any help, I'm not doing anything at the moment."

"Pull up a chair."

There wasn't another chair on the porch, so Clooney settled for sitting on his haunches with his back resting against an upright, within reach of Killough so they could easily pass the bottle back and forth.

After each of them had indulged in a few draughts, Killough said, "So what were *you* doing there that night, Clooney? Keeping an eye on your marshal friend? Or on me?"

Clooney shrugged. "A little of both."

"You think I might be after that ten-thousand-dollar bounty on Payne, don't you?"

Clooney looked him square in the eye. "Are you?"

"If I was, I'd have a smarter way of going about collecting it than this!" exclaimed Killough, gesturing with disgust at his game leg.

"Just doesn't make any sense to me, Jim," confessed Clooney. "You're not the type to do something just out of the goodness of your heart. Why would you care if Creed killed the marshal? What difference would it make to you?"

"You keep asking me that."

"Maybe because you haven't given me an answer I can swallow."

"I told you the first time. I did it because I wanted your marshal to be beholden to me. I figured I might want to stay in Abilene for a while. You know, there aren't that many places left where I'm welcome. Speaking of Payne, I haven't seen him around lately. Thought he might at least drop by and see how I'm doing. The bullet I took in the leg was meant for the marshal, you know."

"Yes, I know. I'm sure Ethan will be along to thank you when he's able. He's not one to forget a favor done him. For now, though, I guess you'll have to settle for my thanks."

Killough took another drink from the whiskey bottle. While he did, Clooney fired up a Mexican cheroot, offered it to Gentleman Jim, who took it with a nod of gratitude.

Clooney took another cheroot from the silver case he carried in an inside pocket of his frock coat, lit it, and for a moment the two men sat there puffing away, savoring the pungent smokes.

"So how is he?" asked Killough.

"Ethan? I'm sure he's doing fine. I haven't seen him, either. But he's in good hands."

"How's that?"

"His wife. She'll take good care of him."

"Wife, you say. I didn't know."

Clooney nodded. "He's lucky to have her."

"Is she pretty?"

"As a picture." Clooney gave Gentleman Jim a sidelong glance. "But you can forget any ideas you might have. She'd have nothing to do with you, even if she wasn't married."

Killough chuckled. "I've been thinking, Clooney. Thinking you need some competition. You've got prime fixings here, and you're making way too much money. Soon as I'm able, I'm going to get a table at one of the other saloons and run a game, just like you are."

"There's plenty of cowboys with plenty of money to go around," replied Clooney. "Just be sure you run a straight game, Jim. Ethan won't tolerate a crooked table. When does the doc say you'll be up and around, anyway?"

"Another week, at least. So he says. But I say give me a few more days and I'll be walking."

Clooney took one more swig from the whiskey bottle before handing it back to Killough and getting to his feet. "Well, when you're able, drop by the Lone Star and I'll buy you a drink."

"Where does Payne and his pretty wife live? When I'm able, I'm going to pay him a visit, make sure it's all right with him if I stick around awhile."

"He lives a few miles out of town. I plan to ride out to see how he's doing tomorrow. I'll ask him if it's okay to bring you out when you can ride."

Killough nodded. "Fair enough."

When Clooney was gone, Gentleman Jim put the bottle down and pushed himself up out of the chair. He grabbed hold of the nearest upright and gingerly tested his wounded leg. Then he slowly scanned the street. The hairs at the nape of his neck were standing on end. He had good instincts, and he knew to rely on them. Right now he had this feeling that someone was watching him, and his thoughts turned to Renny. He'd been wondering for some time now whether the Texan would actually show up in Abilene. He didn't really think that the warning he'd issued to Renny back at Marston's private train would do any good. Killough had never worried too much about Willie Creed. Sure, Creed was a killer, and a cold-blooded one at that, but he was a brash kid, too, someone who was prone to make mistakes. Like being impatient enough to get himself killed. Renny, though, was something else again.

Gentleman Jim considered his own immediate future. Everything he'd done since arriving in Abilene had been to one end, and that was to earn Ethan Payne's trust. Once he had that, he could pick his time and place, kill the marshal when the opportunity presented itself, and get away clean with the ten thousand dollars Ash Marston was offering. But Clooney was the joker in the deck. He was the one person who could scotch the whole deal. It was obvious to Killough that Clooney had strong suspicions regarding his true motives for being so helpful. Maybe Clooney would have to be taken out of the picture.

Gentleman Jim tested his wounded leg again, and decided that in two or three more days he would be able to walk, albeit with the aid of a cane. Then he could get on with the business at hand. He was just going to have to be patient. A *patient* patient. He grinned and eased his lanky frame back down into the chair. If Renny *was* out there, and *was* watching, then it would be best to play the invalid.

The next evening, Clooney showed up again at Doc Fields' home. Killough was sitting down to dinner with the doctor and his assistant, but when the gambler showed up they repaired to the porch so that they could talk privately. It had been raining hard all day, and the streets of Abilene were treacherous strips of mud. A cool wind was gusting in from the northwest.

"Summer's over," remarked Gentleman Jim.

Clooney nodded. "Cattle season is just about over. I think there's an early winter coming this year."

"I think I'll go to Mexico," said Killough, and smiled to himself. He'd already decided that once he'd been paid the ten thousand dollars for Ethan Payne he'd head south of the border. With that kind of money he could live like a king for a good long while. And, best of all, there were plenty of pretty young señoritas down there who would favor him if his pockets were full. "What about you?"

"I'll probably stay here. Just because the cowboys aren't coming uptrail doesn't mean I can't drum up some business. There's always the railroad men, and the farmers, and the army has a new post not far from here, so I can expect some yellowleg customers, too."

"This would have to be a pretty dull place come winter," remarked Killough.

Clooney looked at Gentleman Jim's leg. "I notice you're standing a lot more today. The leg must be healing up."

Killough grinned. "You know what they say. You just can't keep a good man down."

"Well, that's good. I rode out to see the marshal yesterday. Told him you wanted to see him."

"Did you tell him why?"

"No. Thought that was best left to you."

"What did he say?"

Clooney smiled wryly. "Before he could say anything his wife invited you to dinner tomorrow night. The marshal didn't say nay. Just gave her an amused look, and said nothing more about it. So looks like you'll get what you wanted."

"Yes," said Killough. "It sure does, doesn't it?"

"So I'll be around about this time tomorrow evening with a buggy."

"You're coming too?"

"Yeah," said Clooney. "I also got an invite. I happen to know she can cook up a storm. When I first met her she was running an Overland way station pretty much on her own."

"Sounds like quite a woman. And pretty as a picture, you say." Killough was pleased. It looked to him like this job might have some unexpected benefits.

As he had said he would, Clooney arrived at Doc Fields' house the following evening. The rain had moved on, but that cool wind was still blowing in from the northwest, herding shreds of low purple clouds across the darkening sky. Gentleman Jim was waiting for him on the porch. He was dressed to the nines, and he had a walking stick that the doctor had loaned him. The staff was walnut, the knob staghorn. He was shaved, and all the tangles were brushed out of his yellow locks. As Clooney pulled up to the front of the house in a buggy, Killough hiked himself up out of his chair and, using the cane to support his weight, made his way gingerly down the steps to the buggy. Clooney got out and Killough allowed the gambler to give him a helping hand—even though he knew that he could have made it up into the buggy without assistance. He *wanted* Clooney to think he was much less self-sufficient than was the case.

"It's about five miles," Clooney told him. "Are you sure you're up to it?"

Killough grinned. He could tell that Clooney had doubts about the wisdom of bringing him to meet the marshal, and the gambler would have liked nothing better than to hear him say that five miles of bumpy road was more discomfort than he cared to endure.

"I think I'll manage," he said.

Clooney just nodded, and turned away to hide his disappointment. As he went around the back of the buggy to get to the other side, he reached under his frock coat to feel the reassuring bulk of the pistol that was snugged under his belt in the back. Climbing into the conveyance, he took up the reins and whipped up the horse in its traces.

They rode in silence up the road that ran north out of Abilene. A couple of miles out, where the road forked, Clooney took the turn to Plunkett's Mill. This road, noticed Killough, ran along a creek lined with cottonwoods. The leaves of the trees looked silver in the last light of day.

"How much farther?" asked Killough casually, shifting his weight uncomfortably.

"It's just a couple more miles down this road," said Clooney.

"Well, that's good to hear," said Killough—and then swung the cane with all his might, slamming the staghorn knob into Clooney's face. The impact drove the gambler's head back, and then he pitched forward, blood spewing from a broken nose and shattered mouth. He dropped the reins and groped blindly for the gun under his coat, but Killough swung the stick again, striking the gambler in the head a second time. This time Clooney fell sideways with a groan, tumbling out of the buggy. Before the horse could even think about bolting, Killough dropped the cane onto the footboard and snatched up the leathers, pulling with all his might to stop the animal. Once that was accomplished he tied the reins around the brake pull and got down out of the buggy. Once more wielding the cane, he limped back down the road to where Clooney was struggling to get up. The gambler had made it as far as his hands and knees. That seemed to be all he could manage. His head lolled, blood drooled from his ruined face. Killough's second blow had opened up a deep gash just above his right temple, and that entire side of his head was glistening black with blood.

Gentleman Jim stopped a half dozen paces away and, cocking his head to one side, sized up Clooney's condition and shook his head.

"I kinda hated to do that, amigo, if that makes you feel any better. But you've just been way too suspicious of me for your own good."

Clooney mumbled something, but Killough couldn't make it out. He noticed that the gambler was still trying to get his gun into play, and he shook his head, marveling at the man's gumption. He waited until Clooney actually had the pistol in hand before knocking it out of his grasp with another swing of the cane. The pistol went spinning down the road, and Killough marked where it landed before turning his attention back to Clooney, who was sitting down now, grunting at a fresh dose of pain from a dislocated finger.

"You were right about me," said Gentleman Jim, "I *did* have an ulterior motive in telling you about Willie Creed. I *am* here to collect that ten thousand dollars."

Clooney again tried to say something.

"What did you say?" asked Killough, leaning closer.

"W-who?" managed Clooney. It took a huge effort to get his mouth to form the word.

"Oh, you mean who's offering the money for Payne's hide?" Killough thought it over, and shrugged. "I guess it really doesn't matter if I tell you. It's a fellow by the name of Marston. He's a very rich man. Crippled from the waist down. Blames Payne for that. He's been waiting for the day when he could have his revenge. And it looks like today will be that day." Gentleman Jim looked around, then stood up, and sighed. "I hope you don't mind, but I better get a move on. Don't want to be late for dinner."

He swung the cane again, savagely, gripping it with both hands, and the impact was so severe that it splintered the walnut staff. Clooney toppled sideways. Killough tossed what was left of the cane away and then circled the body to limp down the road and retrieve the pistol. Returning to where Clooney lay, he thumbed back the hammer and aimed the pistol at the gambler's head. But then he lowered the gun. Clooney looked dead. Gentleman Jim bent closer. No, he wasn't breathing. He *was* dead. Gentleman Jim pursed his lips, lowered the hammer, and broke open the pistol to check the bullets in the cylinder. Five rounds. Did he really want to expend one on a dead man? That didn't make much sense, considering what he had in mind for the rest of the evening. So he slid the pistol under his belt and dragged Clooney's body off the road into the sagebrush. Then he made his way back to the buggy and continued on his way to Ethan Payne's place, whistling a cheerful tune.

It didn't take long for the scavengers to find Clooney.

They were coyotes, two of them, a male and a female, and the latter had denned not far from the spot on the road to Plunkett's Mill where Killough had left the gambler. The smell of blood, carried on the strong gusts of wind, alerted them. The wind also carried another scent—the scent of man. So they approached cautiously. An opportunistic predator, the coyote preferred game, but the female was raising a litter of five pups, left behind in the den, and she was always ravenously hungry. Curiosity brought them to Clooney's body. They circled it in the darkness for a while. The male occasionally ventured closer—a little closer every time, until it was near enough to sniff an outflung arm. The coyote drifted back into the gloom again, circled a few more times, and then darted in to grab the sleeve of Clooney's frock coat and, shaking it vigorously, ripped the broadcloth with his razor-sharp canines, lifting the arm off the ground. When the fabric gave way and the coyote lost his grip, the arm fell heavily to the ground. The coyote moved in, head down, back slightly arched—and then leaped away. He paused a dozen feet away. The female joined him. They turned their heads and watched the man lying in the dust. They could see quite well in the nocturnal gloom. Well enough to see Clooney's hand twitch. Once, twice. That was all they needed to see. The man was still alive. The coyotes vanished like wraiths into the night.

CHAPTER EIGHTEEN

Ethan Payne stepped out of the sod house as the buggy pulled up out front, and was surprised to see that it had but one passenger.

"Howdy, Marshal," drawled Killough, with his most amiable smile. "I'm afraid Clooney had to back out at the last minute. Something about a big game at the Lone Star. He sends his regrets, and was kind enough to tell me how to get here. He knew how much important this dinner was to me."

"Important," echoed Ethan, nodding. "Well, then, come on in, Mr. Killough."

"Thanks." Gentleman Jim gingerly disembarked from the buggy. Just as he had for Clooney's benefit, he pretended to be less certain on his wounded leg than was in fact the case. Without seeming to, he checked to make sure that the marshal wasn't heeled. And he realized that he could kill Payne right here and now and be done with it. The lawman was unarmed, and Killough had Clooney's pistol concealed beneath his coat. He might not get a better chance. But Jim Killough liked to take chances. And he didn't cotton to the prospect of squandering an opportunity to put one over on Payne. It gave him a sense of power.

Of being in complete control. And of being better than the
famous Abilene lawman.

Ethan watched Killough's progress from the porch. He
didn't move to help the injured man. He'd been ambivalent
about inviting the man to dinner, but he hadn't been willing
to overrule Julie, and he understood that his wife felt beholden to Killough for actions which, in all likelihood, had
saved her husband's life.

Approaching Ethan, Killough stuck out a hand. "We
haven't been introduced," said Gentleman Jim. "And where
I come from, the formalities must be adhered to."

Ethan shook the hand. "And where do you come from,
Mr. Killough?"

"Call me Jim. All my friends do. I hail from Georgia,
sir. Though it's been many years since I left there to seek
my fame and fortune on the frontier."

Ethan smiled faintly. Some men came West because they
were running from their past. Others came for a new beginning, a better chance to find fame and fortune. He, like
Killough, fell into the second category.

"A lot of us came out here to do that. Had much luck?"

Killough shrugged. "Not much, I confess. But you
know, somehow I feel as though my luck is about to
change."

Ethan nodded and gestured at the door. "You're welcome in my house."

Killough preceded him inside. As he crossed the threshold, Julie came forward to greet him, a radiant smile on her
lovely face. She wiped her hands on the apron she wore
over a plain blue gingham dress, then proffered it to her
guest. Gentleman Jim brought it to his lips.

"So this must be Mrs. Payne. I am honored to meet you,
ma'am. Clooney told me a great deal about you. He said
you were a good cook."

Julie laughed softly, charmed by Killough's gallantry.
"And where is Clooney? Didn't he come?"

"He couldn't make it," said Ethan, closing the door.
"Have a seat, Mr. Killough."

It didn't escape Killough's notice that Ethan had apparently declined the offer to use his first name. He sat at the table that stood in the center of the room. A lantern on the table provided the room with illumination. A small but hot fire crackled against the underside of a Dutch oven that hung by a stout hook in the fireplace.

"Whatever you're cooking in there, ma'am, it smells grand," said Killough pleasantly.

"Beef stew. There's a Texas outfit camped not far from here. They brought the beef to us."

Killough nodded, and turned to Ethan. "My compliments, sir. It's not often a trail town marshal can remain on such good terms with the Texans."

"We have come to an understanding. Drink?" Ethan had moved to a rough-hewn hutch, and lifted a bottle of whiskey up for Killough to see.

"Don't mind if I do." Killough could appreciate the sweet irony of the situation. He was going to be served by and drink the whiskey of the man he was about to kill. He noticed that a gun rig was hanging from a peg near the door, and that a Remington Army was snug in the holster. And he was certain now, having seen Ethan front and back, that the marshal wasn't armed.

Ethan poured two glasses, carried them to the table, and sat down opposite Killough, handing one of the glasses to his guest. "I thank you again for what you did that night."

"You were taking a big risk, trying to draw Creed out that way. I'd already figured out you weren't the kind of man who would ask for or want any help. But I couldn't just stand by and do nothing. So I followed you that night. Good thing I did, too."

"I think it was very brave of you," said Julie gratefully. "You took the bullet meant for Ethan."

"Well, as for that—I confess it isn't the first bullet I've taken. But it may be the one I'll be most proud of."

"Clooney said you wanted to talk to me about something," said Ethan.

Killough sipped the whiskey, nodded. "That's right. I

told him that I was thinking about sticking around here for a spell. Maybe run a table, the way he does at the Lone Star. But before I did that, I wanted to make sure you didn't have any problem with it."

"Why would I?"

"I have a reputation."

"Don't we all."

Killough smiled. "But that's just what I told Clooney I wanted to see you about. The truth of the matter is, I'm here for the same reason as Willie Creed."

As he spoke he reached under his coat and pulled the pistol. He figured that he had Ethan Payne dead to rights; even if the marshal didn't freeze, as most men would in that situation, he was still too far away from his pistol. What he hadn't expected was Ethan's lightning-quick reaction. Ethan tipped the table over on top of Killough. This not only knocked the would-be assassin to the floor, it also sent the lantern tumbling. The lantern shattered, plunging the room into semi-darkness—the only light came from the flickering fire in the hearth. Julie let out a cry of alarm. Ethan sprang toward the door and the Remington Army in the gun rig hanging on the peg.

"Julie!" he shouted. "Get out!"

Julie started toward him. But Killough, momentarily pinned beneath the table, had the presence of mind to reach out with one hand and grab her ankle as she passed by. She fell. He kicked out from under the table, holding on to her. She tried to kick free, but his grip was like iron. On one knee, Gentleman Jim swiveled and brought his gun to bear on Ethan, who had reached the Remington and was in the process of freeing it from the holster. The Abilene lawman whirled, ready to fire. But he hesitated, because Julie was in the line of fire. Killough didn't hesitate.

"*No!*" Julie screamed, and kicked out at him again.

It was just enough to throw Killough's aim off by a few inches. His pistol roared in the confines of the room. The bullet smacked into the wall behind Ethan. Ethan realized that he had but one option. If he stayed put he would die, and dead he wouldn't be of much use to Julie. So he dove through the open doorway. Killough sent another bullet chasing after him, but this one missed its mark, too.

Cursing, Killough forgot he was a gentleman and angrily planted the barrel of his pistol against Julie's head.

"Woman," he rasped, "I'll kill you right here if you don't stop struggling."

She didn't doubt him for an instant. And now that her husband had escaped, she was willing to stop. Killough transferred his grip from her leg to her arm. Getting up, he hauled her roughly to her feet, using her as a shield just in case Ethan shot at him through the doorway.

"Payne!" he roared. "I've got your wife. You want her to live, you'll throw down that gun and come back in here!"

"You're as good as dead," hissed Julie.

"Shut up."

"You'll never get out of here alive," she insisted.

"I said shut up!" He shook her viciously.

"Let her go, Killough," called Ethan from beyond the doorway. "When she comes out, I'll come in, and we'll settle this just between the two of us."

Killough laughed. "You must take me for a fool, Payne. I'm not going to give up my ace." He threw a quick look around. There was no back way out. He had to bring Ethan Payne back inside to kill him. His gaze fell on the Dutch oven in the fireplace. Then he grinned at Julie. "I hate to do this to you, ma'am. But your coward husband leaves me no choice."

"He's no coward!" she said fiercely—and then yelped in pain as he wrenched her arm around at an angle it had not been designed to reach, dropping her to the floor, then dragging her over to the hearth. At the last second she realized what he was about to do and gasped "No!" an instant before he laid the side of her forearm against the Dutch oven. The hot iron seared her flesh and she screamed at the pain in spite of her willing herself not to, because she realized, too, why he was doing it. She simply couldn't help herself, though, and her heart sank as she heard her husband's boots on the planks of the porch, and an instant later he was exploding through the open doorway. Killough was waiting for him and triggered his pistol, and almost simultaneously Ethan found his target and fired. The room was filled with gun thunder, acrid gray powder smoke, and the blinding double-barrel flash. Killough grunted as he was slammed back against the stone of the hearth, and he let go of Julie. She scrambled away from him as he fired again. His bullet smacked into the overturned table behind which Ethan had sought cover. A slow smile moved Killough's thick mustache as he came to the understanding that he had lost his advantage, that he was probably going to die. At least he could die standing. He fired again into the table, trying to buy himself enough time to get to his feet, using the hearth to brace against, wondering why his body was so cold, and wondering, too, where he'd been hit. The pain would come later, once the body had recovered from the shock of being torn apart by the bullet. He fired again— and then Ethan showed himself. Killough had a brief second of hope, pulling the trigger again, only to have the hope shattered as the hammer fell on an empty chamber.

"That's a five-shot hideout," muttered Ethan, and put a bullet squarely into Killough's chest.

Killough sat down hard. His left arm flopped into the fire and sent sparks flying. He could feel the searing pain of the flames licking his flesh, and he stared curiously at his burning hand because no matter how hard he tried he couldn't move it out of the fire. His body was going numb. The numbness started in the middle and seemed to spread quickly outward, into his extremities.

"So this is what it feels like where I'm going," he murmured, and then his body convulsed, and he spewed blood before falling over on his right side.

Ethan Payne walked over and sat on his heels in front of Gentleman Jim Killough, and determined to his satisfaction that the man was dead before crossing to where Julie sat, hunched in a corner of the room. He gingerly checked her arm. It was a nasty burn, already blistering. He got up, fetched a can of lard, brought it back, and gently spread the lard on the burn. She buried her head in his chest to muffle her moans.

"I'm taking you into town right now," he said. "Doc Fields will have something better to put on that."

He felt her nod her head against his chest, and he took her head in his hands, tilted it up, and kissed the tears on her cheeks. She smiled bravely.

"I guess dinner is ruined," she said.

"I guess."

She looked across at Killough's corpse. "When is it going to stop, Ethan? How many more men will be coming to kill you?"

"I don't know," he admitted, looking at Killough too, and silently cursing his luck because neither Creed nor this man had lived long enough to tell him who had posted the ten-thousand-dollar bounty on his head. But he'd have to worry about that later. There was more pressing business to attend to. He lifted Julie up in his arms and carried her out to the buggy in which Killough had arrived, then got in himself, gathered up the reins, and got the horse moving.

He was only about a mile and a half down the road when he saw something blocking their way. He checked the horse, told Julie to get down on the floorboard of the buggy, and climbed out with pistol drawn. It was a man, staggering in the middle of the road. He called out to the man to stop, and when his warning went unheeded, raised the pistol and drew a bead. But then he realized that the man was either drunk or seriously injured and might not have heard or understood his warning. So he held his fire. And he was very glad that he did as, a moment later, he recognized Clooney.

Not that it was easy to recognize the gambler. Clooney's face was swollen and covered with blood. Ethan couldn't remember having seen so much blood on a man who was still alive.

"My God," he muttered, shocked, and put away the Remington. "What happened to you?"

Clooney made an incoherent noise with his ruined mouth, and suddenly pitched forward. Ethan was only just able to catch him before he hit the ground. He laid Clooney down gently on his back. Clooney weakly reached up and clutched his shirt. He mouthed something, straining to make himself understood, and Ethan bent down and made out the name "Killough."

Ethan nodded. "I know," he said. He'd already figured out how Clooney had ended up here in the middle of nowhere in such a wretched condition. Obviously the gambler had been bringing Killough out to the house as planned— that Clooney had decided at the last minute not to come had just been one of Gentleman Jim's many lies. Somewhere along the road Killough had gotten the drop on Clooney, and left him for dead. But somehow Clooney had found the strength to get on his feet and had been on his way to the house to try to warn Ethan. The Abilene marshal still wasn't sure why, but he needed no further proof than this that Clooney was a true friend. "It's all right," he said. "Killough is dead. You just rest easy. I'll get you to the doctor. You'll be fine."

He hoped he sounded confident, because he wasn't at all sure that Clooney would live out the night. In fact, he was amazed that the man was still above snakes.

Lifting Clooney up bodily, he carried the gambler to the buggy and managed to prop him up in the seat and then quickly climb in after him so that the half-conscious man was wedged between him and Julie. She did not cringe away from Clooney, as many woman would have done from a man in his condition. Instead, she reached an arm out across Clooney's chest and laid her hand on Ethan's arm, the arm acting as a restraint in the event that Clooney pitched forward.

Reaching Abilene, he drove straight to Doc Fields' house. Along the way he shouted at a man he recognized to find Ed Wilcox, and to tell his deputy to meet him at the doctor's residence. The man went running off to do his bidding. Wilcox showed up in time to help Ethan carry

Clooney, who by now had slipped into unconsciousness. Julie pounded on the door and Fields answered the summons in his nightshirt, bleary-eyed, clearly having been awakened from his slumbers. But when he saw Clooney, the sawbones didn't look sleepy anymore. He had them lay Clooney out on a table and asked Julie to stoke up the fire and put a pot of water on to boil.

"She's hurt, too, Doc," said Ethan. "A bad burn on her arm."

Fields briefly examined Julie's arm, then turned back to Clooney. "He's hurt a lot worse. She'll be fine. Somebody get me some hot water." Fitting a stethoscope into his ears, he took a listen at Clooney's chest. Then he felt the gambler's pulse, and shook his head. "Pulse is weak. We've got to stop this bleeding or he'll die within the hour."

"I'll get the water," said Julie, and before Ethan could protest, she had vanished into another room.

"Jesus," muttered Wilcox, staring at Clooney. "What the hell happened to him, Ethan?"

"Jim Killough happened to him," replied Ethan grimly, and proceeded to succinctly relay to his deputy all that had happened at the house, and what he surmised had taken place on the road.

"So Killough was wanting to collect the bounty on your head, just like Willie Creed," said Wilcox.

"Looks that way. He told Clooney about Creed just to get rid of the competition. And to get close enough to me to do the deed."

"Smart bastard," rasped Wilcox. But he wasn't really thinking about Killough. He was pondering instead who the next would-be-assassin would turn out to be, and he glanced sidelong, pityingly, at the Abilene marshal. "Forgive me for saying so, boss, but I'm sure glad I'm not in your shoes."

Ethan nodded. He knew what Wilcox meant. Creed was dead. So was Killough. But he was still in mortal danger. Worse still, so was everyone else around him.

CHAPTER NINETEEN

When John Tyler White stormed into Kelso's Restaurant early the next morning, G.W. Ransom sighed. He had a real good idea what Tyler was here for. Though he was perturbed, Ransom tried not to look it as he took another bite of egg and washed it down with strong black coffee. White saw him, crossed the room, and sat down uninvited at his table.

"Damn it, G.W.," growled White, "this is it. Payne has got to go."

Mrs. Kelso was waiting on someone on the other side of the restaurant, but White spoke loudly enough for her to hear him cursing, and she shot a scolding look in his direction. White was too agitated to notice, but Ransom, as usual, missed nothing.

"Calm down, John," said Ransom. He said it in a friendly fashion, but there was steel beneath the words, and White knew him well enough to take heed of that. "And mind your manners. There are ladies present."

White threw a sheepish glance around the room. As always, Kelso's was packed at this time of the morning. Nearly every table was taken.

"We'll talk about this outside," said Ransom. He took one last sip of the coffee, put money on the table, and with a smile and a nod at Mrs. Kelso, led White out of the restaurant. Once out in the shade of the boardwalk, Ransom pulled a silver case out of his inside coat pocket, opened it, and carefully selected one of the cigars contained within. He bit off one end and fired the other with a match. White watched him wryly.

"Well, are you ready to talk about Payne now?" asked White.

"Why does he have to go?"

"Because his being here endangers innocent people. Have you heard the news? Payne killed another man last night. It was that Jim Killough, and apparently he was after the same bounty that Willie Creed intended to collect."

"So the marshal has killed two men who came here to kill him."

"That's not the point and you know it, G.W.," said White, exasperated. "Last night two other people got hurt. Payne's wife and the gambler, Clooney. Who knows who might get hurt the next time someone shows up here gunning for the marshal? Maybe my wife—or your daughter— will just happen to be walking down the street at that precise moment, and be caught in the crossfire. You want to see that happen?"

"Of course not," said Ransom, puffing on the cigar and watching the morning bustle on the street. "I'm just a little surprised, that's all."

"Surprised? At what?"

"Your sudden concern for a gambler and a woman that, if I remember correctly, you once called a two-dollar whore."

White's eyes narrowed. "I don't understand you, G.W. There for a while I thought you were as dead set against Payne staying here as I was. Back when he took that . . . woman to be his bride. But now, when I want him out of town, you're bucking me."

"I'm not," said Ransom. "It just gives me pause to send packing a man who has done a lot for this town. A lot for you and me, John." He held up his hand as White opened his mouth to make a retort. "And don't tell me it isn't so. Ethan Payne has done a lot for Abilene. He saved this town from slow death with the way he handled that Tell Jenkins business. Had he handled it any other way all the herds would be headed for Ellsworth now."

"I have no problem with how he handled that situation. It's what he's done since then that bothers me. And I'm not the only one, G.W. You know that."

Ransom nodded. "Yes, I'm well aware that there are some in this town who'd rather someone else wore that badge. But we shouldn't overlook the fact that with Ethan Payne behind that tin star we've had a lot less trouble with the Texans—and no trouble to speak of with those who ply their trades on the Texas Side."

"You never struck me as a short-sighted man, G.W.," said White. "We've had a good year thanks to the Texas trade, I won't deny you that. But that trade won't last forever. We all know it. I'm not sure if you've noticed, but more and more settlers are moving into Kansas every year. That's why the army has set up Camp Sheridan right down the road. And even if—or I should say, when—the cattle trade moves to points west, the railroad will still run right through here. The day will soon be upon us when Abilene doesn't need the Texans anymore. And I think the day has already come when we don't need a man like Ethan Payne as town marshal."

Ransom nodded. "So what you're really saying is, this provides us with a good excuse to get rid of him. Thank him for all that he's done for Abilene—and send him packing."

"I never knew you to be the sentimental type, G.W. We're all businessmen, and there's no room for sentimentality in business. Besides, we have a responsibility to the people of this town."

"But just the respectable people."

"The ones on the Texas Side are transients. So is Payne, when you think about it. He's never been anything but a

yonder man. A drifter. Time for him to move on, I say. I'm
sure he'll find gunwork somewhere else."

"I'm sure," said Ransom.

When Renny entered the hotel room, Elyse was still in bed.
It was where they had spent most of the past week, and
while he had no complaints, the walls had started to close
in on him. That was one reason why he'd been out keeping
an eye on Gentleman Jim Killough while the latter had been
a guest of the doctor's. Up until this morning, though, he'd
had no news to report.

He sat on the edge of the bed and gently brushed her
tousled hair, black as a raven's wing, away from her face.
His touch made her smile even in her sleep. She moaned,
stretched luxuriously, and then rolled over, opening her
eyes.

"Good morning," she said.

"Killough is dead."

Her eyes widened. No longer sleepy, she sat up quickly.
The covers fell away from her magnificent breasts, which
Renny knew so well by now, but she was oblivious to her
nakedness.

"What happened?"

"I don't know all the details. But the talk is all over
town. He went after Payne, and got his toes curled for his
trouble."

"And the marshal?"

"Still alive. Though it seems Gentleman Jim came close
to killing a gambler by the name of Clooney, who is a
friend of Payne's. They're laying odds down on the Texas
Side on whether Clooney lives or not."

"How nice," Elyse said wryly, and swung her long,
shapely legs off the bed. She grabbed a red silk wrapper
from the back of a nearby chair and put it on. Belting it
tightly around her narrow waist, she turned and looked intensely at Renny. "So now what are we going to do?"

"You know what I have to do. It's our only chance. If
I *don't* do it, we'll be just like Ethan Payne. Always looking

over our shoulders. Always wondering if today is the day someone comes to collect the bounty."

"Yes," she said softly, and went to the window.

"You sure you don't have feelings for Marston?" asked Renny.

"Of course not. Apart from loathing, that is. Why do you ask?"

"You look troubled, that's all."

"I have feelings for you, though. I—I don't know what I would do if anything happened to you."

"Nothing is going to happen to me."

"Don't underestimate him, Renny."

"At least now we don't have to worry about Killough being on our trail, coming after the ten thousand dollars he'd have felt was owed him had he succeeded in killing Payne."

She was silent for a moment, standing at the window looking out. He rose and came up behind her, put his arms around her, and pulled her body back against his.

"Something's gnawing at you," he said.

"I'm coming with you."

"No. It's too dangerous."

"Too bad. I'm not letting you go alone. Besides, if you ride up without me, he'll be suspicious. On his guard."

"He'll probably be suspicious anyway. He'll wonder why I don't just take the money from you and be on my way. He'll wonder what other business I have with him."

"I'll take care of that. I'm supposed to send him a telegram when the deed is done. I'll have an explanation for him."

"Will he try to confirm what you tell him about Payne?"

"I don't think so. I think he trusts me."

"Because if he does have some way to confirm whether the marshal is dead or not, he'll find out you're lying to him in that wire, and he'll be ready for me."

"There's a risk," she said, and reached up and behind her to stroke his gaunt cheek. "But it's worth the risk."

"I don't want you to come along, Elyse. I'll have enough

to worry about without worrying about you."

"I can take care of myself," she said sternly, turning to
face him, and jabbing a finger in his chest. "And you're
not going at all unless you take me with you."

Renny had to smile. She was nothing if not a strong-
willed woman, and she was already accustomed to getting
her way with him. That was okay, though. He hadn't
minded, except in this instance.

"Okay," he said, relenting. "When do we leave?"

"This morning. I'll send the wire. And there's one more
thing I want to do."

"What's that?"

"I'll tell you later," she said.

Renny knew better than to argue.

They traveled east on the morning train out of Abilene,
traveling about forty miles before stopping out in the middle of nowhere. The rest of the passengers were perplexed,
unaware that before boarding Elyse had made arrangements
with the engineer. She and Renny left the passenger car
and walked back to one of the boxcars. A Union Pacific
man opened the doors and, with Renny's help, put down
the ramp. Then Elyse and Renny brought out their horses.
She rode up to the Baldwin locomotive and gave the engineer a wave and a smile. A moment later the train was
on the move again, belching a plume of smoke from its
diamond-shaped stack. As the sounds of the train dimin-
ished, Renny could hear the constant whisper of the wind
across the prairie, the rustling of the sea of grass. He was
glad to be out of Abilene, out in the wide open spaces
where he didn't have to smell the effluvium of civilization—or rather, what passed for civilization on the Kansas
frontier.

They continued on an eastward course, following the
iron road that cut across the prairie, the sun warm on their
backs. It was mid-afternoon when they disembarked from
the train. Two hours later they topped a low rise, checked
their horses, and gazed at Marston's private train, which

was sitting on the rails about a mile and a half away. Renny knew it was Marston's—the dark-red mogul and the green passenger car were familiar to him from his first visit. He assumed that Marston had waited out the eastbound train on a siding at one of the small towns that lined the iron road.

Now that the moment was upon him, Renny felt an immense calm sweep over him. He'd been expecting it. That had always been his greatest asset—he never got nervous or excited when action was imminent or under way. He wasn't the fastest gunslinger around by a long shot, but he had nerves of steel, and time and again this had tipped the scales in his favor.

"Okay," he said. "So, what did you tell Marston? How did you explain my being here?"

Elyse smiled. "I told him you had a present for him. Something you wouldn't leave with me, that you wanted to deliver personally to him."

"That's true enough. But somehow I don't think he's going to want it."

"I told him it was the badge of the Abilene town marshal. A memento."

"You figure he bought into that?"

"Absolutely," she replied confidently. "It's just the sort of thing he'd relish. Something that money can't ordinarily buy."

Renny nodded. He drew his pistol and checked the loads. "I wish you'd stay behind until it's all over," he said.

"We've already discussed that. I'm riding in with you."

"Then let's ride."

They headed for the train.

As they drew near, a man emerged from the caboose and walked up to the passenger car to wait for their arrival. Renny recognized him from his previous visit as one of the members of the train crew. He wore grease-stained overalls and, as far as Renny could tell, wasn't heeled. But that didn't mean Renny was going to discount the man as a threat. The crew member was a big, brawny fellow who

looked plenty capable of taking care of himself and of anyone who crossed him.

"Hello, Miss Elyse," said the man. "Good to see you
again."

"Hello, Jake." Elyse immediately climbed down out of
the saddle. Renny did likewise. But he hesitated in following her lead when she handed her rein leather to the crewman.

"I'll see to your horse, mister," said Jake, and held out
a hand.

Renny realized there were no options. If he balked at
this he might lead Jake to wonder if something was amiss.
He figured the situation would play out in one of two ways
after he'd done what he'd come here to do—either the crew
would try to kill him or they would make themselves
scarce. In case the former happened, Renny had wanted his
horse as close at hand as possible.

He handed over the reins, and Jake gave them both a
friendly nod and headed for the back of the train. Elyse
climbed up onto the front platform of the passenger train,
started to reach for the door—and then she froze. When
she looked at him Renny could tell that she was scared.

"Don't worry," he murmured. "He's not going to hurt
you anymore."

She nodded, drew a long breath, manufactured a bright
smile on her face, and entered the car. Renny went in right
behind her.

Marston was just as Renny had remembered him—
seated in a wheelchair, clad in an impeccable red smoking
jacket. A broad smile flashed across his soft, pale face.

"My dearest Elyse! It's so good to have you home!" He
held out his arms, and Elyse dutifully, or so it seemed to
Renny, stepped forward to bend down and give Marston a
peck on the cheek. "I must say, Elyse, it's been terribly dull
around here without you."

"Naturally," she said with a wry smile, and stepped
aside.

Marston turned his attention to Renny. "Well, Mr.

Renny. Somehow, after meeting you and Mr. Creed and Mr. Killough, I *thought* you would be the one to get the job done. And it seems I was correct. Ethan Payne is dead." Marston closed his eyes, as though in the grip of unbearable ecstasy. "Ah, you can never know how good that makes me feel. To know that, at last, I've had my revenge! It is sweet, I assure you. I only wish I could have been there to see him die. But that would have given the game away, now wouldn't it? I trust you've been paid in full?"

Renny nodded, with a glance at Elyse. "She gave me everything."

"Splendid. The telegram I received mentioned that you've brought me a little memento?"

"Yes, I have," said Renny, and drew his pistol, aiming it at Marston's chest.

The smile frozen on his face, Marston stared at the gun barrel pointed right at him as though he couldn't quite comprehend what it was.

"I hate to tell you this," said Renny, "but Ethan Payne is going to outlive you, Marston."

Marston blinked, slowly turned his head to stare at Elyse. "What's the meaning of this?" he asked.

Elyse ignored him. Her gaze was fastened on Renny, and her voice was harsh. "Get on with it, Renny."

Renny thumbed the hammer back.

"Wait!" shouted Marston. "Wait just a minute. I'll pay you anything you ask, Mr. Renny. Name a sum and it's yours."

Renny shook his head. "No, thanks. I don't want money. All I want is Elyse."

Again Marston looked at Elyse, and now he seemed to comprehend what was happening, and why. He smiled coldly.

"So that's how it is. Aren't you the clever one, my dear. You recruited your assassin with your favors, I take it. How is she in bed, Mr. Renny? I can only imagine. But what I imagine is that she is quite extraordinary."

"Shut up," said Renny.

"Damn it, Renny," snapped Elyse. "Just shoot him, for God's sake."

"It's cold-blooded murder that you're contemplating, Mr. Renny. I have many powerful friends, and they'll see to it that both you and my loving wife hang for this."

It felt to Renny as though someone had just hit him, very hard, in the chest.

"Wife?" he echoed.

"Oh, you didn't know? She didn't tell you? What did you tell him, my dear, to get him to murder me? Let me guess. That you were just a slave, a prisoner held against her will, and that once I was dead the two of you would run away together and live happily ever after. Am I close, Mr. Renny?"

Renny was staring at Elyse. "Is he telling the truth? Are you his wife?"

"Damn you," she breathed, and turned angrily to the rolltop desk beside which she stood, pulling open a drawer and brandishing a small hideout pistol, which she swung round to aim at Renny. "Yes, it's true," she said archly. "I am his *loving* wife."

"Then . . . that story . . . how you tried to run away, and he sent those men to bring you back . . . that was all a lie."

"Yes."

"*Everything* was a lie."

"Yes."

Marston was chuckling.

"Shut up, damn it," growled Renny.

"I'm sorry, I simply can't help myself. Is it the truth you want, Mr. Renny? Then let me tell you the truth. I've always loved Elyse. I took her in when she had nothing, and I gave her everything that her heart desired. I gave her as much love as any man has shown a woman. Although there was one thing I could never do for her, I did everything in my power to make her happy. I hoped that one day she would come to love me. Perhaps not as I loved her—I knew I had to be realistic in that respect."

"So what if I *am* his wife?" she asked Renny, a desperate

note to her voice. "That doesn't change anything. We can *still* be together. And we'll *have* everything. Because I inherit it all, you see. Every last dollar of the Marston fortune will be mine. Ours."

Stunned, Renny shook his head. "Well, I never thought I was fool enough to fall for a trick like that. You sure pulled one over on me, lady. Yep, you sure did." He started backing toward the door.

"Where are you going?" she asked.

"I'm afraid your assassin is checking out of the game, darling," said Marston.

"You've called me that for the last time," she snarled.

Putting the barrel of the hideout to Marston's temple, she pulled the trigger.

"Jesus," muttered Renny.

Blood and brains exploded out of the opposite side of Marston's head. The corpse pitched forward out of the wheelchair and the wheelchair fell over on top of it.

Elyse swung the hideout 'round and again aimed it at Renny. "Just so you know," she said, "I was going to shoot you right after you shot him. You see, I really don't care to share the fortune I'm about to inherit. So sorry." She looked at the pistol in his hand and smirked. It was the same smirk he'd seen when they'd first met, when she'd stood on the platform and ushered him inside to meet Marston—her husband—for the first time. *I wish I was back in that Mexican prison,* he thought. "You can't do it," she said confidently. "You can't shoot me. Not after everything we've shared. You can't shoot the woman you love, Renny."

He squeezed the trigger. The impact of the bullet threw her back onto a horsehair sofa, and she rolled limply off that and hit the ground with a dead *thump*.

"The hell I can't," he muttered.

He heard men outside, shouting. He headed for the rear door of the passenger car, stepping over the bodies without glancing at them, looking instead out the windows, with their rich, brocaded maroon drapes pulled back with golden

sashes. He saw no sign of the crewmen, but he wasn't going
to wait around for them. Bursting onto the rear platform,
he jumped over the coupling to the caboose and kicked in
the door. There was no one inside. He went out the back
door and saw, with massive relief, that his horse was
hitched to the rear of the train. But before he could get into
the saddle, a crewman came running, pistol in hand. Renny
got the drop on him.

"Get rid of that smoke maker," he said, and it was man-
ifestly evident by his tone that he was serious, and that he
wasn't going to bother repeating himself.

The crewman dropped the pistol, raised his hands, and
backed away. He threw a quick glance toward the front of
the train, then watched Renny climb into the saddle. The
Texas gunslinger whipped the horse around and kicked it
into a spirited gallop, its hooves churning up a cloud of
dust. Bent low in the saddle, Renny tossed a glance over
his shoulder at the train. The man he'd met at the back of
the caboose was running toward the mogul. Apart from
that, he saw no activity. He allowed himself to think that
maybe he'd gotten clear.

That was his last conscious thought before the .50-
caliber bullet struck him at the base of the neck. Renny
experienced a blinding explosion of light, and then complete and eternal blackness.

Aboard the locomotive of Ash Marston's private train,
the crewman named Jake slowly lowered the Sharps Lead-
slinger, thinking grimly that he hadn't made a shot like that
since his days as a buffalo runner. Five hundred yards if it
was an inch. Two of his coworkers started out on foot to
check the body. Jake knew that was unnecessary. It was
just lucky, he mused, that he'd taken to carrying the long
gun in the mogul, in case there was game along the tracks
that was worth shooting. He hadn't expected to ever have
to use it on a man. Not that he'd spent all those years on
the frontier without having to kill another human. Still, it
had been a while, and he sat down on the iron steps of the

locomotive and rolled a smoke with slightly shaky fingers and waited for his stomach to settle.

The young fireman came running up, pale as a ghost. "They're . . . they're both dead! Marston and his missus, both!"

Jake already knew that, so he didn't bother responding.

"Why'd that feller kill 'em, Jake?"

Jake shook his head. It was just like young people, expecting every question to have an answer. If the fireman lived long enough he would discover in good time that most of life would forever remain a puzzlement.

"I dunno," he muttered. "But he did, and now he's dead, and that's that."

CHAPTER TWENTY

Two days after the shootout with Jim Killough, Ethan arrived at the jailhouse right before six P.M. to start his shift and relieve Ed Wilcox, who was working days. Wilcox was in the office, pouring himself a cup of that morning's coffee from the pot atop the stove.

"Anything happen today?" asked Ethan.

"Not a thing. Pretty quiet. Most of the cow crowd has gone home to Texas. Not but three or four outfits left, far as I can tell. Coffee?"

"No, thanks." Ethan went to the desk.

"How's the wife?"

Ethan nodded. Doc Fields had treated Julie's burn and released her into his care, and Ethan had put her up at the Drovers' Cottage even though she wanted to return to the sod house, claiming, to his surprise, that she felt like it was home. It was the first time she'd openly expressed an affinity for the place, and under other circumstances he would have been pleased. But now he didn't think the sod house was a safe place for her. And he certainly couldn't take her back there until he'd cleaned up—which meant taking care of Killough's corpse.

Which he had done earlier today, burying Gentleman Jim in an unmarked grave on the other side of the creek from the house, piling stones he gathered from along the creek bed atop the grave to discourage coyotes and such from digging up the remains.

"I dropped in at the doc's office this afternoon," continued Wilcox. He could sense that Ethan wasn't exactly in a talkative mood. Usually when that happened he wouldn't make an effort to start a conversation, but this time he didn't want a curtain of silence to descend between him and the town marshal because there was something he felt Ethan needed to know. It was just that he wasn't sure how to broach the subject. "Clooney was conscious. Doc says he's going to be all right. Says it's nothing short of a miracle. Of course, he's never going to look the same. I think Clooney knows that, too. He told me he thought the days were gone when he wouldn't have to pay for a lady's favors."

Ethan was staring at a letter on the desk. It was addressed, in a woman's hand, to "Marshal Payne, Abilene." A cold chill ran up and down his spine. Was that Lilah Webster's handwriting?

Wilcox sighed and came over to the desk and set his cup of coffee down. "Been hearing some talk today, around town."

"What about?" asked Ethan, paying only the most cursory attention to what his deputy was saying.

"About you. Rumor has it that the town council is going to vote you out of office, Ethan."

"Really."

The marshal's relative lack of interest in that news surprised Wilcox. Ethan had always expressed a strong interest in keeping his job, particularly since his wedding day.

"Rumor is probably all it is," continued Wilcox. "'Course, I've been thinking. Considering what's happened, and us not knowing when the next Willie Creed is going to show up, maybe it wouldn't be such a bad thing if you did leave Abilene."

Ethan raised his head and smiled at Wilcox. "You bucking for my job, Ed? Is that what this is all about?"

"Hell, no!" exclaimed Wilcox, jumping to his feet. "I wouldn't take it if it was offered to me. And personally, I'd hate to see you go."

"I didn't know you cared so much, Ed."

Wilcox grimaced. He could tell, belatedly, that Ethan was pulling his leg. "I don't care two bits about you. It's your wife I'm thinking about. And I figure you're thinking mostly about her, too. How it isn't safe for her, long as there's a price on your head."

"That wouldn't change just because I left Abilene."

"It might—if you two went far enough away from here. Changed your name and everything. And took up a peaceable occupation that won't bring you to the attention of the public. This is a mighty big country, and most of the time folks don't care what you call yourself, or what you've done in the past, long as you don't muddy up their water."

Ethan looked at him for a moment without saying anything—long enough for Wilcox to start feeling uncomfortable.

"What did I say?" asked the deputy, worried.

"Nothing. You're right about one thing. I have been thinking a lot about Julie. How to protect her. I haven't been doing a very good job so far." He shrugged. "I don't know, maybe you're right . . ." He looked again at the letter. "Where did this come from?"

"Boy brought it over from the post office this morning. That's all I know."

Ethan drew a long breath. Then he picked up the envelope, opened it, extracted the letter contained within, and read it. Wilcox waited expectantly.

"Well," said Ethan, after a while, "that explains it."

"Explains what?" asked Wilcox, slightly exasperated. "What does it say?"

Ethan handed him the letter. Wilcox had to fish spectacles out of his pocket and hook them onto his ears before he could read it.

To Ethan Payne, Marshal, Abilene, Kansas.
The man responsible for sending Willie Creed and

*James Killough to kill you was Ash Marston. I say
"was" because by the time you read this, he will be
dead, and you may rest assured that you will have
no more trouble on his account.*

"There's no signature," murmured Wilcox. "Got any
ideas about who wrote this?"

"A woman. That's all I can say for sure."

"Who is this Ash Marston feller?"

A ghost from my past, mused Ethan with a sigh. *Come
back to haunt me.*

"An Englishman I met a long time ago, on a Mississippi
riverboat," he said. "He was robbing passengers. I was a
member of the crew. I caught him trying to leave the boat
one night with a bag full of loot. There was a struggle. He
fell overboard. I was never sure if he survived. I guess now
I have the answer."

"He must have been crazy," said Wilcox, "to go to all
this trouble just to pay you back for something that happened a long time ago."

"Sometimes people just won't let go of things."

"So you believe that letter? Maybe it's just a ruse. To
get you to lower your guard."

"Maybe," said Ethan. But he doubted it. Call it intui-
tion—he felt as though the letter was genuine. He told himself not to worry about the identity of the person who had
written it, or how she could be so certain that Marston was
dead. There was reason, he supposed, for him to investigate
further, to try to determine whether that was, in fact, the
case. Or he could take it on faith. There were some things
you just had to take that way.

He rose, took the letter back from Wilcox, returned it to
the envelope, and put the envelope in a drawer of the desk.
"Time for you to go home, Ed," he said, "and for me to
start my rounds."

"Reckon so. If I'm late for supper I'm made to pay for
the transgression ten times over. But you know how that
is, being married and all."

Ethan was at the door when a thought occurred to him, and he turned back to Wilcox. "You know, Ed, if they ever do offer you my job, I'd want you to take it."

"I couldn't do that, Ethan."

"I'd feel better knowing that it was in your hands." Seeing that the deputy was prepared to argue the point further, Ethan held up his hand. "Just so you know." And with that he left the jail.

As was his custom, Ethan did not stick to a particular route as he made his rounds. When you wore a badge it wasn't a good idea to be too predictable. That was why it took G.W. Ransom about an hour of searching to locate the marshal. When a bartender at the Lone Star told him that Ethan had been in only minutes earlier, Ransom hurried out to the corner of the street and thought he saw the lawman's tall, black-clad frame moving in the shadows of the boardwalk on Houston Street. He started after him, then saw that Ethan was turning onto Jefferson. Hoping to make up some ground, Ransom cut through an alley, turned down another, and then another, just in time to see the marshal cross the mouth of the alley. He called out—and had a bad moment when Ethan whirled, the Remington having materialized in his hand.

"Ease up," said Ransom hastily. "It's me, G.W."

Ethan lowered the pistol as Ransom stepped forward.

"Didn't mean to startle you," said Ransom. "I was wondering if we could talk. I'll buy you a drink."

"We can talk here."

Ransom had hoped to buy himself a little more time. He'd pondered how to break the news to Ethan all day long, and he still wasn't sure of the best way to go about it. The problem, he'd decided, was that his heart wasn't in it.

"How's Mrs. Payne?" he asked.

"Fine. But that's not what you came looking for me in the middle of the night to talk about."

"You're right. It's about this damned business with killers like Creed and Killough. That's got a lot of people concerned. They don't feel . . . safe. Now, I know what you're thinking. That you're the one these men are gunning for, and yet *they* don't feel safe. But it's true. No one knows if they or their loved ones is going to get caught in the crossfire the next time a hard case rides into town looking to kill himself a marshal." Ransom paused, looking at Ethan hopefully, thinking that maybe the marshal would let him off the hook, would tell him he knew what was coming. But Ethan just stood there, looking right back at him with a stony expression on his face and not saying a word, not making it one whit easier for him. *Even though he knows. He must know how this is going to play out. Because Ethan Payne is no fool.* "Anyway," said Ransom, with a sigh, "the town council met in emergency session earlier this evening. A decision was made. I have the unfortunate duty of relaying that decision to you."

"You can't fire me," said Ethan.

The blood ran cold in Ransom's veins. He wasn't a man to scare easily, but there was something about the marshal that had him spooked.

"Now look here—" he began.

"You can't fire me because I quit."

Ransom stared. "What? You quit?"

Ethan took the badge off his coat and held it out to Ransom. "I'm done."

For a reason he did not quite comprehend, Ransom was reluctant to take the badge. "When did you decide to quit?"

"I think it was when I saw Killough put a pistol to my wife's head," said Ethan.

Ransom nodded. He took the badge. "I want you to know, I voted against firing you. But the sentiment against you is just too strong. It was a battle I couldn't have won. So I didn't try. Hope you understand."

"It wasn't one that was worth fighting."

"This business with the hired killers, that wasn't the only problem they had with you, you know. You brought law and order to Abilene. And now Abilene doesn't think she needs you anymore. You've become a liability."

"That's fine. Ed Wilcox would make a good replacement. But you'll have a hard time talking him into it. And as for any more hired killers riding into town, you don't have to worry about that."

"How come?"

Ethan thought about the letter in the desk drawer back at the jail. He might have used it had he wanted to fight to keep his job, as evidence that the good people of Abilene needed to worry no longer about crossfires. But he'd realized, even without Ransom spelling it out for him, that the Marston business wasn't the real reason he was being let go. That was just an excuse.

"Just take my word for it," he told Ransom, and left it at that.

"Where will you go? What will you do?"

"Does that really matter to you?"

"I don't blame you for resenting me. All of us."

"You're just doing what you feel you have to. I don't blame you for that."

Ransom nodded. He thought more ought to be said, that it shouldn't end so quickly, but he couldn't figure out how to say it. Ethan Payne was getting a raw deal, but he couldn't lay the responsibility for that on someone else; he was just as culpable as John Tyler White. He was unable to pinpoint exactly when, but at some point in the last year he had learned to respect Payne. He considered telling the ex-marshal as much, but he didn't figure it would be of much comfort to the man.

"Well," he said, "if there's anything I can do for you, all you have to do is ask."

Ethan didn't say anything. He walked back to the Drover's Cottage. Instead of going directly up to the room where he hoped Julie would be asleep by now, he sat in one of the rocking chairs that lined the porch, listened to the cattle in the half-full stockyards across the way, and watched wisps of ghostly clouds skudding beneath the moon. The cool night wind held just a hint of the winter that would soon be sweeping across the prairie. It wasn't the best of times to pull up stakes. Where would he and Julie go? What would he do? Ethan was at a complete loss. At least he had a good sum of money saved up. First thing in the morning he would go to the bank and withdraw all of it. And he needed to buy Julie a horse. Ned down at the livery had some good deals. One thing was certain; now that he was a married man he couldn't go back to being an aimless drifter. That had always been good enough for him before, back when he'd had only himself to look out for. But it wouldn't be right now that Julie was depending on him.

He was reluctant to break the news to her, too. Not that it was his fault—he realized that this was just one of those things that happened to you in life that you had no control over. Tonight's events had started many years ago, aboard the Mississippi sternwheeler called *Drusilla*, when Ash Marston had first come aboard. The threads of the past were woven into the fabric of today as well as the future, and no man could control that, or even predict it. The consequences of the choices a person made reached a lot further than anyone could readily imagine. Still, he felt bad about it, for Julie's sake. All she needed—or wanted—was stability. As long as he'd known her she had never had that, not even with Cathcott at the Wolftrap Station, and certainly not with Ethan Payne when he'd been Overland's troubleshooter. Here, though, he had started to build a future for her, and now he was going to yank it right out from under her. She wouldn't complain. She wanted him to take off the badge. Julie wasn't made that way. But even though she'd try very hard to conceal it from him, she would be worried. And that was why he was reluctant to go upstairs.

Finally, though, he steeled himself and went inside. The desk clerk had his feet propped up and was snoring loudly. Ethan climbed the stairs, turned down the hall, and went to the door of the room he'd rented. He had the key in his pocket, as he'd thought he would be coming in early in the morning, when Julie was still sleeping. But as he turned

the key he realized that the door was no longer locked.
Opening the door as quietly as possible, he slipped inside.

Julie wasn't in the room.

The covers lay in a tangled heap on the floor beside the
bed. Her clothes were gone. But nothing else looked dis-
turbed or out of place. Pushing away the fear that was
building inside him, Ethan racked his brain for a rational
explanation. Maybe Julie had been unable to sleep, or
afraid, and had gone out to look for him. Or maybe she
had run away, unable to cope with the stress of being wed
to a man with a price on his head. No, she wouldn't do
that, he told himself fiercely. That was just the fear talking.

He closed the door, went downstairs, and reached across
the counter to roughly shake the clerk awake to ask him if
he had seen Julie. The clerk assured him that he had not.
Ethan went outside. If Julie *had* been looking for him,
where would she go? To the jail, but unless she was content
to wait for him in the office, no one was there to tell him
whether she had come by. Still, it was as good a place as
any to start, and he bent his steps in that direction.

She wasn't at the jail, however. Ethan spent the next
hour aimlessly wandering the streets, hoping to catch a
glimpse of her. He asked several people he knew whether
they had seen her, but always the answer was the same,
and not the one he had hoped for. Returning to the hotel,
he asked the clerk if she had returned. The answer was no.
He ended up back in the rocking chair on the porch, at a
loss as to what to do next.

He had thought sleep was impossible, but he found himself waking with a start as the sun peeked over the eastern
horizon and bright light stabbed like daggers at his eyes.
Rising stiffly, he went up to the room. Julie wasn't there.
Swallowing the lump in his throat, Ethan took a closer look
at the room. And he saw something that he had missed the
night before, when the room had been dark. A strip of cloth
that he was sure had been torn from the sleeve of Julie's
chemise. There had clearly been a struggle. Her shoes were
under the bed; she would not have left the room barefoot

to go about Abilene in search of him. No, she hadn't left the room of her own free will. Someone had come in and taken her. But who? Someone she knew, perhaps, as she'd had to unlock the door from the inside to let them into the room. Or someone who had played a ruse clever enough to lure her into opening the door to a total stranger.

Ethan left the room and went to the end of the hallway. Here were narrow stairs leading down to a door at the back of the hotel. If Julie and her abductor had come this way the clerk would not have heard or seen them. Descending the stairs, he went out the back door and began to search the ground. After a while he concluded that two horses had been tied up at the back of the hotel at some point last night. And he clearly saw the footprints of a woman.

He noticed something else. One of the iron-shod horses had a nail missing from a shoe. That would leave a distinctive trail—and, with any luck at all, the horse would throw the shoe, and slow down the man who had taken his wife.

And who could that be? Ethan bleakly scanned the horizon. Another of Ash Marston's hired guns? Possibly. Maybe he'd been wrong to put so much faith in the mysterious letter that assured him the threat posed by Marston no longer existed. But it really didn't matter *who* it was, decided Ethan. Because if he harmed a hair on Julie's head, he was going to die.

CHAPTER TWENTY-ONE

Julie was afraid, not just because she had been kidnapped, but because the kidnapper was someone she had trusted for many years. It was hard to understand why Manolo would do this, and that was an important element of the fear she experienced because it meant she had never known the young mestizo, as she had thought. Still, she thought it was important not to show that she was afraid, and this she tried to do. Once upon a time, at Wolftrap Station, she had been in a position of authority over Manolo, and she didn't know if it would be possible to reestablish that authority, or some portion of it, in the present circumstances. But it would not be possible if he knew she was terrified of what he might do.

What had transpired back at the Drover's Cottage was a blur to her. Manolo had knocked on her door, rousing her from a deep sleep. She had thought at first that it was her husband, before she remembered that Ethan had taken the key with him. She had called through the door, and Manolo had identified himself. She'd been overjoyed; his sudden disappearance some weeks earlier had left her mystified and worried. Now he was back, and she threw open the door without a second thought.

But it was not the Manolo she had expected. This one

was vicious, threatening her with his knife, forcing her to get dressed, and when he had grabbed her she had misunderstood his intentions and began to fight back. As it turned out, all he wanted to do was take her out of the room and down the back stairs to the horses waiting outside. "Do not try to run away," he had warned her. "If you do, I will kill you." And she believed him.

They rode through the night, and by the arrangement of the stars in the sky she knew that they were headed in a southerly direction. She knew her geography well enough to be confident that the land south of Kansas was known as the Indian Territory, a lawless land filled with fugitives from justice, who had little to fear from the tribal police of the Cherokees, Choctaws, Chickasaws, and Creeks. And she despaired of ever seeing her husband again. It would be morning before he returned from his shift to find her gone. Would he figure out what had happened to her? Were there any clues? Her dress was torn, and she thought that this had to have happened in the room. But even if Ethan came to the correct conclusions, and even if he found a trail to follow, would he be able to catch up with them? Manolo was traveling fast, and he showed no inclination to stop. Her only refuge was the thought that sooner or later he would have to. The horses were tiring more and more with each passing hour.

Finally, after sunrise, they did stop, at a remote sweetwater spring. Manolo let the horses drink slowly. He filled his canteen. He allowed Julie to drink, as well. Then he bade her sit on the ground beside the spring, and squatted nearby, holding on to the reins of the horses.

"My husband will kill you for this, Manolo," she said. "Let me go now, and I'll make sure he lets you go."

"He will not catch us," said the mestizo flatly.

"A good many outlaws said the same thing, I'm sure, when he was troubleshooting for the Overland. If you remember, he never failed to bring his man back. Though sometimes it was across the saddle. Dead man's ride."

Manolo just stared at her blankly.

"Why are you doing this?" she asked, deciding to try a different approach. "I thought we were friends."

"We are," replied Manolo. "I do this for you."

"For me?" She was incredulous. "You steal me away from the man I love and you think you're doing me a favor?"

A flash of anger animated his face. "You say you love him. Maybe so. But he does not love you."

Julie pondered the implications of that remark, trying to read between the lines to get a handle on Manolo's motives.

"I heard what was happening," he continued. "The men coming to kill your husband. You were in danger. I could not bear to think of it. So I have taken you away from that. One day you will thank me."

Julie refrained from uttering a bitter retort. She had to be smart, and antagonizing her abductor wasn't the smartest thing to do. "I understand why you did it. We've been friends for a very long time. You think you're just helping out a friend. Back at the hotel I didn't realize this. And the knife scared me. That's why I resisted. I'm sorry."

Manolo looked away. "I do not wish to scare you. We are friends. One day maybe we will be more than friends."

Julie tried desperately to mask the shock and horror she experienced. So that was it! Manolo wanted more than friendship from her. He was in love with her. How long had he felt this way? Perhaps since Wolftrap. And she had been too blind to see it. Julie cursed herself for a fool. This explained why he had suddenly disappeared from Abilene; he had run away because he was unable to accept the fact that she had agreed to marry Ethan. It suddenly made perfect sense to her.

"Where are we going?" she asked, as calmly as possible.

"Mexico," he said.

Mexico! To get to Mexico they would have to pass through the Indian Territory, and then—even worse—Comancheria, the uncharted domain of those fierce warriors of the southern plains. For all his skill with the knife, Manolo would not be able to fend off a Comanche raiding party.

And Julie knew that she would be better off taking her own life rather than allowing herself to fall into Comanche hands. *God help me!* she thought, beating down the panic that threatened to overwhelm her. *God, please let Ethan find me.*

"Manolo."

He looked at her.

"Manolo, I will go with you. But not to Mexico. I don't want to go to Mexico. Do you understand? We can go to Colorado. Or California. And I won't try to run away. I give you my word."

He studied her in grim silence for a moment, and Julie began to hope that maybe, just maybe, he would listen to her, and abide by her wishes. If she still exercised any sort of authority over him, he would do as she asked.

"No," he said, at last. "We go to Mexico. And you will not run away. We will never be separated again, unless it is by death."

Julie shuddered. She couldn't help herself.

"Come, we go," said Manolo curtly, and rose. She got up, too, and though her body screamed complaint, she pulled herself back into the saddle. Though they had ridden all night, Manolo seemed tireless; with cat-like agility he leaped into his saddle. She cast a quick glance northward, hoping against hope that by some miracle she would see Ethan coming over the horizon. Manolo saw her glance that way, saw the expression on her face. It angered him, and he savagely jerked the reins of her horse, starting it into motion, and leading the way southward.

Ethan knew he had a lot of ground to make up—Julie and her kidnapper had at least a six-hour head start—so he gave Ned, the livery man, a note for a second horse, and picked a chestnut gelding that looked like it had plenty of bottom. He was about to leave Abilene when Ed Wilcox caught up with him at the Drover's Cottage.

"G.W. Ransom was waiting for me at the jail this morning," said the deputy. "He told me he was about to fire you last night but you quit."

Ethan nodded. "Did he offer you the job?"

"Yeah. He said you recommended me."

"That's right. You going to take it?"

"I told him I needed a little time to think about it. You leaving today? Where you going, do you know?"

Ethan glanced at Wilcox, considered telling the deputy what had happened with Julie—and decided not to. Ed would insist on coming along, and Ethan was sick and tired of people getting hurt on his account.

"Wherever the trail leads me," he replied, then swung into the saddle strapped to the chestnut's back. He figured Wilcox would assume that the second horse was for Julie, and not think twice about it.

"Sorry to see you go, Ethan."

Wilcox wasn't a very demonstrative man, and it was a struggle to make such a personal comment. Ethan understood this, and appreciated the sentiment all the more. "Take the job Ransom offered you, Ed," he advised, and with a so-long nod, rode out of town, leading his coyote dun, and following the trail that began at the rear of the Drover's Cottage.

He maintained a steady pace throughout the day, and by early afternoon had arrived at the sweetwater spring where the sign informed him that Julie and the man who had kidnapped her had stopped for a while. He let the horses drink a little, but the chestnut was winded and he didn't want to take the chance that it might become waterlogged. Closely checking the ground, he saw where someone had written a single word in the dirt. MEXICO. That had to be Julie's doing. Somehow she had managed to leave this clue for him without her abductor being aware of it. At least now he knew where they were headed. But it raised new questions. If the man was one of Marston's hired killers, why was he taking Julie all the way to Mexico? The purpose of the abduction would be to bring Ethan into killing range, and he wouldn't have to travel all the way to Mexico to do that. So if this didn't have anything to do with Marston and the bounty on his head, it could only mean that the target was Julie. Someone was stealing her away, literally. But who?

Ethan thought of Manolo. Could this be the mestizo's handiwork? He knew that Manolo had vanished because he couldn't bear to see Ethan and Julie wed. Now, perhaps, the mestizo had returned to claim what he thought rightfully belonged to him. That would explain why Julie had opened the hotel room door. Ethan cursed himself for having refrained from sharing his suspicions about Manolo with his wife. If he had, this might not have happened.

He didn't linger long at the waterhole, pressing on, following the tracks southward. An hour or so later he switched over to the roan and led the chestnut, and by the end of the day he calculated he had ridden over one hundred miles, and closed some of the distance. He wondered if Manolo—or whoever the kidnapper was—would make a night camp. They had traveled through the previous night, and their horses could not last forever at that rate. Ethan could only hope so. He stopped for a couple of hours, tying the reins to both horses around his wrists and lying down on a blanket, trying to get some sleep while he waited for the moon to rise. Sleep eluded him, however. There was some dried beef in his saddlebags, and he ate some, washing it down with water from his canteen. And when the moon finally did rise above the eastern skyline he was on the move again. This time, though, he remained afoot, kneeling often to check the ground, to make sure he had not strayed from the trail left by Julie and her abductor. At this rate, he figured, he wouldn't make but ten, maybe twelve miles before sunrise, but that was better than nothing, and certainly preferable to sitting around waiting for daybreak.

Shortly after sunrise he came to the place where they had made a cold camp in a dry wash. He saw where Julie had laid on the ground, resting, and over there the man who had stolen her had sat with his back to the cutbank. Ethan was encouraged. They could not be more than a couple of hours in front of him now.

Switching back to the chestnut, Ethan pushed the horse hard. An hour later, the chestnut's gait slackened, and the animal made a wheezing sound. It was windbroke. Ethan stopped, stripped saddle and bridle from the cayuse, and let it go with a soft-spoken "Thanks." Then he was aboard the coyote dun, galloping southward. The chestnut, accustomed to running with the dun, tried to keep up but couldn't; before long it had ceased to try, and turned to make its way back to the spring.

The prairie gave way to broken country, arid hills covered with scrub; Ethan crossed a wide but shallow river he assumed was the Cimarron. If he was right, that meant he was entering the Indian Territory. As a lawman, he knew only too well that the Territory was a haven for long riders—only United States Marshals exercised any legally constituted authority in the Territory. It was just that much more important that he catch up with Julie as quickly as possible, because the longer she remained in the Territory, the greater the danger.

Night fell before he caught up, however, and this time he made a cold camp and stayed put until dawn. He was guessing—and hoping—that Manolo, or whoever it was who had kidnapped Julie, would be doing likewise. Only a fool would travel at night in this kind of country, perfect for ambush, and chock full of cutthroats. Ethan settled down in a bosque of stunted oaks and managed to get a little shuteye. He felt confident that at some point tomorrow the chase would be over.

Dawn found him on the move again, following the sign deeper into the hills. Now he had to worry about whether the man he was pursuing would double back to watch his backtrail and bushwhack anyone that happened to be following. That would have been difficult to do on the wide-open prairie, but there were countless excellent hiding places in these hills. But that consideration did not slow Ethan; he dared not slow his pace.

It was nearly noon when he saw them, two riders cresting a rocky slope less than a quarter of a mile ahead of him. He assumed it was Julie and her abductor, and spurred the weary coyote dun forward, hoping he could get close enough for a shot before the man became aware of his presence. A moment later the pair of riders disappeared down the far side of the slope. Ethan pressed on. When he reached the crest of the slope he checked his horse and scanned the broken country in front of him.

The riders were nowhere to be seen.

He waited, impatiently, expecting them to break cover, but when they didn't, and he could wait no longer, he kicked the dun into motion and headed down the rocky slope, scanning the ground for sign.

For that reason he was seconds late in seeing Manolo, who burst suddenly from a thicket and in three long strides was in front of the coyote dun, which snorted and jerked away. Ethan reached for the Remington at his side, saw the flash of sunlight on the blade of Manolo's knife, and watched helplessly at the mestizo slashed open the coyote dun's throat. Dark red blood geysered across the stones on the slope as the horse reared back and then fell sideways. Ethan desperately kicked his feet clear of the stirrups and tried to fall the other way, hoping to avoid being pinned beneath the dying horse, or knocked unconscious by its flailing hooves. He succeeded, but just barely, and landed poorly; pain shot through his left arm, and he bounced his skull off a flat piece of shale, not hard enough to knock him out, but enough to send the world spinning crazily. It was the instinct for self-preservation that sent him rolling blindly down the slope in an effort to buy himself a few precious seconds. Rocks gave way beneath his body and he found himself rolling farther than he had hoped, and unable to stop himself from tumbling down the slope. The tumble ended with a short fall as he pitched over the verge of a cutbank into a dry wash located at the bottom of the hill.

He lay there for a moment, on his back, flinching away from the blazing orb of the hot sun directly overhead, groping instinctively for the Remington, and relieved to discover that it was still in its holster. He thumbed the leather loop off the hammer and drew the pistol, rolled over on his left side—and nearly shouted at the pain shooting through his arm and shoulder. Something was broken, or dislocated. He rolled the other way and got to his knees, then to his feet, and in a stumbling crouch made it to the cutbank, placing his back against it. His vision finally clearing, he checked the rim above him and to either side. No sign of Manolo. No sound, either. It was as though the whole world was waiting with bated breath to find out who was going to live, and who was going to die.

Nervous about staying in one place too long—especially when he had no idea where his adversary was—Ethan moved to his left, noticing that the height of the cutbank lessened in that direction, and going far enough so that when he stood straight he could see over the rim and scan the slope. He saw the dun, lying on its side, about forty feet up the hill. Its life lay in a crimson pool that leaked serpentine rivulets down over the gray shale. Manolo was nowhere to be seen. Ethan had to hand it to the mestizo. He had played it smart; rather than going for a man on horseback he had put his enemy afoot, equalizing the odds. Or, if he chose not to stay and fight, making it virtually impossible for Ethan to continue the pursuit. Ethan could only hope that Manolo would want to finish it here and now. If he made off with Julie, all was lost. There was only one thing to do: tempt him into doing the former, and not the latter.

With that in mind, Ethan clambered over the cutbank and started up the slope toward the dead horse. He had no idea if the mestizo had a gun, but even if that turned out to be the case, Ethan didn't figure he had the luxury of laying low in the dry wash and waiting for Manolo to come to him.

"You can't have her, Manolo!" he shouted. "No matter what you do, she'll never be yours. She loves me. And she'll never love you. So just let her go. Let her go and maybe I won't kill you."

He was answered by the clatter of shod hooves on stone, and whirled to see Manolo and Julie, on horseback, at the crest of the next hill over, on the other side of the dry wash. For some reason Manolo checked his horse to look back at Ethan; perhaps it was a taunt of sorts, his way of saying *Take one last look at the woman who loves you.* But it was a mistake; one Ethan knew he had to capitalize on. He slammed the Remington back into its holster, turned, reached the coyote dun and whipped the repeating rifle out of its saddle boot, silently thanking the Good Lord that the horse had fallen on its left side and not its right, the side where the scabbard was tied to the saddle. Realizing what Ethan was about, Manolo whipped his horse around and made to drop down the far slope, out of sight. Down on one knee, Ethan raised the rifle to shoulder one-handed and got off a snap shot. He was rewarded by the sight of Manolo's cayuse going down.

"One good turn," muttered Ethan, "deserves another."

Julie saw her chance; she sawed at the reins, turning her horse quickly and kicking it into a headlong gallop down the near slope back toward Ethan, who immediately broke into a downhill run. Halfway down he scanned the rim of the far hill and saw Manolo there, and what he had in his hand wasn't a knife.

"No!" roared Ethan—a shout of impotent rage drowned out by the loud crack of Manolo's rifle, and Julie and her horse went down together, a tangle of human and animal that rolled breakneck to the edge of the wash and separated right at the instant that both went over the edge to plummet to the bottom of the dusty, rock-strewn gully.

Choking on his fear, Ethan stumbled the rest of the way down the slope and tried to jump down the cutbank, but he couldn't keep his footing when he landed, and hit his left shoulder again as he went down. The pain nearly made him pass out. Then a bullet kicked up a geyser of dust inches away, and he looked up to see Manolo scurrying down the far hill, trying to shoot on the run. Ethan turned his attention to Julie. She lay still, facedown, beside the horse, which was trying to get up but couldn't—shattered bone had pierced the flesh on its right back leg. Ethan no longer cared about Manolo; all he cared about was finding out if Julie was alive or not, and he got to his feet with a groan and staggered toward her. He was nearly to her when Manolo reached the rim of the cutbank and with a scream of rage launched himself through the air. Ethan drew the Remington and fired, but the shot went wide.

Manolo's hurtling body hit Ethan squarely, knocking him down, knocking the wind out of Ethan's lungs and jarring the pistol out of his grasp. Manolo bounced to his feet and tried to lever another round into his rifle's chamber. But the rifle jammed, and Ethan kicked out in desperation, knocking the mestizo's legs out from under him. Manolo came up again, quick as a cat, and this time he had the knife in hand, having discarded the rifle. With a snarl he hurled himself at Ethan, who had gotten up on one knee. Ethan met the attack with one of his own, throwing his body at Manolo, consumed by his own blind rage. Manolo hadn't expected this; it threw his timing off, and Ethan was able to pull up and avoid the slashing stroke of the knife, a stroke that might have disemboweled him had it been a few inches closer. Manolo was thrown off balance and Ethan threw a quick punch that grazed the mestizo's face and knocked him down. He lashed out with the knife to keep Ethan at bay; Ethan dodged the blade and moved in, only to get a faceful of dirt for his trouble. Stumbling backward, partially blinded, he tripped over a rock and fell. It saved his life—Manolo was already on his feet again, lunging again, and would have gutted Ethan but for the latter's misstep. As it was, Manolo stumbled over Ethan's body and also fell, giving Ethan time to blink some of the dirt out of his eyes. He groped for, and found, the rock, and when Manolo came at him again, he struck with all his might, slamming the rock against the mestizo's skull. Manolo went down onto hands and knees, blood streaming

down one side of his face. Winded and in immense pain,
Ethan managed to stand up. He put one foot on the knife
in Manolo's hand, and kicked the mestizo in the ribs with
the other. Manolo rolled away, leaving the knife behind.
Ethan picked it up. He took a step toward Manolo—and
then a sound made him whirl. It was Julie. She was moving.
She was alive. He rushed to her side, put down the knife,
and rolled her over gently to cradle her in his arms and
wipe dust and blood and a tendril of yellow hair from her
face. Her eyes fluttered open, and he saw the movement
reflected in them. Mustering his final reserve of strength,
he snatched up the knife and twisted around and drove the
blade to the hilt into Manolo's belly. The mestizo had
picked up the jammed rifle and had it raised like a club;
now he let it slip from his fingers as he looked in amaze-
ment at the knife. With a snarl of exertion, Ethan twisted
the knife and made an upward cut. Manolo lived long
enough to give the man who had killed him a look filled
with hate—then he died on his feet, his body hitting the
ground as lifeless as a sack of grain.

Ethan sat there for a while, holding Julie to him with his
one good arm, but the horse that lay nearby was suffering,
and he could only take so much of that. He located the
Remington and put a bullet in the animal's brainpan, ending
its misery. The gunshot roused Julie. She sat up, looked
about her, and her gaze lingered for a moment on the
nearby corpse of the mestizo.

"Are you hurt?" asked Ethan.

She shook her head, and with his help she stood, testing
her body, amazed that nothing had been broken in the fall,
and then she noticed the way he was holding his left arm.
"No," she said. "I'm fine. But you're not."

"I am now," he said.

She knew what he meant, and smiled, and touched his
face. "I love you, Ethan Payne. I was so . . . so afraid I'd
never get another chance to tell you that."

"And I love you, Mrs. Payne." He glanced at the dead

horse. "But I'm afraid I don't have much to offer you besides that. Don't even have a horse for you to ride." He looked at her, sheepishly. "Or a job in Abilene, anymore."

"No?" She smiled. "Good. I'm glad you don't have that job any longer."

"So, where would you like to go?"

She put her arms around him and pressed her body against his, laying her head on his shoulder. "I think I'll stay right here."

That suited him just fine.